The Second Coming

Doyle Thomas

Outer Banks, North Carolina

2009 by Doyle Thomas
All rights reserved.

ISBN 1449958389

Printed in the United States of America.

This book is dedicated:
First to my parents, for teaching me to think and question.
Then to my brothers and sisters, for their encouragement.
To my wife for her invaluable help, and my children for their patience.
And finally to the friends who have read my stories and offered their encouragement, ideas, and criticisms.

THE SECOND COMING

April 1985

I

    Rob Wheat pulled Rios' car off the road on to the clay and shell driveway in front of O'Connor's house. The rasping sounds of the tires stopping on the surface stayed for a while in his ears. He sat with both hands on the steering wheel and tried to calm himself. Then he got out and leaned against the car, his breath coming hard and scraping against the silence and the cool night air. His heart was still beating violently and his chest and throat were still constricted though it had been an hour since he left Rios' house, and he thought the quick beer he had at the motel where he stopped to pick up his things would have calmed him.
    Above him the random stars were high and far, and the blurred, chaste wheel of the Milky Way turned silently. The moon was getting fuller and it was tinged with violet and blue. There was something about it that made the normal sounds of the night seem slow and heavy and far away. Though it was chilly, his palms were moist, and a little rivulet of perspiration ran down the hollow of his breast. He opened the door again and pulled the satchel across the front seat. With careful steps he walked toward the silhouette of O'Connor's house. He was glad they lived out behind the groves where he didn't have to worry about prying neighbors. As he approached he saw the silver-blue reflections of the television screen jumping like dervishes against the curtains in the back bedroom. He stepped up to

The Second Coming

the house and pressed the doorbell, and when it didn't work, he opened the screen door and knocked. After a moment he heard O'Connor's halting, uneven steps, and he felt the clumsy, tripping fear of the man behind the door as if it were in conjunction with his own.

"Rory," he hissed at the door when he felt the other man's presence behind it. "It's Rob Wheat, Rory. Open up."

"Who?"

"It's Rob," he repeated, and he heard the sleepy man's fumbling with the lock. The door opened and a pale yellow light broadened into the yard.

"Man, you're going to get your ass killed," the man in the house said, his long silhouette filling the doorway. The overhead light behind him shone off the dome of his thinning crown, and Rob could just make out the wrinkles at the corners of his eyes as he squinted behind his glasses. He and Meg must have fallen asleep in front of the television. "What time is it anyway?" Rory asked him, finally opening the door wide enough for Rob to know he would let him in.

"It's late, real late. Look, Rory, I need a favor and I don't have time to explain it all now. I need to borrow your car."

"Whose fucking car is that?" O'Connor asked with a violent nod of his head toward the road.

"Rory, who is it out there?" Meg called from the bedroom. The floor creaked as O'Connor shifted his weight and turned around.

"It's alright, honey. It's Rob...he's drunk."

"Well, tell him to go be drunk somewhere else. You can't miss no more work. You start drinking with him and you know you won't get up in the morning."

"Tell her I'm leaving," Rob whispered.

"He's leaving, Meg. Go back to sleep," he yelled into the darkness, and then stepped aside to let Rob come in. He took a few shuffling steps back in the tight little kitchen. He opened the refrigerator and pulled out two beers. "She's pissed at you 'cause of Jane and Kelly. She got a letter a couple of weeks ago and I know they've talked a few times on the phone. Jane said she hadn't heard from you or gotten any child support in a while. She was trying to track you down and wanted to know if we'd seen you. If I was you, Rob, I'd catch up on my payments, and fast. Meg isn't the only person she's called, and you don't want her singing that same song to everyone else. Man, that's one castrating bitch I wouldn't want looking around for my ass. And you know Meg. She likes to get worked up about things, which is alright, but I don't want to be the one to have to hear about it. Where have you been, anyway?"

"Around. Rory, I need to borrow your car, just to go to Jacksonville. Just let me leave the other one in the shed for a few days. I'd take it if I could. I just don't know if it can make it to Jacksonville."

"Can I drive it?" Rory asked.

"No."

"Rory!" Meg called from the bedroom.

"What's in the bag, Rob?"

"Don't say no, Rory, just don't say no."

"Rory O'Connor!"

"Shut up, Meg, for Christsake! I told you he was leaving, and you better not get out of that fucking bed." He turned around and looked at Rob again, resting his elbows on the table. His hands fluttered to the top of his head which was sunk down between his shoulders. "I can't do it, Rob," he said, straightening up suddenly. "I'm sorry. Things are quiet for me now, and that's the way I need them. She doesn't bug me too much. She's good for me, man. She keeps me going. You know how it is." He looked down at the table and quickly picked up his beer.

The movement was clumsy and abrupt, and the light in the kitchen was suddenly too bright. Rob looked over at the clean, floral dishrag draped over the edge of the sink.

The Second Coming

There weren't any dishes in the drainer, and there was new wallpaper, and curtains on the window above the sink. Everything was neat. Rob heard the springs squeaking on the bed down the hall in the dark.

"I don't even care what's in the bag, man. You know how it is."

Rob was already standing. He wasn't angry, but he didn't say goodbye. O'Connor walked him to the door. Rob knew how it was. Everyone just wanted to get through it.

He heard the other man throw the latch as he walked across the lawn. At least he wasn't as jumpy as he had been. The night seemed a bit warmer, and the stars winked behind a slowly rising haze. Clouds stood low and dark in the west, brooding before momentary flashes of orange lightning. As he slid behind the wheel he smelled the cloying stink of the rotting oranges that lay gray and deflated on the ground.

He put both hands on the steering wheel and took a deep breath. He could be in Jacksonville in three hours. That would be six o'clock. He had to be careful. If he was stopped, that was it. He turned the ignition. The engine started, then choked and died. He turned it again and shifted into first. Fucking Rios.

As soon as he got to Jacksonville he would call Andy and John. They would get him a car. They were younger. He should have known better than to have bothered Rory. There had always been that hesitancy in his nature, and now it had an anchor. It wasn't cowardice exactly. Hell, he didn't care what it was. Rory was like everyone else, and he was right, Meg was good for him.

Rob had first met him in Mexico. It was on the trip he took after he and Jane split up. He had gone because he knew the pace and the lifestyle would help him forget about things. Also, Mexico had somehow crystallized his desire to marry Jane in the first place, and it was natural to suppose it could also help break the bond. He had lasted almost three months in Oaxaca, surfing, smoking pot, drinking cervesas.

Rory had been there for a month with a couple of friends from Florida. After a two week flat spell his friends lost patience and decided to go down to El Salvador and check out La Libertad, even though the rumor was that government soldiers were throwing bodies off the cliff there. Rory didn't want any part of it. He was ready to go home, and as Rob was too, they decided to travel back to the states together.

They took the bus to Vera Cruz where they'd heard there was a cheap ferry they could catch to Corpus Christi. But when they got there they found that the ferry was much more expensive than they had been told and neither could afford it. They resigned themselves to take the train to Brownsville the next morning. They got a room in a hostel, and then went down to the waterfront, found a bar, and ordered tequila.

After a couple each they began to relax and the idea of taking the train didn't seem nearly as bad as it had. They were sitting back a little more comfortably finding out about each other's lives when two other gringos came in. It was early afternoon and they were the only ones in the cantina so naturally they began to talk, and before long they were all buying each other rounds. It turned out the two were from Nova Scotia and they were cruising in a thirty-five foot trimaran one of them had built in his back yard. He was the more voluble of the two and he quickly recounted their adventures and laid out their plans. They had brought the boat down the east coast in the Intracoastal Waterway. They sailed around south Florida and the Keys, and when they felt comfortable with her, and fairly confident she would hold together, they had begun to hop from island to island, first through the Bahamas, then south to the Virgin Islands, and down to the Leewards.

Their first plan was to follow the chain down to Tobago, cross the Caribbean, and then go through the Panama Canal and up the Pacific coast. But Tony, who had built the boat, got sick, and they'd gone back to Nassau for

The Second Coming

him to recover. Then they decided to sail between Florida and Cuba into the Gulf of Mexico, drop through the Yucatan Channel, and sail south to the canal from there. They made it to the mouth of the channel easily, but there they ran into an oncoming gale. They tried to motor through, but their engine failed. When they had been close enough to see the lights on Cuba's western coast they turned back and sailed into the Bay of Campeche to make repairs and wait for more favorable weather.

They were leaving the next morning. They were going to try the Yucatan Channel again. Once through they were planning to stop in the Cayman Islands for a few days and then sail for the canal. After four or five tequilas they took Rob and Rory to the marina to look at the boat. Although Rob didn't know much about sailing or boats, it appeared seaworthy from the outside. The only thing he could remember about trimarans was that they had a tendency to pitch-pole in high seas, and if you were on board one that did you had bought it. The cabin was three times larger than anything he had seen on a monohull, and the craftsmanship in the interior was phenomenal. The more Tony and his friend talked about building the boat and sailing it, the more Rob wished he could go with them. And after burning a joint down below, they invited Rob and Rory to come along.

Rob was ready to jump at the chance. He'd love to go through the canal and sail up the Mexican coast and disembark in San Diego or L.A. Money was tight, too tight. But he thought he could get some wired to him in Panama. He looked over and Rory was shaking his head. He didn't have the money. He didn't have the time. Rob didn't really owe him any consideration. He had only known him for a few days and he wasn't tied to him in any way. But somehow Rory's reaction dampened him enthusiasm, and in the end Rob just said he'd think about it. They all went back to the cantina and picked up where they left off.

Doyle Thomas

By sunset none of them could walk or talk very well. The Canadians wanted to look for some women, and after some drunken indecision Rob and Rory agreed to tag along. The bartender directed them back to the docks. There were girls, very nice girls, he kept repeating in Spanish, but they couldn't get him to be any more specific than that. Rob had a pretty good idea what kind of girls he was talking about and he wasn't interested. But he had almost decided to take the Canadians up on their offer, and he didn't want to lose track of them.

Tony spoke good Spanish, and as they got closer to the waterfront he began to stop and question some of the men they passed. "Digame, por favor. Donde esta la casa de punta sublime machimbo?" They began to see some rough characters and Rob didn't like the looks they gave the group when they were asked the question. Tony got uglier about it each time he asked until finally he grabbed a little Mexican by the collar and hissed the question through his clenched teeth. "Donde esta la casa de punta?"

"Take it easy," Rob said.

"Donde esta?"

"En el Calle Ramos," the man said, shaking himself free and pointing. "En la casa della porta verde."

"Gracias," the Canadian whispered, leaning forward, his breath in the man's face.

They found the Calle Ramos, and the house with the green door was in the middle of the block. The front room was just a bar with four small tables looking out on the street. They took one of the tables and the three of them sat while Tony walked over to question the bartender. Before long his voice got loud and demanding, but the bartender wasn't backing down. He spoke just as loudly, and to emphasize his words he began flailing his arms. The other locals in the bar became interested in the conversation and began to mumble among themselves and look from the argument at the bar to the table where Rob and Rory and the

The Second Coming

other Canadian sat.

"We better get out of here," Rob said as fear began to sober him.

"Donde esta la casa...?" Rory mumbled, smiling and looking around. "Where's my drink?"

"Come on, Rory," Rob said, lifting him under the arm. "Let's go. How about it, mate?" he said to the other Canadian after he had gotten Rory to his feet.

"Yes, I'm with you. Let's go." They went to the door and called to Tony. He and the bartender were still arguing, pointing fingers at each other and shaking their heads, but their voices weren't as loud as they had been. "Tony, you coming?"

"Not until I get an answer from this old woman," he said in English.

"We're leaving," the other Canadian said. "We'll see you back at the boat, eh?"

"Alright, alright," Tony said, and he thumbed his teeth at the bartender as he headed for the door.

Rob helped Rory down the steps. When he reached the street he looked up and saw the little guy Tony had manhandled standing at the corner. He knew something was up when the man ducked around the building.

"Come on," Rob said, heading in the other direction.

"The boat's this way."

"You go that way if you want. We'll meet you at the boat later."

A half dozen men, led by the little one, came around the corner and began walking toward them.

"Run, Rory," he said, and they began to trot. They went awkwardly at first, but then he knew Rory understood what was going on and they increased their pace, holding on to each other and running in tandem. Rob guided Rory across the street and at the corner they headed up the hill, Rob looking over his shoulder as they went. Rob knew they could not outrun the Mexicans for long, especially when he realized how slowly they were laboring uphill. But he was counting on the Canadians not following them, and he was hoping the Mexicans would realize who it was who had insulted them.

At the next intersection they stopped just long enough to see the pursuing Mexicans rush through the intersection below. Rob was doubly relieved because he thought he noticed the shadows of sticks and clubs in their hands. It was lucky because Rory couldn't have run much longer and he was too drunk for either logic or fear to be of any use to move him. They trotted a few more blocks just to be safe, and by the time they slowed to a walk he realized Rory was chanting in time to his steps, "Donde esta la casa de punta? Donde esta la casa de punta?" and giggling sometimes between his recitations. They got back to the hostel and he helped Rory upstairs and put him to bed. Rob went to the marina the next morning before their train left, but the Canadians and their boat were gone.

That was how Rob had gotten to Florida, because not only had he taken the train to Brownsville with Rory, but he'd also taken the bus with him back to his home near Orlando. After that night Rory always acted as if he owed Rob a debt. Rory sponsored him, helped him find a place to live and a job, and for a while they were good friends. Rob always knew he could crash at Rory's place for a few days when he got back from a trip, and if he needed work Rory could usually find him something. But then Meg came along, and things changed after that. It didn't bother Rob. He had introduced them. She was an old friend of Jane's who had gotten in touch with him when she moved to Florida. Rory was smitten the first time he met her. They were married within a few months, and she had changed him. That's just the way it was.

He wondered if Jack Pruitt still had his Mustang. He'd love to have that car back. It was something else he had abandoned. He had left it in pretty good condition, and

The Second Coming

now he wondered if it was still together, or if Jack had cannibalized it for parts. He had the key in his pocket. It was funny when he thought about the things he kept and the things he left behind. He wondered what other figurative keys he had, and what he was still willing to unlock if he did have them. He let the metaphor drop. Anyway Andy and John would get him a car. And then he would go to Baltimore.

Jane's brother Chick lived there. Rob hadn't seen him in almost two years, but he knew he was just what Chick was looking for. Rob looked down at the satchel on the seat next to him, wondering how much, how pure? He wondered how much he could walk on it. Chick would know. The main thing was to turn it over fast. Once he had the money he could maybe run out west somewhere. He'd liked what he'd seen of Arizona and New Mexico. What was the name of that girl who lived in Albuquerque?

There wasn't much traffic and he stayed in the right lane. Now and then a car would pass him and he would check his speed again in the unfamiliar dashboard. He wasn't tired, but he didn't feel very alert. His mind wandered, occasionally latching on to something like the Mexican episode with Rory, but mostly it flitted, hopping like a hungry little bird looking for seeds in the grass.

Kelly began to creep around the periphery of his mind as he passed through the Ocala National Forest. He didn't want to think about her. He always remembered the same things; her warm, purring form on his lap, smelling that funky little girl smell, trying to unbutton his shirt, and then pushing her blunt little fingers through the hairs on his chest. She would be coy with him and know it, looking up at him with those serious gray eyes, eyes that shouldn't have belonged to a little girl. The look in those eyes she should have been allowed to grow into. She was only four then, and last month she had turned twelve. He hadn't written or talked to her in months. He hated to write, and he never called because he couldn't stand to hear Jane bitch, especially when he knew she had a point. He had gotten behind on his support payments, and hadn't caught up. In fact the further behind he got the more it sometimes seemed like the best thing to do was disappear and forget about it altogether. He had good intentions about it at first. He was always planning to make it up to Kelly. But instead things always seemed to be slipping further away. It was the attrition of time, and he hoped she understood. But in his heart he knew better than to expect a child to understand the friction of moments when he still didn't properly understand himself. He remembered the two of them that last day. For months he and Jane had played "Hills Like White Elephants," and then they finally and calmly decided to end it. Jane stood there nervous and apologetic and a little frantic because she still wasn't sure what she wanted. Kelly was still and silent next to her with those large cool gray eyes. Which was the child and which was the parent? That was a mystery he still hadn't solved. He had been businesslike and straightforward. Then for a long time afterward he wished he could make things different and put them all back together again. But he didn't wish it anymore.

The first hint of the white of dawn drew itself above the black Atlantic as he climbed over the St. John's River bridge into Jacksonville. Small strands of motion and life formed themselves and threads of light thrust into the knotted gray shadows. He got off the highway and followed the grimy cobbled street running next to the river past sinister black creosoted pilings and bulkheads that lined the shore. The warehouses gradually gave way to faded clapboard houses. Though it was just dawn he saw the dark forms of men fishing and crabbing off docks, and smoke curling from little stacks and leaning, cracked chimneys. Here and there were small trellised garden patches, and flowers planted in boxes next to abandoned, rusting cars.

Andy and John lived down the road after the gray

shanties gave way to the green of the country. Rob pulled off the street in front of the cottage set back by the river behind a row of cedar trees. There was still some darkness in the recesses and corners of everything, but the birds were awake and singing. He heard the muffled conversational sounds of the river behind the house and they grew louder as he followed the path around to the dock that walked on its pitched pilings out into the current. The wind was slack and in places the water swirled beneath the cypress roots like an animal's moving skin over the flexing of its muscles. Mullet rose and jumped blindly. Palmetto leaves and water lilies, dislodged by recent thunderstorms, rushed by in the brown water. He recalled a longer and older river with a child hidden among the reeds on its bank, and he remembered that the child had been delivered. He smiled because whenever he drew religious analogies he embarrassed himself even when he was alone because he didn't know the gods or prophets very well and in their company he was truly a stranger in a strange land. He sat on the end of the dock with his legs dangling above the river, smelling crabs and periwinkles, mud and decaying leaves drifting downstream. The water swirling among the pilings below was almost black. Bowing his head and putting his chin on his chest, he felt the double strand of knotted muscle in his neck loosen and the blood pressing on the inside of his skull slowly began to recede.

Gradually he became aware of sounds from the house, the ordinary, muted sounds of John and Andy's shabby morning benedictions. He stood and walked to the back door.

"John," he called quietly through the screen. The broad back of a large figure moved in the interior shadows and turned its gray prognathic profile into the morning light. Rob could tell he recognized his voice.

"Rob Wheat. Come in, man," he said, hocking into the garbage pail next to the stove. "I'm a hungover mother."

He shook his big head. "What are you doing up the way? I heard you were in jail." There was an ambient feeling of unconcern or disassociation he dropped with each remark. People were sometimes almost ashamed to answer his questions. No one worried about the threat of his intelligence. But there was something in his earthiness, some primal chord he could strike that cracked away any façade or affectation without even acknowledging it. It was useless to lie or even exaggerate.

"I was in for a couple of weeks, but now I'm out."

"We heard it was ninety days for not supporting your kid."

"It was ninety days," Rob said, wondering if Jane had gotten hold of them too. "But it was for assault. I got drunk and hit a guy."

Rob didn't want this conversation. He didn't want to think about saying too much or too little. He wanted them both to trust silence to sift for the value of the situation. John seemed to agree. He shook his head again and walked over to the cabinet, his feet slapping on the linoleum floor.

"How's Andy?"

"Same as he ever was. He'll be hungover too when he wakes up. You want some coffee?"

"No," he said, sitting down at their kitchen table. After a few minutes he heard Andy hacking and growling from the bathroom. Through the wall his whole body was making dangerous noises. "He sounds great."

John rolled a number, and after he got it right he lit it up. When Andy came in from down the hall he ignored Rob and went straight for the joint in his brother's outstretched hand.

"How are you, Andy?"

"Static," he answered and chitz, chitzed as he tried to hold in his hit. "You want some of this?"

"No. I had to give it up. It made me stupid."

Andy shrugged.

17

The Second Coming

"Do you know if Jack Pruitt still has my Mustang?"

"I guess he does," Andy said. "He did the last time I talked to him. He keeps saying he's going to fix it up." He rummaged through the cabinet looking for a clean coffee cup, ignoring the dirty ones standing on the edge of the sink. "What are you doing up here anyway?"

"Business. I'm going to Baltimore. But I need another car."

"Want some coffee?" Andy asked. John was out of it. He had looked interested at first, but by the time the joint was gone he wasn't. Anyway, Andy made the decisions. Rob would have to deal with him. John drank the last of his coffee, rose from the stool at the sideboard, and left the room. It was full of morning now.

"No. No coffee. But how about a beer? I didn't get any sleep last night, and I'm kind of jagged." He was. His eyes burned, his jaw was set hard, and his neck was sore again. He didn't feel like explaining anything, or making anything up, or asking for favors. He wished he had gone straight to Atlanta and dumped the car there, or maybe left it in some lot in town and taken the bus. Andy handed him a can of beer from the refrigerator. He pulled the tab and put it to his mouth and drank. No, this was the way. He was going to think things over carefully and do them right. No hesitations, no shortcuts, no wild hairs. He was doing business, so he had to be all business.

"What's wrong with the car out front, Rob?"

"It's hot."

"What does Jack's car have to do with it? Do you expect him to trade even up for a hot car, or do you expect him just to give it to you?"

"I don't expect him to do either. I want you to get it for me. It's not really his car. He never paid for it. I guess he figures it's his now because he's had it for so long."

"It seems to me like the easiest thing would be for you to explain this all to him." Rob shook his head. "But you don't want to do that. You want us to get it for you. What are you going to do with the other car?"

"Park it somewhere," Rob said. He knew Andy would do it. "You won't be stealing it, Andy. The title is still in my name, and I have a key."

"How much?"

Rob tipped his beer. He had hoped to keep everything packed and sealed until he was in Baltimore behind the locked door of Chick's apartment. What an asshole! He had expected favors based on barren old friendships and the philanthropy of his drug acquaintances. He had forgotten what decade he was in. But Andy's narrowed eyes and anticipatory smile jolted him back. He wished he had stopped somewhere on the road and cut it up, but he hadn't.

"White bag," he said. "Clean white man's bag. An ounce." He had to do a lot more thinking. He was only four hours from serious retribution and he was already making mistakes. What was he thinking? Andy didn't give a fuck about him. Rob could already see the machinations behind his eyes.

"Let's taste," Andy said.

"A small taste, that's all. I need a room where I can work for a while."

"How much do you have, Rob?" Andy asked, and Rob began shaking his head. "John and I can get rid of some of it for you. Marcia's boyfriend has some triple beams. He could turn some of it for you too."

"Look, Andy, I don't want anyone else to know about this. Understand?"

"Alright, Rob. Don't worry, we'll be cool. If you didn't think we could be, you wouldn't be here, right?"

"Right," Rob answered wearily.

"Use the spare room," Andy said. "Relax and take it easy for a while. You can crash in there if you want."

Rob just nodded. He went out to the car, reached in

The Second Coming

the window, and pulled out the satchel and his bag. Coming back into the house, he went without a word into the spare room. It was musty and dark. Faded curtains hung limply from the windows. They must use it more for storage than for guests, he thought, because there were boxes on the bed and an old rug rolled up on the floor against one of the walls. The bed had an old tubular steel frame painted black with scabs of rust breaking out on its surface. Rob pulled a mirror from the wall and wiped its surface with an old shirt from one of the boxes. He opened the satchel and took out a package the size of a large loaf of bread wrapped in a Spanish language newspaper. Inside the paper was a heavy, translucent plastic bag sealed by melting the edges together. He didn't want to open it, but he didn't have a choice now. He took the razor out of the satchel and carefully slit across the top of the bag. Immediately the heavy soapy smell of the cocaine's ether base rose to his nostrils. The powder was tightly packed inside. Spreading the mouth of the bag open, he ran the blade through the surface of the drug. It was flaky with some small rocks, and on some surfaces it had a barely discernible pinkish hue.

He looked into the bag and tried to concentrate, hoping for good decisions. But he was suddenly very tired. He heard the buzzing and dull thuds of a fly behind the curtain bumping against the window pane. Through the door he heard John and Andy moving around, and sometimes when they stopped he could hear their muffled voices. He put the blade into the bag and shoveled two piles onto the surface of the mirror. After a moment's hesitation he repeated the motion and heaped out a third pile. He began working the blade through the piles, chopping at the little rocks methodically, listening to the rhythmic rap as the blade struck the glass. He worked slowly and intently, the blade screaming across the mirror, until he had drawn three long, sweeping lines. His bowels loosened as he drew the small straw from his breast pocket and leaned over the mirror.

When he did he caught sight of the reflection in the glass below him. Gravity made the skin fall away from his cheeks and created heavy lined pouches below the recesses where his eyes sat in the cavities of his skull. There was no trace of youthfulness in it.

He inhaled part of the line. It was clean and astringent as it attached itself to his sinuses behind his eyes. In an instant he felt the rush all the way to the center of his gut. He shuddered and then ran his forefinger through the ghost of the line's trail and absently pulled it across his gums. His face, from below his eyes to the roof of his mouth, was already numb. Jesus, he thought, how did Rios get hold of this?

He pulled zip-lock bags from the satchel along with a spoon and began to fill the smaller bags from the larger one. He wished he had scales because he was anxious to know exactly how much he had. The sun sent long angled shafts of light through the gaps in the curtains, and motes of dust he had awakened in the little-used room danced in the air. He began to feel something in him, something beneath his ordinary carapace of feeling, something deeper and not quite physical, but still attached to his body. He could pull it off, he knew it. A low-key euphoria began to stand in place of the initial jolt. This was the best it got, the best it would be, he knew, and he wanted to hold it as long as he could. His anxieties dissolved, reformed, and dissolved again. He already wanted more.

He filled the zip-lock bags carefully, slowly spooning the powder from the larger bag. His hand trembled slightly in its path from bag to bag, but he didn't spill any. He filled each bag to what he judged by sight to be a quarter pound. When he finished he had eight bags, more or less the same size, though he could tell there were recognizable weight discrepancies among them. After a little arithmetic in his head he guessed he had a kilo, maybe more.

He took out two more zip-lock bags. Ounces were

The Second Coming

easy. He had seen enough of them to get it close. One of them would be good payment for John and Andy, more than enough. He could still hear them prowling behind the door. He wanted to get back on the road, and he had to keep reminding himself to take his time. There were too many things that needed to be decided in this room, because as soon as he opened the door there would be no turning back. He approximated two ounces by pulling them from the larger looking of the quarter pound bags. When he was satisfied he rolled them up and put them in his jacket pocket. Then he took the eight larger bags and put them in the heavy plastic bag the coke had originally come in. He tried to wrap the whole thing in the newspaper, but it was torn and feathery and not much use. After looking around the room, he decided on one of the faded pillow cases instead. He picked it up and shook it by the end. A stained, lumpy pillow fell stillborn on the bed. He put the stiff plastic bag in the pillow case, rolled it up, and replaced it in the satchel along with the spoon and the empty bags. He sat in the empty room. The mirror and the lines lay next to him on the bed a little out of focus. He was thinking there was something much more than irretrievable about yesterday. It wasn't the first he'd burned a bridge behind him. It wasn't the first time he'd taken an irreversible step. But in this there was much more. He felt like a patient admitted to a medieval hospital, entering a realm of the living and yet not living. He took the rest of the line he had drawn for himself and then part of one of the others. Then he evened up the two remaining lines and went into the other room.

Andy and John were like kids waiting for Christmas, leaning forward in their seats with pale, shining eyes. They both took their lines greedily.

"This is for when you bring me the car," he said, dropping the oblong bag on the table in front of them. Andy picked it up and unrolled it, fingering the powder through the plastic.

"How much is it?" John asked.

"An ounce."

"It looks a little light to me," Andy said off-handedly, looking at Rob with his head cocked at a peculiar, submissive angle. His thin brown hair fell into his eyes and he swept it back.

"That's how much you get. I'm not negotiating. If you're not interested, tell me now before I waste any more of my time." His teeth ground silently against each other. "Well?"

"How about another line?" John asked.

"No."

Andy sat forward in his seat and shot a look at his brother. "We'll do it, Rob," he said, handing the bag back to him. "But you need to relax. When do you need the car?"

"After dark. Here's the key. Take the other car and park it someplace, a mall or something, somewhere it won't be noticed for a couple of days. Make sure it's clean." He stood up. "I need some rest. I'll see you this evening."

He went into the empty bedroom and closed the door. It was much warmer and the room was stuffy and stale. He opened the curtains and tried to get the window up, but it was painted shut. Lying back on the bed, he closed his eyes, but everything was moving much too quickly.

He wondered what condition his Mustang was in, but he figured that Jack had taken good care of it. Machines were Jack's religion. He worshipped at the altar of the internal combustion engine. No, he wouldn't have any trouble making Baltimore in that car. He would drive to Raleigh, spend the day with JP, leave after dark on Friday, and be in Baltimore early Saturday morning. He closed his eyes again. He wanted another line, but he knew he had better get some sleep. He heard Andy and John moving around. They seemed very far away. They put some music on. He couldn't really hear it, but he felt the dull thud of the bass through the wall. Then he was dreaming.

The Second Coming

The dreams disappeared when he awoke. They seemed close, but there were no handles to them. The room was dark and the house was quiet except for a steady, droning buzz. He got up and went into the living room. They had forgotten to turn off the stereo and there was feedback coming through the speakers. He pushed the power button, and in a second it jumped from the speaker box like a released spirit and was gone. Rios' car was no longer in front of the house. He walked back into the kitchen. The sky was salmon and cabbage-colored above the river and the mullet were doing their silly jumping dance routine. He opened the refrigerator. Everything inside looked old and forgotten. No beer. He went back into the living room and flipped through a stack of old albums. They had a lot of classics, but most were in pretty poor condition. He found a Captain Beefeart album he hadn't seen in years, but it was virtually unplayable. "I'll let a train be my feet if it's too far to walk to you." He loved that line. He finally settled on an old Neil Young album. As he listened to it, he tried to remember what it was like to be fifteen.

It became dark quickly, and he waited a while before he turned on one of the lamps. He went into the bedroom, collected his things, and set them on the couch. In his jacket pocket he had an ounce for Andy and John, and an ounce for himself. He was still a little worried that Andy might try something, and the longer he had to wait the more the apprehension gnawed at him. He was hungry, and he finally went into the kitchen again. The clock above the stove read a quarter to nine. He took a dark banana from the top of the refrigerator. The smell made him a little queasy, and the meat was soft and slimy, but it tasted good.

He saw the reflections of the headlights on the wall as he walked back into the living room. He had the sudden almost irresistible urge to grab the satchel and run out the back door to the river and along its bank until he was far away in the darkness. But he didn't. He wished he had a gun. He heard voices and footsteps coming up the walk. As the doorknob began to turn he quickly put his right hand in his pocket.

Andy came in first. His eyes flashed down, and then back up to Rob's face. Rob didn't like the way he moved away from the door so quickly. But then John came in, and though the darkness seemed to give him more size, he was smiling such a big, open grin that Rob relaxed, and guessed Andy was just a little jumpy.

"It was easy," John said. "No one was home. It was sitting out back all by itself. He was taking good care of it. He even had it under a tarp. It started up the first time we tried it."

"What took you so long?"

"We were nervous so we went and had a couple of drinks," Andy said, dropping on the couch.

So that was it, Rob thought.

""It was a piece of cake. Nobody saw us, no one said anything…"

"Give it a rest, John."

"Where are you going anyway?" John asked. He was radiant, with perspiration glistening on his forehead.

"New Orleans first, then out west."

"I thought you said Baltimore."

"I changed my mind."

"It's too late for Mardi Gras, isn't it?"

"Yes," Rob said. "It's almost Easter. What did you do with the other car?"

"We left it at the mall. We even waited for a space up close so it wouldn't look so alone and lonesome."

"Whose car was that?" Andy asked.

"Nobody's," Rob said. "I've got to get going. Thanks…and remember, you haven't seen me, if anyone asks."

"We can turn some of it for you, Rob," Andy said. "You know we could be cool about it."

The Second Coming

"It isn't that I don't trust you. It's just that I need to get further away, much further."

He flipped Andy the bag, and Andy tossed him the keys. He picked up his bag and the satchel.

"Be careful, Rob," John said, and stepped aside to let him walk through the door.

He went out to the car. It had been painted with gray primer, and Jack had been doing some body work where it had rusted under the rocker panels. It was clean inside, cleaner than when he had left it. The engine sounded smooth and chortled steadily. Something was tapping, but very evenly. The night was damp, humid, like the one before it. He pulled out from John and Andy's house and searched out the highway that headed north.

II

It had been a long, tedious drive. Emma looked again at the back of her husband's head as he wheeled the car across the lanes of traffic into the motel parking lot. She had stared at the back of Ben's head for much of the eight hour drive. It was a novel vantage point for her. She had never noticed the short white hairs that stood straight out from the back of his neck, nor the dry pink skin rolling gently over the edge of his collar. They had taken many car trips before, but she had always sat up front next to him. But now with the other couple, the Frosts, along she had been relegated to the back seat. James sat in the front passenger seat with Ben, his broad forearm draped over the seat rest. Emma could see in his profile the curl of his disinterested smile, how he nodded politely at all the proper points in the conversations, or added a few stenciled remarks at the proper time. Most of the time though he ignored the rest of them and stared out at the vast expanses of tidal lands they rolled through.

His wife, Gert, sat in the back with Emma and had kept up a steady line of chatter through most of the trip. No, it wasn't chatter really. It was mostly an intelligent monologue, and it was entertaining and witty most of the time. But Emma somehow got the feeling that Gert was making fun of her. She was sometimes caught listening for second meanings that probably weren't there. Or sometimes she felt slighted because she thought Gert was directing her remarks only to the men in the front seat. But that wasn't it either. She knew Gert was just being herself, and that she was excited, and Emma kept telling herself not to be so sensitive. What was really bothering her was that she was angry with Ben for inviting them. These had always been special trips for her, when she could have Ben to herself. She didn't want to share him with the other couple, especially because they didn't really know them well.

The Second Coming

The Frosts had moved into the Delaney's house next door the previous December. Emma had heard the moving truck rumble up to the house early that morning. It was one of those days after a snow when the sky was a uniform, leaden gray. She had peeked through the curtains a little guiltily, trying to glean some clues to the personalities of their new neighbors as their possessions were hauled, tentatively and angrily, up the icy walk by two large and slow black men. Emma could just hear the echoes of their resonant voices as they cursed the cold and the ice and each other. But she guessed by the way they looked over their shoulders on the way from the house back to the truck that the real object of their wrath was the small woman who would appear at the front door as they struggled up the walk with each new load, and hesitate with her finger to her chin, making them stop and wait in the cold until she decided where would be their burden's destination. Emma had strained to get a better look at her. Her hair was pulled back and trained under a scarf, although she was continually pushing errant gray wisps of it back from her face. Emma wondered how old she was. She moved quickly and energetically, but she seemed to have a slight limp. There was something familiar about her even at a distance, and as Emma had gone back about the business of her day, she wondered what it was.

The movers left in the late afternoon and Emma had gone over with a coffee cake to formally greet her and welcome them to the neighborhood. Gert had introduced herself and invited her in and made tea which they drank amid the crates and boxes and rumpled paper. Emma noticed that the furniture was very modern; simple, abrupt, Scandinavian designs that didn't appeal to her at all. But Gert could sit in the chairs in a way that softened their geometric austerity. They talked for quite a while, until after dark. Gert explained that she and her husband, James had moved to Buck's County from central New Jersey where they had lived for all their married lives. James had been involved in the manufacture of something. Gert was rather vague about it, apparently because she wasn't interested and didn't expect anyone else to be. She was very open about everything else.

"You must watch out for me," she said, "because I don't hold back on anything. I think it's important to have opinions on issues. Sometimes it makes for short friendships, but it if does, I don't care. I want people to know who I am. That's why I also read the papers every day, even the ones I don't agree with. Because, as Hegel said, 'it's a realistic benediction of the day.' And I'm a strong supporter of a realistic outlook."

She had gone on to say that she had a theory that realism formed the basis of penance and guilt suppression in the Teutonic mind, but Emma somewhere lost the thread of her conversation, if there was one. After all, she considered herself fairly well-read and try as she might she could remember no more about Hegel than his name, although she vaguely felt he had had a pessimistic outlook on life. But she liked Gert immediately. Many of her friends had fallen away over the last few years once the activities of their children no longer brought them together, and she was glad for the new infusion of personality. Because of Gert's opalescence and Emma's curiosity as to the roots of it, they passed quickly from the first strains of acquaintanceship into a probing friendship.

They were very different. Emma had always had strong religious feelings. She had grown up in the Catholic Church, and been educated in it. She had gone through the usual hormonal crises of youth, and the doubts that the concrete realization of mortality brought on in middle age. But she had developed a system of faith that had succored her until this, her sixtieth year. The church, her idea of the church, remained the same. The Angelic Doctor had built an unassailable wall of logic around her deity, and she, with her

The Second Coming

quiet emotional faith, kept him there.

"Don't you miss the old liturgy?" Gert asked during one of their frequent morning discussions. Yes, she did. She missed the rich vestments and the arcane Latin phrases. Her conservative nature objected to what she thought was the cheapening of the ceremony by switching it to the vernacular and turning the priest so he faced the congregation, although she couldn't say all that.

"I thought so too. Of course, I'm not a Catholic, but I've always been interested in comparative religion. I thought the changes took away the feeling of mystery and initiation, which is the unconscious appeal of religion anyway. Until those changes you Catholics had it made. Are you familiar with Carl Jung? He was on of the founders of modern psychology, and I've always been fascinated by him. While Freud believed that an individual's psychological history was personalized, and his unconscious was made up of things that had been suppressed because they couldn't be satisfactorily neutralized by the libido, Jung believed there was a whole body of unconsciousness that was shared and common to all men. The concept is called the collective unconscious. Let me see if I can remember how it goes. First of all, you have a personal unconscious and it's made up of feelings, ideas…contents, he called them, that were once conscious, but either through lapses of memory, or repression, they have become unconscious. They are yours personally. Up to this point Freud and Jung are in agreement. But the contents of Jung's collective unconscious have never been conscious in you individually, because they haven't been individually acquired. They're inherited. They are supposedly the remnants of the titanic struggle of mans' passage from instincts to consciousness. Jung came up with his theory through the study of mythological similarities that run parallel in societies without regard to race or time or environment. He also saw corresponding symbols in the dreams of his own patients.

Of course, it dispels the idea of 'tabula rasa,' but I could never stomach that anyway. Getting back to religion, Jung believed that dogma takes the place of the collective unconscious by systematically formulating its contents on a grand scale. The whole collective unconscious is channeled into dogma and is controlled by the symbolism of creed and ritual. I always thought that if that were true, then Catholics must have very uneventful dreams. My, I haven't tried to put that together in quite a while."

"I don't think I could believe that," Emma replied after a moment, "especially the idea of the collective unconscious. It could too easily be used as an excuse for a person to escape the responsibilities of his actions. We all have to make our way through this life individually. I have to believe that."

In some secret ways though, Emma did agree. Aquinas could make God and his powers a logical reality. But the stained glass and the candles, the tinkling of bells and the tabernacle shielded beyond the broad, silk-draped shoulders of the priest, the incense and the genuflections, they were symbols that appealed to and touched the very core of one's emotions. In the end though she resented Gert's intrusion into something she took so seriously.

They spent more and more time together. Emma sometimes felt a little out of her depth because of the ease with which Gert could speak on so many different subjects. But even when she was most confused, she knew she had an important contribution to make. And she tried to wait patiently for her opportunity to make it.

One morning in early February they sat in Emma's kitchen drinking coffee and talking.

"But you didn't ever have children," Emma said, leaving it somewhere between a statement and a question.

"No, thank God," Gert answered emphatically.

Her response stung Emma. She couldn't help taking it personally. She was about to say what a joy her two

The Second Coming

children had been, what an education, but she couldn't. Instead, in a pained instant, she saw them as unremarkable and plain. The anecdotes she had kept and repeated about their developing personalities now left them as nothing more than caricatures. She thought about the running disagreements she had with them now, which the forms of convention just barely managed to conceal. Yet she loved them deeply, she knew. Gert couldn't understand. She couldn't understand because it was the struggle of birth and motherhood that developed finally into the ultimate feminine joy of pain.

Suddenly they heard something crash into the window above the sink. They both went to the window, and in the snow below, they saw a tiny crumpled form. Emma went out in her sweater and slippers and returned with a small bird cupped in the hollow of her hand.

"It's a Cape May Warbler, I think," she said. "I'll bet it's going to have a terrible headache."

"Is it still alive?"

"Yes, I can feel it twitching. It's just stunned, I think."

"It's very warm," Gert said, prodding its yellow and black breast with her forefinger. "What did you call it?"

"It's a warbler, a female Cape May Warbler. I'm almost positive. You can tell by the yellow patch behind its ear. I don't know what it's doing up here this time of year though. It should be much further south. They usually winter in Florida or the Caribbean."

"Shouldn't we all? But how did you know what it was?"

"There's nothing so odd about it. Ben and I watch birds. We have for a number of years, since the children grew up anyway. It's fascinating. We spend our lives surrounded by these animals. We see their nests in the trees. We see their forms in the skies. We hear their songs. Just think about their songs. Aside from their reproductive and social functions, did you know that some ornithologists believe there are birds that sing just to perfect their songs, for the pure joy of it? It's miraculous. Their songs, their shapes and colors and habits, and I never properly noticed them until I was forty years old."

"You must have a keen eye."

"Well, Ben does. He would almost get in accidents in the car when we first got interested, trying to get a better look if he thought he'd seen something new. We're a little calmer about it now. Look, it's starting to move. We better take it back outside."

Emma covered the bird with her free hand. Gert opened the door for her, and they both went outside. As she walked, it began to peck gently at Emma's palm. It was bright outside with a small white winter sun shining on the snow. She could see how the bird had become confused. She bent down and let it out of her hand on to the snow. After a few clumsy hops it gathered itself and flew up to the bare branch of a tree. It perched on the branch for a moment, a tiny black silhouette in front of the sun, and then it flew away.

Afterward Gert was full of questions. Emma lent her some books that she read and returned quickly with a plea for more. She picked Ben and Emma's brain, and Emma realized that she asked astute questions, and remembered the answers. Emma began to change in her attitude toward Gert. She knew that Gert was quick-witted and glib, and from their conversations she knew that she possessed knowledge on a wide variety of subjects. To Emma her knowledge had usually seemed to be of the parlor sort, aimed mainly toward the development of lively conversation and repartee, but now she saw that her new friend had a truly incisive scientific mind. Emma imagined she was glimpsing something of what Gert had been like as a young woman. And she wondered at what point Gert realized life was not going to reward her erudition? Essentially it had to be a defeat of the

The Second Coming

will, and that thought was a guilty balm to Emma because she had to believe that faith was more important than knowledge or will.

Ben noticed Gert's interest and aptitude too, and Emma became a little jealous, especially when he loaned Gert a pair of binoculars and patiently told her how to use them, explaining how to focus, telling her of the importance of using small glasses that you could move quickly if you were trying to catch sight of a bird on the wing. Emma's jealousy came because Gert's new enthusiasm infected and animated Ben, and around Emma lately he had been so uninspired.

He had retired the previous summer. Although they had been looking forward to the time they would spend together, once it actually came it had been a letdown for both of them. Ben had always been a tinkerer, but now even a screwdriver seemed too heavy for him. He moved through the house like Marley's ghost, ephemeral and shackled. He sat for hours in his chair by the window watching the lives that skimmed by. At first Emma thought it was a stage. She even imagined she had read about it in one of her womens' magazines. But she could not shake him from it. He was uncommunicative and resentful of intrusion. She finally decided it was best to step back and let the thing run its course. They settled into a quiet truce where habit stole the sting from silence. Sometimes though, especially in church when she would catch him staring vacantly at the stained glass, she would become afraid and pray for him. The nuns at school had taught her well and she still prayed with her whole heart. But she knew that somehow now, because of the compromises of life, her heart was smaller.

Gert began to draw him out of it. He was politely sullen to her at first, but she pressed on. She didn't only ask questions, she demanded answers. And if he was too slow with them, she ran roughshod over his reticence. She became preoccupied for a while with the ages of birds. She had given no thought to it before and was amazed to discover that a robin could live to be ten years old. One morning she ran over flushed with excitement to ask them if they knew that the oldest known banded specimen of Canada goose had lived to be twenty three. Soon she was able to tell Ben other things he didn't know or had forgotten. When talking about birds her eyes became alive and earnest. And when it came to birds at least, she laid aside the barbs of her wit. She became the incarnation of John Burrough's epigram, 'If you take the first step in ornithology, you are ticketed for the whole voyage.' She rekindled Ben's waning interest, and Emma noticed resentfully how much more effective Gert's efforts were than hers had been.

Winter wore on slowly. One evening in the middle of February Emma felt herself catching a chill. The next day she took to her bed. She had always been healthy and could brag that she had not been sick a day in all the years of raising her two children. She tried to shake it off, but she could find no resistance within her. On Sunday, for the first time since she had been in labor with her second child, she missed Mass. Ben did not go without her. She could hear him moving around downstairs. Even through the waves of nausea she recognized the familiar measure of his paces. He was solicitous to her needs and made her soup and hot tea and brought it up on a tray, but she didn't feel the comfort she needed to feel having him so close.

Gert came over to the house for a ride to their usual Monday night outing to the Audubon Society meeting. After Emma refused her offer to have James come sit with her, protesting that she was feeling much better, Ben and Gert went to the meeting without her. It was after eleven when Ben got home, and the meetings always ended at nine thirty. Emma pretended to be asleep when he came into the dark room, undressed, and slipped beneath the covers. The next morning she got out of bed. Her legs and back ached, and she was weak and cranky, but she felt better by Thursday,

The Second Coming

and by Saturday she was almost herself again.

She and Ben usually made a winter excursion to North Carolina's Outer Banks. They had been in all seasons, but they preferred to go in December or January because it was located in the middle of the Atlantic Flyway and they could drive down to the Pea Island refuge and view all the waterfowl that wintered there. Then there were all the other birds resting there on their way further south. Emma loved it, the wild ocean sending bits of threatening, brown storm scud over the tentative protection of the dunes, the salty north wind knifing through her clothes no matter how many layers she wore, and she and Ben all bundled up, trudging through the muddy marshes in high rubber boots, trying to get a better look at something.

She loved crossing the bridge to Pea Island. On a clear day from the top you could look south and see the long sickle of Hatteras Island slicing between the ocean and the Pamlico Sound. Once on the refuge there was only one road running through the middle of the barrier island. Everywhere were birds. Complaining gulls wheeled overhead, flocks of disdainful crows draped heavily like omens on bayberry or yaupon bushes, or rising together on their sinister black wings. She had never seen so many different kinds of ducks in the same place, canvasbacks and mallards, pintails, wood ducks and buffleheads. If you were lucky you might see a pheasant moving uncertainly next to some heavy brush. And lately the brown pelicans had been making a good recovery in their population. There were kingfishers and nee swans and Canada and snow geese. The snow geese were her favorites when they first arrived each fall, with the contrast of the black tips on their white wings beating fiercely and evenly to keep their thick bodies aloft. There was nothing more beautiful than the sudden brightness of a flock turning on the wing and catching the full reflection of the sunlight. After they settled though and began to graze they seemed to change. Emma would see them through the car window as she and Ben drove through the refuge, standing dumbly by the side of the road eating the grasses and roots in shallow puddles until their white feathers were spattered with mud.

In the fall when she had expected they would plan their usual winter trip, Ben had not been interested, and after a few careful nudges she had let it drop. Just after the New Year they received a letter from Colonel Wheeling in Nags Head. He was a founding member of the local ornithological society in Dare County, and they had met him many years before on one of their first trips to the area. He was a loud and unapologetically obscene man, fond of wearing those fatigue military caps with insignias on them. But he had been very helpful in his precise military manner, telling them where to go and what to look for, and over the years they had become good friends with him and his wife. Whenever they were down they would call the Wheelings, and it would usually end up that he would arrange some sort of itinerary and invite them to dinners and social functions.

The colonel wrote with a proposition. He lived in Colington Harbor, a development back on the Albemarle Sound that had been recovered from an area of pine-topped sand hills and boggy marshland. A population of ospreys had long spent their summers there and continued to return each spring in spite of the human intrusion. For a while their population had been decimated because of the use of pesticides. But in the time since the federal government had banned DDT they had steadily increased in numbers, until there were over twenty family groups and more than fifty total birds summering in the Colington development area.

On the vacant lot adjoining the colonel's property was a large dead tree crowned with an elaborate, sprawling osprey nest. The colonel had long enjoyed the nest himself and now he proposed that members of the local society and visiting enthusiasts pool their efforts in order to closely observe the nest and its inhabitants from the time of their

The Second Coming

arrival, usually in mid-March, through the period when they rebuilt the nest, and from that time through mating and all its rituals, then brooding, and hopefully, if interest and support continued, through the raising of the chicks.

He had developed a schedule which would allow for continuous observation during the daylight hours. He proposed to outfit a spare bedroom in his house facing the nest with provisions and equipment to make it an efficient observation post and amateur laboratory, providing it with reference books, logs to record the comings and goings of the ospreys and other birds in the area, a telescope trained on the nest to view their behavior there, and field glasses for more mobile observation. He would also furnish the room with an ice box and coffee maker. He had corresponded with the National Audubon Society to see if there were any references he could use concerning similar projects in the past. From the information the colonel received he decided it was best to have observers work in teams of two for four hour periods. He ended by saying he hoped they would come and that he was looking forward to seeing them. He also asked that they present his proposal to their local group to see if there was any interest there.

Emma was impressed with the colonel's letter and filled with his enthusiasm. He had taken the time to write them personally, and because it was obvious he had put a lot of time and effort into developing the project, she felt honored. She showed the letter to Ben thinking automatically that he would share her enthusiasm. She was flabbergasted when he read it without reaction or comment, and then said they should wait a few weeks and think about it.

When Emma returned from church on Ash Wednesday evening a few days later, Ben was waiting for her. He told her that he had decided that they should go after all, and then said that he had invited James and Gert. Emma was tired and a little feverish again. It had been cold and damp in the church, and the service, though short, had been uninspiring. The priest had droned on monotonously and the congregation had coughed and shuffled its feet. Emma's legs and lower back ached as she went forward in the long line to receive the ashes on her forehead, and she had longed to go home so she could take some aspirin and go to bed. She was not happy with the news. She thought they should have discussed it before he invited them, and she told him so.

"Em, I didn't start out trying to invite them. The other night on the way to the meeting I mentioned we were thinking about it and Gert asked some questions and started getting excited about the idea. So I offhandedly said that maybe she and James might like to go. I didn't think it would go any further than that. You know James. I thought he'd scotch the idea and that would be that. But I'll be damned if she didn't talk him into it. And then I thought it might be nicer for you to have someone along besides me. You know she likes you, and you're the one who got her hooked on the birds."

Emma turned and left the room and went upstairs. She thought Ben would follow her, but he didn't. She went to the medicine cabinet and shook two aspirin out of the jar. She helped them down with a sip of tap water, and then went into the bedroom where she undressed and sat on the edge of the bed rubbing her tired legs. Why did he think she would like someone else to go along with them? He knew she didn't. Sometimes she thought there was something very far inside her like a star, and that its light is what animated her. Now she wondered if, like a star, it had gone out, but it was just so deep inside that the remnants of the light still shone, and that lagging light was all that was left of her life. She was angry at Ben, and she was angry because she didn't feel well and still she had dutifully gone to church and had been allowed to leave so uninspired. She looked at the photo on the dresser of Ben and her, and her children, and her

The Second Coming

childrens' children. She loved them, but still she was on the verge of thinking they weren't enough. She crawled under the covers and pulled them up tightly to her chin. Slowly her fingers relaxed and she fell asleep.

Ben had been right though. Gert was excited. She was over frequently in the next few days asking questions about the colonel and the area, and if there were other activities or sights to see. She seemed concerned about Emma's health and volunteered to help if Emma needed it. Emma noticed that when she expected Gert to say something critical and caustic, or make a sarcastic remark, that remark didn't come. But sometimes Emma saw that Gert had to make an almost conscious effort to hold her tongue, and Emma began to enjoy watching her struggle.

It was decided they would go down for two weeks, and they chose the weeks before and after Easter. Emma would have preferred to spend Easter at home, but it fell early, and they wanted to be there for the ospreys' arrival if they could, and the rebuilding of the nest. Emma and Ben also made tentative plans for another trip in late spring to try to catch the chicks' first attempts at flight. They decided to sign up for six shifts during their two-week stay, thinking that would give them enough time to make their observations worthwhile, and still allow them time to shop and walk on the beach. She told Gert that when she and James decided how many shifts they wanted to let her know so she could write the colonel and inform him of their plans.

The first day of March struggled to dawn with a loud and violent snowstorm. The wind blew wickedly, piling snow in high drifts. It was biting cold and everything stopped for a day or two. But the storm lost its punch quickly and by the weekend it was almost warm. The mantle of clouds opened and a soft breeze from the south stirred the tops of the empty trees. The snow melted into patches and then disappeared entirely, leaving a tight brown skin to cover the earth. In the mornings the ponds were crowned with mist and the first intrepid buds began to spring forth from the branches.

The colonel called that weekend to make sure they were coming. He told them that the storm had also come through the Carolinas with winds up to seventy five miles an hour. The ospreys' nest had been completely destroyed, but he was still confident they would return, and encouraged because he hoped it would give them the opportunity to witness the entire process of nest construction. Emma noticed that his voice was hoarse and at times his conversation was interrupted by a persistent hacking cough. He admitted edgily that he might have a touch of the flu, but that on the whole he was feeling better than he had in years.

One morning the next week, as Emma was at the kitchen sink doing the breakfast dishes, she saw Gert come out of her back door and through the gap in the hedges. She walked quickly and seemed to hop because of her limp. Her lips moved as if she was talking to herself.

"Emma, I'm so mad I could spit," she said when she came in. "I'm sorry. I wish I had your tranquil outlook on things. But that man," she said, waving in the direction of her house, "that man makes me so angry sometimes."

"What happened?"

"This morning, out of the blue, he told me he didn't know if he wanted to go. Well, I went right through the roof because he knows how badly I do want to go. And then, to calm me, I think, he said he wasn't backing out, but if we were going to Nags Head he didn't plan to spend his time sitting in a room watching birds roost. A friend of his told him the surf fishing was good, and he said he thought he'd like to try that. That man wouldn't know the front end of a fish from the back. But he pulled out a magazine he'd gotten from somewhere and started reading about a bluefish blitz or something."

"Don't worry, Gert," Emma said, wiping her hands on a dish towel. "I'm sure the colonel can line someone up

The Second Coming

for you. There are probably a lot of people without partners."

Ben came in from the den where he had spent the morning wrestling with the newspaper. "What's the matter in here?" he asked.

"Gert's just a little upset. James apparently isn't interested in our birds. Seems he'd rather be fishing."

"Yes, he mentioned something about it to me. The Outer Banks is a great place for it."

"But it means I don't have a partner."

"I'm sure we can take care of that," he said, nodding to Emma, who nodded back. "The colonel is usually prepared for any contingency. I'm sure he has a pool of talent to choose your partners from. As a matter of fact, we could always split up some of our shifts. The way you could work a couple of shifts with Em, and a couple with me, and you could probably get as many more as you wanted. Wouldn't that work, Em?"

Emma wanted to explode, but all she could do was nod. She always prided herself on her composure. She had learned that open anger never served her will. Where other people could get away with displays of temper, she knew it only made her look silly, like a spoiled child stamping her feet. She was much more likely to get her way by keeping a cool head and quietly manipulating the other players and events. Now though events were conspiring against her. She felt at a disadvantage because she had quite recovered her equilibrium since her illness. Not a week before she had shown her displeasure at Ben for making decisions without discussing them with her. And here he was, doing just that, smiling benevolently and offering a solution which she should have offered herself. But she knew that if she had been given a little time, and Ben had held his tongue, she could have worked things out differently.

She did not want to share Ben's attention with Gert or anyone else. He was hers now, a possession, and she needed to possess him on every level. She had shared him with his work, and shared him with their children, always waiting for this time they would have alone together. He had finished working, and the children were gone in body and understanding to a world she didn't want to know. In the bright, sunlit kitchen she realized that her heart was really very provincial in the scope of its desires.

She realized it again sitting in the car looking at the back of Ben's head. Perhaps she should trim those errant hairs. Of course she had nodded and smiled and agreed with them that morning. Ben had continued to smile blithely back at her, and Gert had called her a saint.

Now Ben switched off the ignition, and the four of them went to check into the motel.

III

Rob picked up 95 and headed north. He still had it in the back of his mind to go to Atlanta or New Orleans though he had only told Andy and John that to throw them off the track. He knew though he had to develop a plan and stick to it. If he allowed himself to be distracted he would end up hurting himself or someone else. Baltimore had been his first impulse, and it was the correct one. He knew with Chick's help he could make his money quickly and anonymously. The coke or money alone would be reason enough for Chick to do it. But Rob knew he would do it mainly to be able to say he did. It would be a way of insinuating himself into a position he wanted to be in, and for that reason he would be especially careful to make sure he succeeded. Rob knew the group that Chick lived on the fringe of, Italians mostly, caricatures with big cars and gold chains, dealing drugs for the easy profits. They tolerated Chick because he could turn a quarter pound for them, or do just about anything else they wanted him to. But the real reason they put up with him was the most obvious one, it was because of his reputation with women.

Rob didn't know anyone who really understood Chick's success with women, himself included. His looks were part of it, but their contribution didn't go nearly far enough to explain. He remembered going to parties with him in high school and the first year they were all in college. He and JP and Chick would enter a house together and Rob would watch Chick spend the first five minutes picking out a girl. She might not have the prettiest face or the best body, but she always had that something that all of the men wanted. He would catch her eye and find a way to whisper something to her to let her know he was interested. It didn't matter to him if she had come with someone else. He had no respect for relationships because he knew how fragile they were and why. If the girl had come with someone, after her date had left her to take a leak or something, she'd find herself out in Chick's car wondering why she was giving him a blow job. There were few preliminaries, no residue. Most likely, he wouldn't even talk to her the next time he saw her. He never went on many dates, but the phone used to ring off the hook for him. And more often than not he wouldn't be able to recognize who it was on the other end of the line by their voice alone.

Rob didn't understand it. To him it was just one of those things. But he remembered how much it used to bother JP, though JP never said anything about it. Rob knew that JP felt he had a lot more to offer than Chick in terms of sensitivity and understanding and respect, and Rob knew that he was right. But maybe women didn't want more. Maybe they felt safer within themselves offering and giving less. Women had always been mercenaries with their hearts, and now that they had gained so much they had to be careful not to sell off anything too cheaply. But because of that thinking they could sometimes give away what really didn't matter.

Rob sometimes wondered if people thought he was a misogynist. There was distrust, he would admit, but no hatred. There was a fear of the unfathomable and unimaginable depth, but there was nothing overt in any of his feelings. He thought and spoke of them the way he saw them. It didn't bother him if he didn't understand it, but it ate away at JP. JP would go on offering everything, and most women, even the soft-hearted ones, would take it and return no more than they would have given to Chick. There he went again.

It used to make Jane crazy too because of Jane's ideas about emotions. She thought emotion was the most important thing in life, and that life's quality was in direct proportion to what one felt, good or bad. Chick's attitude was an affront to that. He would not allow a woman to rise above the physical level. As long as it remained on that

The Second Coming

level he would give her anything. But at the first sign of an emotional attachment he would back off. Most knew to get away. But some, especially the younger ones, would try to stay on for the ride. Eventually, because of the rapid heating and cooling, something would crystallize in the solution. Rob thought it was probably just the raw desire, which was all Chick was after anyway. He also thought the brother and sister were more alike than Jane wanted to admit. He had seen that look in her eyes when she was numbing herself in one emotional sphere as a necessary prelude to putting herself on edge in another. He thought that what really bothered Jane most was the fear that if she had not been Chick Gandil's sister, she might have one night found herself in a cold car with her head buried in his lap.

There was a stinking ozone yellow in the night where the lightning lit the sky above Savannah, but it never rained. Rob knew a truck stop across the border in South Carolina, and he decided to wait until he got there to eat. Afterwards he could do a few lines to keep him awake until he made Raleigh around dawn. He spun the dial on the car radio, cocking his ear, trying to pick up some music, but nothing would hold.

Forty five minutes later he came upon the truck stop, its well-planned lighting throwing stark rays out at the scattering night. He parked amid the groaning exhalations of the diesel tractors and walked inside. After taking a leak in the cavernous antiseptic lavatory, he went into the coffee shop and took a stool at the counter. He still wasn't hungry, but he knew he had to eat. Something about the woman behind the counter reminded him of Jane. They both offered the same vulnerable cockiness in their smiles. He didn't smile back. He ordered the special, pork chops and butter beans and rice, and ate it quickly before the gravy could congeal on the plate. He kept his head down and his eyes on the food, ignoring the small knots of truckers sitting in the booths with their legs stretched out on the benches or their boots thrust into the aisles, carrying on subdued conversations beneath the brims of their feathered cowboy hats. When he finished he ordered a piece of chocolate pie from under the plastic dome. It was sweet and good, but old enough that the sugar had begun to crystallize on its surface. He paid with a twenty he had taken from Rios' coat. Typical, he thought as he walked across the parking lot. Only Rios would have that much coke and only one twenty dollar bill.

Rob had spent November and December in Aleuthra. He had saved five hundred dollars and he was sick of work, so he just went. There were only three good days of surf in the two months so he mostly swam and snorkeled and walked on the beach. He grew brown and lazy and began to siesta more and more in the shimmering heat of the afternoons. He camped next to an English couple for a while and got off on their music, most of which he hadn't heard before. But it got weird when the girl started finding ways to be alone with him and hinted that they should all sleep together. Then one night she got drunk and began to flirt openly with Rob and taunted her boyfriend with insults that, like the music, he hadn't heard before. So the next morning he packed up and moved into a shack in town. His money ran out after Christmas and he went back to Florida.

He hung out in Cocoa Beach for a while, but there was nothing going on so he went to Orlando and got a job pounding nails. He told himself it was only temporary, and he thought about saving money and going down to Mexico, or maybe lining up something on a shrimp boat down in the Keys.

Fucking Rios! Hate and loathing given a face, dark and oily, his hair fine and black as a crow's back. That first morning waking and gradually realizing where he was, being so inwardly shamed. He had looked up and seen that face and hollow smile, the tight cavern of that mocking mouth as it laughed at him, the memory of the night before coming

The Second Coming

back slowly and incompletely from somewhere behind his throbbing temples.

He had cashed his check and stayed all evening in that one place because it reminded him of a good northern bar. But then he had gotten too drunk, and the horrible ugly girl had teased him. He saw her full, taunting face too close to his and he remembered pushing her. Then there were other faces and voices, voices of Friday-night men trying to make themselves terrible with indignant rage, but really just looking for an easy target. He felt the pressure of their blows, but no real pain. He sat like an animal in the corner when it was over, and then there were uniforms and more blows. In the morning his ribs ached and his back was bruised near his kidneys.

"You look terrible, man. They beat the shit out of you, eh? I almost had to put a pillow over your face last night you made so much noise crying and whimpering in your sleep. Why did they have to put you in here?"

Rob was silent in front of the magistrate. He decided not to call anyone so he was in until the following Thursday. The judge gave him ninety days minus the six he had already served. It turned out that the ugly girl was connected with the owner of the bar, and they had both shown up anxious for justice. When he looked at her after the judge called him to the stand she sat forward gripping the back of the bench in front of her, wearing a look of victimized indignity. Rob wondered what he had said to her. One of the arresting officers described the scene, pointed him out formally, and apologetically explained the necessity of the use of force. Rob's ribs still hurt after a week, but at least there was no more blood in his urine.

He didn't care what any of them said. He knew after the sentence he would get a private cell. He would get away from Rios and ignore everyone else until they let him out.

It would give him a chance to calm himself and make some long range plans. He had always wanted to live out west. What was the name of that girl in New Mexico? It was biblical, Rebecca or Rachel...Sarah, that was it. She was quiet and sweet and always, always stoned, living in an enclave of old hippies in a commune in the hills outside Albuquerque. They lived on the cusp, eating cleanly and simply, polishing their turquoise jewelry. Before meeting them, when he thought of the southwest, he imagined dun villages carved into the cliffs, populated by Indians with flat faces and somber eyes, worshipping the sun of the summer solstice, patiently hammering away at pieces of silver ore.

This hippie group was wary of strangers, but they fed Rob and shared their weed and gave him a corner of the loft to sleep in. They preached a kind of soppy, diluted Buddhism, but not with much conviction. The Age of Aquarius had long passed, so he guessed that explained their Piscean indecision. They were clearly on the defensive. Most of them were reactionary in their resistance to change, which was odd considering their origins. The men had become strident and womanish, twirling their silver-gray ponytails as if wondering if they should cut them off. There were only a few children, and they wandered around dirty and unkempt, ignored.

Sarah, with her long straw-colored hair and sweeping skirt, had been warm and pliant, like a geisha. But he knew it wouldn't work now. If he did return, he doubted he would find anything more than their fossilized remains. But something in him cried out for a change. And maybe all he needed was a change of humidity after all. It seemed his soul was like a desert already, empty of life now, but the aridity preserved well what had once been there.

After the judge sentenced him he was taken back to the same cell.

"Man, I thought I was rid of you," Rios said disgustedly when he came in from the yard and found Rob there again. "You know, I'm worried you're some kind of closet faggot. And because we live in this closet, I'm afraid

The Second Coming

you might try to come out."

"Shut up, Rios."

"Look, man, I'm just telling you my fears, alright? I'm not long for this place, and I want to get out with my cherry intact."

Rob turned on his bunk and faced the wall, but he couldn't get rid of the image of Rios' face, with its cocked eyebrow and cynical smile, its shoddy machismo.

"My cousins, they're coming to get me. They got bucks, man. They're out of the country now, you know what I mean? But they're coming. They'll drop the money for my bond and I'll be history. We're family, man, and because we're family, the money ain't nothing to them. They can use me and they know it. I know my way around the business, you know?"

"I'm not interested, Rios."

"Hey, besa mi culo, man! Why are you going to sit in here? Are you stupid? You act like you don't have anyone to call. But it is just your pride. You can't ask for no money because you're afraid, right? But maybe it's not fear or pride. Your skin is white. Maybe your blood is white too. You won't bleed for anybody and nobody will bleed for you, right? But maybe I can help you."

"Look, Rios, I don't want your help."

"Ah, there is that pride again. But don't pretend with me. There is nothing in your life, no vessel, which can hold your pride without it leaking out like piss down your pant leg. Tell me what you have to be proud of."

He grabbed one of his snatch magazines and lay on his bunk. He wasn't waiting for an answer. Rob could tell he was angry by the way he flipped through the pages and muttered under his breath.

Rios' cousins didn't come for him before his court date, but he didn't seem to worry. He had arranged with his lawyer to get a continuance. He dressed carefully that morning. He wore a suit with a silk shirt and tie, and snakeskin boots. His clothes gave him an air of dignity which somehow shabbily fit him as if he were some shilpit Don petitioning the Crown for a lost title. He came back that afternoon grinning and full of praise for the American system.

    Rob found less and less time to plan, or even to daydream, because Rios never shut up. He was a social creature from the underbelly of society. He required forms and rituals. He loved to talk about his family and the greatness of its ancient members, their names rolling in interminable syllables off his tongue. He claimed they had preserved their pure Spanish heritage for hundreds of years in Nicaragua. But Rob thought he saw a blunt softening of the aquiline nose and an underlayer of ruddiness to his skin that belied that fact. He would become winsome when he spoke of Nicaragua, and then angry, but he always spoke of it with a glistening in his maddeningly steady eyes.

    "It is a beautiful place. I know you think it is just talk, but we have a business, my family, and it is very profitable. We have warehouse and planes, three, until one went down in Panama. Adios, Raoul y Juan," he said, making the sign of the cross. "Somoza was not so bad. At least he admired enterprise. We could fly to La Paz or Colombia, and then back to Managua. He wasn't too greedy. But then those fucking Sandinistas! They threw us out…until they could decide which officials they wanted us to bribe. You see, they liked the idea of poisoning the minds of the American youth. But they were still fucking bureaucrats, and with their fucking economy. But it's back to normal now."

    "I'm not interested, Rios."

    "Well, I'm going to talk anyway, Wheat. What kind of name is that anyway? Look at you, man. You have nothing, no one. No phone calls, no visitors. I can see it. Looking serious all the time, staring at the walls or the ceiling, pretending to think, to plan. But you have no plan.

The Second Coming

All you have is guilt. You see, I know about your daughter, and I'll tell you. Your guilt is just bullshit to me. It is just cowardice because you are afraid to go on."

Rios was pacing, glancing around recklessly, speaking to Rob and himself and the stillness. When Rob caught his profile, it was liquid in the hesitant light. His fine black hair was wet and matted against his forehead.

"Listen to me, Wheat," he said, stopping in the center of the cell. "I can help you, and I will. Don't kid yourself. You are nothing to me, but I want to give you a lift anyway. My cousins are here, and my brother, Tomas. They will come for me tomorrow. I will give you an address. When you get out, come, and I will help you. You hate to think it, but I can help you. Now you just want to hide your head. Your pride and your guilt, they are the same things. They come from the same place. You're dying, man, drying up and dying."

Rob said nothing and Rios shook his head, lay down on his bunk, and began to sing softly in Spanish.

Why were there some things that the memory retained so clearly, while others, some of them probably just as important, drifted into the mist? Driving now he could still see the silhouette of Rios' recumbent form and hear the faint suggestion of a lisp as he sang.

Rob was just leaving South Carolina. He pulled into a rest stop and did a couple of lines. His head was packed with the stuff. He felt the pressure of it behind his eyes. It was way too late to buy beer. Instead he bought a half gallon of orange juice from a buck-toothed girl waiting to be robbed at an all-night convenience store, and pulled on it as he drove north.

Rios was released the next morning. He was called away after breakfast and didn't return. He didn't say goodbye. After he was gone Rob found a small piece of paper with an address written on it on the table between their bunks.

Rob had exercised steadily since he'd been in jail, sit-ups and push-ups in the cell, a little weight lifting in the day room, and some jogging in the yard. But now he stopped. He tried to make himself read. The jail didn't have a library, but it did have boxes of donated books. If you wanted to read they would bring you one of the boxes and let you choose from it. A lot of the books had inscriptions and dates written on the title page, and he would think about who had written the inscription and who they were writing it to, and he rarely got past that point in any of the books. He couldn't find anything to hold his interest. He went less frequently to the dayroom or outside, preferring the solitude. Outwardly he became more relaxed because he was at peace with himself in the cell, and the others noticed.

"I bet you were glad to get rid of 'la boca grande' Rios."

"Yes."

"That pervert, you can bet he'll forfeit his bond."

"What are you talking about? He told me he was in here for writing bad checks."

"No, man. They caught him dicking a ten year old girl, and he was proud of it. He claimed it was her idea."

That evening Rob stood watching the sky through the grated window in his cell. Mars was red above a crescent moon, and both sank slowly into the neutral pink of the dying sunset. It came upon him slowly. It didn't rush to him. The rage welled up and broke over him like a wave. He looked out the window wishing only to be able to reach up and crush the horns of the new moon. He spun around, expecting to see Rios on his bunk, but he was alone. He stood in the room listening for something as it grew dark.

He went before the magistrate on the third Monday of March, and they released him on Tuesday, the last full day of winter. After he signed his release forms they gave him a brown manila envelope containing his watch, which was broken, and his wallet, which to his surprise held more than

The Second Coming

a hundred and fifty dollars. He knew he had cashed his check that Friday, but he hadn't been able to remember if he had any money when they arrested him. When he questioned them as to how his watch was broken, they showed him the form he had signed in an almost unrecognizable script stating that the watch was already broken when they processed him. He dropped it into the waste basket on the way out.

When he was outside the gate waiting at the bus stop he took Rios' crumpled address from his pocket and put it in his wallet. He went into Orlando and checked into a downtown hotel. After a shave and a shower, he went out for a drink.

IV

Mary didn't want to go to the mountains. It was the first thing she thought when she woke up. She wanted to see the ocean and feel the warmth of the sun and remind herself that summer would follow the lingering winter and tardy spring. She didn't want to take the chance with the altitude that she might see snow again. She didn't want to go to the mountains, and now she didn't have to.

Tony had just left. She was tired of him making himself so at home. She still liked to sleep alone sometimes, but now she rarely did unless she purposely stayed in bed after he left. She didn't have enough time to herself. He was always too close now. Even as they slept he crowded her, pushing her to the edge of the bed and holding her there. She couldn't be mysterious and pretend she had other lovers because he was around so much he knew she didn't. He paid rent for his own apartment, but now it seemed he only went there for a change of clothes or to pick up his mail. Her roommates hadn't said anything yet, but they wanted to.

She had shared a peculiar equilibrium with them. Their emotional relationship was like a colloidal suspension, with their individual needs and contributions floating in the fluid medium of their household. But now Tony had oversaturated the solution. It had taken the three girls months to get their timing down, in the bathroom and the kitchen, and their signals set for when they didn't want to be disturbed, or when they did. It had taken Tony only since Christmas to destroy it. Not only did he monopolize most of Mary's time, but now he had begun to blunder into Cindy and Dianne's lives, kidding them about their boyfriends and making off-color comments about their sex lives. It was all harmless and fraternal, but it was wearing thin. Dianne was never one to hold her tongue and lately Mary had seen her getting that

The Second Coming

look in her eyes.

Mary didn't get out of bed. She stretched and spread her arms and legs across the width of the double bed enjoying the touch of the cool sheets on her skin. She had a nine o'clock class, but she had already decided to blow it off. After all, it was the last day of class before the Easter recess. It wasn't going to make or break her.

It was Tony's idea to go to the mountains. He wanted to drive along the Blue Ridge Parkway and watch spring bursting into bloom, and then go white water rafting in the swollen streams. No thank you! She had made that mistake once already. The water was icy, it never stopped raining, and there was a layer of mud on everything, herself included. She was surrounded by macho, bearded pseudo-mountain men who openly leered at her and spoke in a jargon that might has well have been a foreign language. At least they had a motel room to escape to last time, but Tony had in mind to camp this trip.

Until yesterday she had been resigned to going, but then she had been given an option. In February her biology instructor had asked for volunteers to go to the Outer Banks to take part in an experiment that had something to do with watching birds. It sounded dull and she hadn't paid much attention. Apparently no one else had either. The instructor brought it up half-heartedly a few more times during the term, and Mary thought wryly that he managed to make it sound duller than it probably was.

He was an odd one, Mr. Richardson. He was probably only thirty or so, but he already seemed bored to death with his work, and he was completely unsuccessful at hiding it. He covered the material quickly and superficially and left it to the initiative of his students to dig any deeper. Most of the time he was egotistically self-deprecating and cynical, but then suddenly he could be alarmingly touched by the wonder of some natural phenomenon. All in all, he didn't seem much like the usual scientific type. She thought he would be more comfortable with poetry than with logarithms or the Krebs' cycle.

Most of the girls liked him and he played on it. Mary noticed the halting winsome look he had for them, herself included, which had probably been effective in its day, but seemed a bit washed out and unconvincing now. She had heard that he could sometimes be found at one or another of the student hangouts, insinuating himself into the group by no more overt device than his presence. He would sit alone and wait for the attention to come to him. But he could be quite voluble and entertaining once it did. She still didn't know quite what to make of him.

In class the day before, Mr. Richardson had made an announcement. It seemed that the school had come up with funds to provide room and board for any volunteers for the observations. He explained that the responsibilities would not be too demanding, and there would be plenty of time to sample the beach and the night life. The department was leaning on him to supply some student participation, he said, and though there had only been short notice of the new financial conditions, he hoped that some of them had been considering the possibility even before they became known. Mary volunteered after class.

"Good," he said. "Now, counting me, that makes two. Do you need transportation?"

"No, Mr. Richardson, I have my own car."

"Call me JP," he said smiling, "and it doesn't stand for anything, if you're wondering. The observations should be fairly straightforward. All I need is a commitment for four hours a day. Some of the time will be spent on the observations themselves, and depending on the number of volunteers, there may be some organizational work involved, but nothing too strenuous. We'll be inside so you won't have to worry about the elements. Are you familiar with ospreys?"

"Not really. I thought I'd run over to the library this

The Second Coming

afternoon and see what I can find out."

"It couldn't hurt. Let's see, is there anything else? Here's the name and address of the motel. I'll leave your name at the desk so they'll have a room for you. There will be a meeting Saturday morning at eleven at the motel, so I guess I'll see you then."

Tony would just have to understand. But he had left so early she would have to leave a note explaining everything to him. After all, she was in school for an education, she thought, and it made her guilty. Jumping out of bed, she picked up her towel from the arm of the chair and ran into the bathroom. She caught a glimpse of her reflection as she ran past the mirror and couldn't help being pleased with her young nude form. She turned on the water in the shower. She could just make her class if she hurried.

V

JP lived in an old residential neighborhood on a street below the university. It was a warm morning when Rob got there. The azaleas and dogwoods were in full bloom and the wisteria climbed the trees, their purple flowers dangling heavily with nectar like ripe bunches of grapes. Buds were opening on tree branches like the green stalked eyes of crabs. The earth smelled dark and sweet and heavy, and the birds knew it and sang. Rob passed an old woman already working in her yard, wearing a straw hat tied under her chin with a scarf. She walked brittlely, carrying a little spade in her hand, and where she stabbed the earth it bled anemones.

JP's house sat back from the street behind a row of poplar trees that looked like they could have come out of one of Dali's early androgynous nightmares. There was a cool dark porch in front of the house with heavy, old-fashioned lawn furniture. Rob got out of the car and stretched. He went up the brick path and sat in one of the old rocking chairs on the porch and breathed the cool moist air.

He hadn't seen JP in three years. They had an old and easy friendship that flowed beneath the surface of events like an aquifer. It was based on remembered adolescent images of each other, though sometimes now the images seemed cartoonish in their simplicity. They didn't see each other often any more. When they did, their visits would usually culminate in a drinking frenzy filled with sentimental pinings for the dreams and ambitions of a fugitive past. He had been surprised to learn that JP had taken the job at State because JP had always adamantly maintained the he was on the Outer Banks to stay to anyone who would listen. Then he would go on to give his theory of why people who lived at the beach were different.

Rob sat for an hour, alternately nodding out and taking in the bright morning until he heard sounds from

The Second Coming

inside the house. He stood and knocked at the door.
"Rob?"
"Yeah, man."
"You're looking older."
"I am older. We all are. How are you, JP?"
"Good," he said, holding open the door. "Come in."

It was dark inside and smelled of old carpet and pine oil. The furniture was heavy, dark. JP had hung some framed prints on the wall. Rob immediately recognized Kandinsky and Klee. They were brilliant, vibrant, and intellectually inaccessible. He considered what a long discussion that would have provoked when they were in school. It would have started with a question of artistic responsibility. Must an artist appeal to the emotions or the intellect, or both? And if it were decided he must appeal to the intellect alone, must his work be universally reducible on that level? From there they would have probably jumped to ethics. Should an act be universally, morally reducible? All acts? They would have called up the ghosts of Napoleon and Raskalnikov, and would have ended up going to bed drunk and agitated because JP always had one more point he desperately needed to make.

"Help yourself," JP said, when he noticed Rob looking at the fruit bowl on the table. "An apple...anything. If you don't eat it, no one will." He knelt down and flipped through his CDs.

Rob took a grape from the bunch and popped it into his mouth. The skin was tight and dry and tasted like dirt. The fruit was tart as he chewed, but when he swallowed his mouth was still left with the taste of dirt. He didn't recognize the CD JP played.

"What are you doing in Raleigh?"
"Traveling," he said, plucking another grape, "business. I'm on my way to Baltimore to see Chick, and I thought I'd drop in on you."

"Chick isn't in Baltimore," JP said, adjusting the

volume knob. "Jane told me on the phone the other night. He's on the Outer Banks. Apparently he had some trouble up there, so he left. I'm not surprised. Did you ever meet any of the group he was hanging out with? They were too heavy for me. He's fishing right now, but Jane says he has some big plans in the works. You know Chick."

Chick was on the Outer Banks.

"When was the last time you talked to Jane? I think the real reason she called was to find out if I'd heard from you. She asked a lot of questions, and we had a long talk about a lot of different things. She said she'd heard a lot of contradictory rumors about where you were and what you'd been doing, but she hadn't heard anything concrete. We also talked about Kelly. I think she's worried that Kelly is growing up too fast. You want some breakfast?"

"No, I ate on the road last night."

"Look, Rob, I'm going to Nags Head this afternoon. Why don't you drive down with me? It would be a good chance to see Kelly, and get things straight with Jane. And Chick is there. Think about it. I have a couple of classes this morning, and a lab this afternoon, but I'm going to try to leave by four o'clock. Why don't you sleep on it. You look like hell, you know."

"Maybe I will come with you. The weather's pretty enough. And you're right, I could use some sleep. Wake me when you get back and we'll talk."

"There are clean sheets on the bed in the front room. Just make yourself at home."

Rob realized how tired he was when he went out to the car for his bags. He was also jittery, but he didn't know if it was from the coke or the driving. The brightness of the climbing sun stung his eyes.

He had hoped to make his money in Baltimore where he wasn't known. He had wanted to send Jane enough money to take care of Kelly for a couple of years at least. Now he didn't know what to do. Chick was the only person

The Second Coming

he knew who had the connections to deal with the amount of coke he had. He was sick of thinking about it. He went into the front room and dropped heavily on the bed. He wondered what kind of trouble Chick had gotten into in Baltimore. He heard JP moving around in the kitchen, and he heard the drone of the shower through the wall, and later the final slam of the front door when JP left to walk to the university. It was quiet then except for the birds outside, a little traffic, and his heart beating much too quickly. It took a while, but he was finally able to sleep.

He awoke at noon feeling much better. He went into the bathroom and undressed and stood under the shower, washing himself and rinsing the road grime away, and finally lying in the bottom of the tub under the steaming pounding water, cleansing and emptying himself. He thought about masturbating, but he knew he couldn't get it up. After he dried himself and combed his hair, he dressed in some rumpled clothes from his bag. In the kitchen he made himself an omelet filled with vegetables and cheese and ate it with a glass of his warm orange juice.

For the first time in months he felt comfortable and safe. It had something to do with the driving of the last two nights. The darkness and the fact that he had been alone had been part of it. But something else had given him an almost mythological feeling of rebirth. The shower had cleansed him of the feral memories of the last months, and the meal had completed the sacrament. He knew he was going to the beach, but suddenly none of it seemed important, not the coke or the money, not even going out west. The nights of driving had removed him from the danger. They wouldn't catch him now. They couldn't. He wandered around the house. It was clean and dusted, and all the plants were healthy. There was almost something effeminate to it. If he hadn't known JP so well he would have wondered about him.

JP walked in at one thirty. "I cancelled my one

o'clock lab," he said. "I have a lot to do to get ready, and none of them would have been interested anyway. So are you coming or not? Everyone's been wondering how you are. Here's your chance to show them in the flesh."

"I'm coming," Rob said. He knew he could trust JP, and it would probably take the two of them to control Chick. "You want to do a couple of lines?"

"Sure."

JP pulled a picture off the wall and Rob drew out his bag and blade. He fluffed and chopped and carved until he had drawn four generous lines on the glass.

"Where did you get this from?" JP asked, picking up the bag and looking at it closely.

"Florida. I have some I need to get rid of, and I was hoping Chick could help me out."

"He'll know what's going on down there if anyone does," JP said as he leaned over the first line. "Clean," he whispered, pinching his nostril.

Rob smiled at the studied nonchalance. Everyone worked it. He traced his first line with the straw, watching it disappear and then tapped the straw against the glass. "Go ahead," he said, pointing to the remaining lines. "I need a break from this stuff."

"What a kick. What's it cut with?"

"Nothing, that I know of. That's another thing I need Chick's help with. I don't want to ruin it, but I want to stretch it as far as it will go."

They spent the next hour talking while JP packed. Both had a good buzz. JP explained why he was going to the beach, telling Rob a little about the ospreys. But he didn't think he would be interested so there was no life in his voice.

Rob had never understood why JP had made the switch from English and History to Biology. It wasn't that he had more aptitude for one than the other, but it was obvious where his enthusiasm lay. Rob had been pleased

The Second Coming

when it happened though. He had become so uncomfortable with JP's over the top emotionalism that he was happy for any relief.

Rob knew though that JP had a way with words and a real feeling for history. He had the ability to reduce information to its essence. He was able to recognize and describe the patterns that lay beneath the building and destruction of social systems. He could weigh the contributions of historical events and personalities in the development of art and religion and society. One minute he could be quoting de Toqueville or Spengler, and from them he could float effortlessly to the psychology of Eliade Mirdea or the social commentary of Jonathon Swift. He would have been comfortable in a salon, subsidized by some cultivating feminine patronage. He needed that kind of faith and encouragement, and the opportunity to form his ideas at ease and at leisure. He was one of those intellectual types who worked better at a slow relaxed pace, knowing there was someone compassionate near at hand to second and approve his efforts. He hadn't faith enough in his own merits to produce under the pressure of deadlines. Of course, that attitude was not destined to get him very far in life. He was a dreamer with a shifting cache of dreams, who pretended that he could only realize them through the circuitous and arbitrary machinations of his unconscious. Rob wondered what condition his dreams were in now.

They were ready to leave by three. They had planned to take two cars, but then JP decided to ride with Rob in the Mustang, saying he could get a ride back with friends. They were mostly silent the first hour, both of them wound up by the drug. But after they stopped and bought beer and drank a few they began to loosen up.

"Do you still write?" Rob asked as they were approaching Williamston.

"I haven't written anything on paper lately. I know all the impetus is there, and I think about it all the time, but I find it easier to write in the summer when I don't have the pressures and distractions of school. I'm not lacking for inspiration though. A lot has happened in the last couple of years, but I haven't quite made the step of committing any of it to paper. Sometimes I feel the way Coleridge described himself, 'indolence capable of energies,' not that I'm comparing our talents. Somehow the time just isn't right yet." He laughed. "That even sounds like BS to me, but it's not. Can I tell you a story?"

"Sure. It's a long drive."

"It's a long story too. Before I start I want to preface it by saying that I am capable of viewing it objectively now, although I couldn't initially.

"It begins a couple of years ago. I was still in Nags Head then, basically spinning my wheels, drinking too much, talking too much. For a year or so my emotional life had been pretty barren. I would hit on the coeds who came to the beach for a tan or for the summer, but most of them were so vacant and easy that I had just about lost interest. You know how I am. I have to make something epic out of a relationship, even if it's only for one night.

"One night in a bar I noticed this woman. First of all, she looked to be about my age, which was an immediate attraction after the college girls I'd been spending my time with. I'd seen her around and thought she must be married. I just assumed she wasn't available. But I asked around and found out that she had been married, but her marriage had been an on-again off-again thing until her husband had killed himself the year before. Somehow that knowledge became the nexus for some compassionate synapse in me. Unconsciously, it was the fact of his death, more than anything else, that made me decide to meet her.

"It took a couple of days to work up the nerve to call her, but I finally did. To break the ice, I asked if she had a boyfriend, and she laughed over the phone and said, 'Not on this coast.' We were immediately at ease with each other.

The Second Coming

We made a date for dinner and had a great time. The moon and stars cooperated, and she was attractive and lively and open. We talked about a lot of different things that night, and one thing about her stood out very clearly in my mind. It was the determined attitude she had not to let herself take anything too seriously. She wasn't going to let herself be bothered by anything petty or inconsequential. Is this boring you?"

"Not yet," Rob said. "Go on."

He did. What followed was a lengthy indictment against himself. It was the story of a trap only he could have fallen into. He spoke of a relationship based on sex and pseudo-intellectualism, and the clutching greed of his neurotic libido. It had all the elements of drama; suicide, lust, love maybe, abortion. But the carefully proscribed limits of JP's paltry soul, and his wretched acknowledgement of them, were almost physically sickening to Rob.

"We traveled, went down to Charleston once, and up to DC for the museums and plays. I'll never forget one room on the second floor of the National Gallery. It was only twenty feet square, but it was hung with some of the most beautiful impressionist paintings I had ever seen. On one wall was one of Rousseau's jungle scenes, on another was a stippled Van Gogh, on another five or six Renoir's and Monet's side by side, and on the last wall was a Seurat and a Gauguin. I was overwhelmed. I've wondered since then why I was so affected by that room, and you need to understand its impact on me. I think that 'room full of impressions' was a good corollary to the state of my unconscious mind at the time. I wasn't seeing things with anything like photographic realism or clarity, because I didn't want to. I wasn't seeing Leslie, that was her name, with the studied dark realism of a Rembrandt, or even through the slightly elongated gaze of a David. I wasn't content with just adding an extra vertebra to her reclining torso. I wanted to paint her as Monet would have, in a landscape with flowers not too real, and with features soft, but not too plainly distinguishable. I thought there was some kind of magic to what was happening between us, and I wanted her to fulfill what that magic required of her. I know this had to bore you. Anyway, when I look back on it, there was one moment in that room that was the highlight."

Rob looked sidelong at him. Much of what he went on to describe had to do with their sexual adventures. Unbelievably, they hadn't used any kind of birth control.

"One night she told me she thought she was pregnant. The next morning we bought one of those home pregnancy tests. The result was that she was pregnant. I was afraid, but I was also happy. The woman I loved was carrying my child. Her response was a sarcastic, 'That's just great.' She wanted to know what I thought we should do. But just by the way she asked I knew she was going to attack no matter how I answered. I was ready to commit to anything, but I ended up giving some non-committal answer about respecting the sanctity of a woman's body. I told her I loved her and would be supportive no matter what she decided to do. I didn't know what else to say.

"We had discussed abortion before, and I told her I thought it was wrong. I now think that a man can't be more chauvinistic about anything than he can in his opinions about abortion. It is something completely beyond our domain. It's easy to have an opinion one way or another, but we can never experience that frightening potential for beauty and sorrow and pain growing within us. Are you listening, Rob?"

Yes, he was listening.

"Her determination not to let little things bother her disappeared. She started having various physical complaints, colds and coughs, and she began to have trouble sleeping at night. But when I tried to calm her, she would become hard and belligerent. Her husband started to make his presence felt. She would become upset and say I couldn't love her like he did. No one could. She told me I didn't know what it was like to deal with the guilt of that kind of death, wondering if you were at fault, or if you could have done something to change it.

"She told me I didn't understand death at all. I had to admit that no one close to me had died, but I always thought that some understanding of death was inherent in the human condition. After all, we weren't so far removed from our precursors who walked with death every day. I believed that every parting was a death or a rehearsal for death in some sense. She said that that kind of philosophical bullshit just proved how right she was.

"It finally came to a head. I knew it would. She had talked to her west coast boyfriend on the phone periodically. I never worried about it. Now he came to visit his parents in DC. She went to him. We'd been living together, and I never considered that she wouldn't come back. After a few days, she did…to get her things.

"I watched her park in front of my house late the next afternoon. Where nothing that had happened had been able to convince me it was over, the way she got out of the car, just that one action, and I knew it was. She came in and hugged me, and smiled a smile that went from her hairline to her chin. But when it dissolved the look on her face was made of the impregnable steel of contrition. At that moment I got my strongest impression that you can't share a person's sorrow. Maybe I thought I could understand death, but she couldn't allow me to understand her sorrow.

"The next day was a concentrated lesson in the imprecise laws of the science of mortality. She had gone for the abortion. She wasn't coming back. I don't know why I thought the things I did that day, or remembered what I did. The thoughts and the memories were both inconsequential and disconnected. I guess they were a defense to keep my mind out of the present. She called me in the evening. It had been a long day, and there were complications, as I knew there had to be. She tried to explain things over the phone, but none of it registered. It was over.

"I heard from her a couple of days later. She and her boyfriend were in Mississippi on their way across country. She was sick. Five weeks later I got a short collect phone call. Three months later someone told me they were married.

"I had to make sense out of everything. The more I thought about it, the more I realized I needed to explain to her and to myself that I did understand death. I hadn't written anything in a while, but the germ of a story began to grow in me.

"I know you, Rob, and I know what you're probably thinking. Some wiggy cunt gives him the bum's rush and all he can think to do is try to turn it into poetry. Maybe you're right. Anyway, I began writing again. I ended up with a short story that had essentially written itself. I tried to be as honest with myself as possible, and develop my feelings about death as far as I could, and when I finished I was satisfied, too satisfied.

"Two weeks after I finished it my father died. What I had written in no way covered how I felt when he died, because I didn't feel it in any of the forms I anticipated I would. I didn't feel much of anything. I thought about what Thomas Wolfe had written about 'the great silence between father and son, which goes beyond motherhood, beyond death,' but somehow that didn't cover my ambivalence. I thought some more about my father, who hadn't lived well, and about Leslie, and about her husband who hadn't wanted to live, and I thought about the unborn child who never had a choice, and they all began to seem less and less real to me. They were all just ciphers. They weren't individuals. They didn't have souls or thoughts or motives of their own. They only lived through me. I don't know…good story, eh?"

"Yes, why don't you write it?"

The Second Coming

"I can't."

They were driving through the woods east of Columbia. The road was lined with the oaks and pine trees of the Union Camp forest. Just within the border of the trees were wild dogwoods in full bloom, shivering in the night breeze, looking, in the young moonlight, like virginal brides with tiny white uplifted hands. Occasionally and vaguely they smelled smoke. On the car radio they heard that the trees in the forest not far from the road were burning.

JP told Rob that it hadn't rained in eastern North Carolina for months. Somehow a fire had started. It burned the trees above the marshy ground and they fell, crossing like fingers above the earth's dark mounded belly. After they controlled the fire above ground it reached down to the roots and the layers of peat below. Now it burned slowly and monotonously underground, burned like love in the womb of a simple woman. Rob didn't guess there were any more simple women. He had never known any. But he protected himself. He looked at JP. JP was another story. The wife of a suicide, that was typical. JP was always attracted to women who were essentially flawed. There was a hidden silent challenge in any of his women. You could see it in their eyes. He couldn't. The attractions were always spontaneous and irresistible, but Rob knew it wasn't just at the urge of some latent masochism that JP sought these women or they sought him.

They drove on in silence. In another hour they were checking into the motel. Rob needed sleep. His eyes stung and his muscles burned. But before he went to the room he borrowed ten dollars from JP, went into the motel gift shop, and bought a big stuffed bird for Kelly.

VI

The beach at Nags Head was different than Gert thought it would be. Unaccountably she had imagined it would be similar to the shingled beaches of New England. She thought that she would be high above the ocean watching the waves breaking against the cliffs, and she pictured large smooth stones squatting in the shore break. She was a little embarrassed at herself. There were no cliffs to be seen anywhere, nor were there any rocks. It was just as Emma had described it. Gert found herself on a slowly shifting barrier island, a thin finger thrust out into the belly of the Atlantic Ocean. The beaches sloped gently to the ocean, and the sand was a neutral drab dun color.

After they settled into their room and had a light dinner with Ben and Emma, she and James went for a walk. He was anxious to see if there were any fishermen on the beach, to see what kind of equipment they were using, and what kinds of fish, if any, they were catching. As soon as they were over the dune line he spotted a couple fishing fifty yards down the beach, a man and woman holding their rods high, looking out past the breakers. James walked on ahead of her, kicking up plumes of sand. Gert was in no hurry. Evening was coming on and the shadows were lengthening, but it was still deliciously warm, and winter already seemed just a distant memory.

She saw two crows hopping in the dunes among the dancing sea oats, and tried to think what she knew about them. They were so large they must be ravens, she thought. Another flew down and joined them. She had read somewhere that it was unlucky to see them in odd numbers, but she couldn't remember why. What else did she know about them? She scoured her mind for information. Two crows had originally been the companions of Apollo, but they and all their kin had been condemned to be thirsty in the

The Second Coming

summer because one had taken too long to fetch him water. There was another version, it was German she thought, that said they were condemned to thirst because they were the only animals not to weep at the crucifixion of Christ. Another legend held that it was because a raven had failed to return to the ark to tell Noah it had found land. The ancient Greeks had thought that a raven's egg could restore blackness to graying hair. But you had to be careful and keep your mouth full of oil as you applied the eggs to your locks, or your teeth might turn permanently black as well.

When she caught up with James she found him and the fisherman leaning over the man's bucket. The woman cast her weighted rig out and stood with her back to them, staring out at the blue gray expanse.

"Look, Gert, he has a gray trout and a couple of small bluefish."

"Those are called taylor blues, the small ones," the man said. "Although it won't be long before the choppers get here. It's just a matter of the water temperature."

"What is a chopper?" Gert asked.

The man looked disgusted. "A chopper is a big bluefish, ten or twelve pounds, or more. This time of year the blues are migrating up the coast. When the water temperature gets near sixty degrees the choppers start blitzing the beach. They'll eat anything. I've seen trout swim right up on the sand to get away from them. Some years you can stand in the shore break with a gaff and fling up enough fish on the beach to fill your cooler, and your neighbor's too."

"I've heard they put up a good fight," James said.

"Yes sir, those things are mean as hell. They'll straighten out your hooks and tear up your leaders, and I've broken more than one knife trying to get my tackle out of their mouths. These little ones, they're good eating, but the big ones ain't worth a damn...just catch 'em, and throw 'em back."

"How long is your rod?" James asked.

"Nine feet. You need the length to get your stuff to the holes out there past the shore break."

James and the man talked some more about tackle and bait and Gert lost interest. When it became obvious that the woman didn't have anything to say to her, she walked further down the beach. She kept within the littoral zone where she could bend over to examine bits of shell or clumps of seaweed. She found some black pods she thought were skate eggs, but she wasn't sure. The ocean turned a deeper blue with each passing moment, and the lulling sound of the waves breaking was a gentle cathartic. Eventually she became aware of James' voice far behind her. She hadn't realized she'd walked so far. He was still with the fisherman a hundred yards behind, waving his arms to call her back. She couldn't see either of their faces, but she had the feeling they shared some mutual impatience toward her. She waved back at them, and signaled for James to go back by himself. Then, before he had a chance to answer, she continued on her way down the beach, quickly falling back into her reverie.

The sky was a lovely violet by the time she got back to the motel, and the stars were just beginning their slow, steady promenade. The lounge crowd from the bar upstairs had spilled out on the deck because it was so warm and inviting. She heard many young voices, college kids she realized, out of school for their Easter break. When she got back to the room James was sitting at the desk making a list for the tackle shop. There was a shiny copy of "Salt Water Fisherman" on the bed. He barely acknowledged her entrance so she pulled her nightgown from the suitcase and went into the bathroom to get ready for bed. She tried to read in bed, but nothing held her interest so she crawled under the covers and quickly fell asleep.

She awoke early the next morning, excited that things were about to get underway. They met Ben and Emma for

The Second Coming

breakfast. James quickly drank a cup of coffee, and then asked Ben if he could borrow the car. Gert tried to tell him he'd better eat something, but he ignored her and jumped up as soon as Ben handed him the keys.

As the remaining three ate their breakfasts, Gert noticed that Emma seemed preoccupied, and finally she asked her what was on her mind.

"It's the colonel. Miriam Wheeling called last night. She told me Cal has been sick for the last couple of weeks, and she couldn't get him to slow down. He insisted he was fine and continued to try to coordinate everything. On Wednesday he almost collapsed, and he was so weak she finally had to put him to bed. She wants him to go to the doctor, but he's being very stubborn and insists it's only a bug. She said that when he tried to get up yesterday morning, he couldn't. It's ironic the way things have happened because the ospreys arrived on Wednesday too. He made Miriam turn the bed and prop him up so he could see the nest site."

"Do you think they'll cancel the observations?" Gert asked.

"No, I'm sure they won't. He wouldn't allow it. You'll have to meet the colonel to understand. Miriam said he dictated a letter to her yesterday afternoon, and he wants me to read it at the meeting. I don't know why in the world he picked me. I hate speaking in front of people."

"You'll be fine, Em'," Ben said.

"I hope so. I'm going upstairs to read it over again."

"I'll be up in a minute," Ben said, draining the last of his coffee and signaling the waitress for more.

Gert watched Emma get up from the table and walk through the dining room, moving with her precise, determined steps. She felt like walking on the beach, but she was afraid Ben would want to accompany her, and she had seen the look Emma gave him when he didn't go upstairs with her. Gert was quickly tiring of Emma's jealousy. She hadn't encouraged Ben, and she wasn't going to. But unless he really got out of line she couldn't confront him about it either. It was harmless, and she would make sure it stayed that way.

She liked Emma though, which surprised her. Until recently she would have found her an awful, narrow-minded bore. Though Gert prodded her about the elements of her faith, and made comments about her myopic meliorism, those things didn't bother her any more. She thought she must be getting soft in her old age.

That morning when she first saw the tiny bird in Emma's hand something had changed in her. She had always been interested in new things, but now not only more of her time, but more of her emotions became involved in watching the birds. The more she learned about them the more the miracle of their lives filled her with awe. She knew unconsciously it had to do with their ability to fly, and she first directed her interest to the many and marvelous physical refinements that allowed them to. She read about the lightness of their hollow bones and the fact that they had eliminated teeth and heavy jaws and jaw muscles. She learned that over time they had developed a method that allowed them to eliminate concentrated uric acid and therefore didn't need a bladder to store their urine. She read that most birds had only one oviduct, and that their sexual apparatus could grow six hundred or even a thousand times in the mating season.. Their choice of foods, the functioning of their lungs, their streamlined features, their balance, these were all miracles. But they were miraculous in the most logical and precise sense, and they gradually altered the way she viewed the rest of life.

Almost all the books she read made strong mention of the concept of homeostasis, the necessity of an organism to avoid too great a change in internal and external aspects of its physiological existence. Gert began to relate it to her own emotional homeostasis, if there was such a counterpart,

The Second Coming

and the quests for equilibrium that caused her sometimes to take off on her own unconscious wings.

She fell on the birds as she hadn't fallen on anything in years. Her eyes became more keen for them, and in turn more keen for everything else. When she was out shopping or for a drive, her eyes continually searched the bare fillagreed branches against the background of the gray winter sky, hunting for perched silhouetted forms. She learned to recognize birds first by knowing their forms within their larger groups. From there she moved to their songs and colors, and she had lately been striving to learn more about their individual and collective behaviors.

She set up a feeding station in her backyard, some sunflower and niger seeds in a store-bought feeder, and suet hung in a mesh bag from a tree branch. She kept her identification book and small field glasses on a table under the window, and she would go there four or five times a day to see if there were any birds, and what they were eating, and what kinds of activities they were engaged in. Sometimes the squirrels raided her station, and she didn't know quite what to do because though they were easily shooed away, they would usually persistently come back. Emma told her that Ben kept a loaded air pistol by the back door, and he was quite ruthless when his station was encroached upon.

She recorded all her sightings, but she noticed that with each new sighting there came a letdown, and that each letdown was a bit more severe than the one before. It was a silly depression she would find herself in, but her recognition of it's silliness didn't ease it. It didn't impede her though, because she felt she was moving toward something larger. With each new sighting, with each new insight, along with the letdown came a balancing strength and a determination to know and see more. More of what she wasn't quite sure.

She would have liked to walk on the beach, but instead she went up to the room and sat by herself. After a short time James came in. He had spent a hundred dollars on his fishing gear. He left the rod leaning on the wall outside the room, but he brought in a tackle box filled with leaders, sinkers, hooks, and shining silver lures, and some plastic monofilament line on a spool that he rigged on one of the bedposts so he could wind it on his new spinning reel. She smiled as she watched him, but she didn't pretend to be interested.

She returned to the dining room a bit before eleven, feeling guilty because she hadn't checked to see if Emma needed any help. The room was filling with all kinds of people. There were the older, experienced birders, a type familiar to her from the meetings at home. She wondered why most of them seemed more alive than other people their age. There were many more young people than she expected. Some of them appeared to be of the young professional class, but there were one or two young enough that she thought they must be college students. A tall man who looked to be about thirty, with the tousled hair and hollow-cheeked look of an academic, appeared to have something to do with the organization of it all. He moved from one group to the next, smiling and nodding to each with the same neutral look. He seemed to have the same bland encouragement for everyone.

Emma came in with Ben a few minutes later. Ben came over and sat with Gert, and Emma walked to the front of the room, looking pale and nervous, clutching a thin bundle of papers in her hands. Gert felt a small twinge when Emma reached the front because the tall man put his arm gently on her shoulder, and it was obvious that he genuinely wished to soothe her and put her at her ease. After a few more minutes everyone had found a seat, and he quieted them finally by tapping a glass with a spoon.

"Good morning everyone. I'd like to welcome you all here today. My name is JP Richardson. I am a biology instructor at North Carolina State University, and I have

The Second Coming

been asked to help coordinate these ornithological observations which are the brainchild of Colonel Albert Wheeling. Colonel Wheeling has graciously donated the use of his home as our main center for these observations, and if you have received the informational letters from him on the subject, I'm sure you realize the extent of the preparations he had made in order to make the task of our observations both efficient and comfortable.

"Unfortunately Colonel Wheeling has been feeling under the weather this past week, and so he is unable to be here today to brief us himself. Instead he has written a letter and asked his good friend, Mrs. Emma Corcoran, to read it to you. So, Mrs. Corcoran, if you will be kind enough, please let us hear what the colonel has to say."

There was scattered, polite applause when the man finished, and some of the people who didn't know Emma shifted their positions to get a better look at her. Emma stood with the sheaf of paper held in front of her and positioned herself behind the narrow podium. Gert also wondered why the colonel had chosen Emma to read the letter for him. She seemed very nervous and uncomfortable when she began to speak. Her voice was high and reedy when she began, but after the first few sentences she calmed herself and wound up speaking deliberately and effectively.

"Dear friends,

"I am glad you were all able to make it, and I hope those of you who made a trip have had a pleasant journey. I am sorry I cannot be with you today. I am temporarily indisposed, as they say, but I have all confidence that I will make a quick and complete recovery. You need have no worries that my indisposition will interfere with the business at hand. All arrangements have been made according to plan and schedule, including, I am happy to report, the arrival of the ospreys. Observations began with their arrival on Wednesday morning and have continued, albeit with a skeleton crew, until the present.

Doyle Thomas

"Let me first give you a little background as to what has transpired so far. As most of you know, these two birds have returned each spring for the last eight years, and the site was occupied by another pair for many years before that. Professor Simon Jones, a noted ornithologist from the University of Georgia who visited last year, estimated the age of the female at twelve years, and that of the male to be a year or two younger.

"Each spring when they return to the nest, some amount of repair and reconstruction has been necessary. In most years the birds were able to affect these repairs within a day or two. This winter however a severe storm demolished the entire nest. Not only that, but the winds were so violent they knocked down one of the limbs that had served as a basic support on which the nest was built. We had already put a good deal of time and effort into the development of this project, and I became concerned that the birds might not be able to rebuild the nest at the same site. I contacted Professor Jones and he responded that he thought the odds were good that they would return, but whether they would stay or not depended on the feasibility of their rebuilding under the new conditions. It might also depend on the number of other desirable sites in the area, and the amount of competition for those sites among other birds in the area. Even if our particular pair of birds didn't choose to or couldn't rebuild there, it seemed probable to him that another pair, possibly offspring of the first, might attempt to take their place. I checked on alternate sites where we might move our observations in case the nest was abandoned altogether, but there was really nothing else to do but wait.

"This past Wednesday morning, a little after dawn, I was awakened by the short, high-pitched cries that have become so familiar to me from springs past, although on Wednesday morning they seemed a good deal more persistent than I remembered them. I looked out my window and across the way, perched on a limb, were the two ospreys.

The Second Coming

The female is a grand regal thing only marginally larger than her mate, and it was she who was making most of the racket, although they both seemed, for lack of a better word, confused.

"They continued this racket for over two hours. Finally the male flew away toward the woods to the north and out of sight. He returned ten minutes later carrying a stick which he tried unsuccessfully to wedge in place to begin the nest. In the past the nest has been constructed among three limbs which extended from the trunk at a height of about eighty feet, and with roughly ninety degrees between them. Two limbs extended out on opposite sides and the third emerged between them. Unfortunately it was the middle limb that the storm removed. If it had been either of the other two I don't think it would be presenting the problems it has.

"The male could not get his stick wedged properly and they have had trouble getting others to hold since. Although they have not given up yet, and they appear determined to stay, I guess we'll have to wait and see.

"On a brighter and perhaps more philosophical note I think it is important now to say a few things about our goals in these operations. First of all, it would be a mistake to take ourselves too seriously. All of us, for one reason or another, have been drawn to this field. There is something about these animals and the miracles of their lives, the freedom granted them by their ability to fly, the beauty of their forms or their songs, something, beckons us. We have chosen the osprey. We could as easily have chosen any of the other 8600 species of birds that grace the earth with their presence. What is important is that we dedicate our concentration and effort to making these observations as precise and our recordings as accurate as possible. We will probably not make any important scientific discoveries. But if we are careful…and patient, we may find that we discover some things which are personally far more important.

"We begin tomorrow. With the information you have given me, I have tried to develop a schedule that I hope will be agreeable to everyone. Of course, it is not etched in stone, and I'm sure we can make modifications where they are necessary.

"One final note. If you are on duty and you happen to see an older man shuffling around in his pajamas, let me warn you, before my wife does, that it would probably be wise to ignore him.

Signed,
Col. Albert Wheeling"

When Emma finished reading the letter Mr. Richardson again took the podium. He thanked Emma and launched into a cursory lecture on the ospreys. Within minutes he had lost most of the audience. The group had listened attentively to Emma, but it was obvious that they viewed the letter as the most important piece of information, and now they were impatient to find out what the schedule was so they could make their arrangements and get on with their vacations. The sunlight was angled out low on the sand outside the awnings of the dining room windows. It looked warm and inviting.

Ben had seemed nervous and embarrassed the whole time Emma was reading the letter. He drummed his fingers and played with the silverware and glanced around to the door as if he were expecting someone. He only gave Emma a nod and a weak smile when she returned to the table.

The schedule was posted on a large cardboard rectangle and placed on the easel that usually displayed the restaurant's lunch and dinner specials. When he finished his short lecture the man from the university stood next to the easel in front of the shifting knot of people, smiling and nodding, shaking hands with some of the men, and handing out directions and copies of the schedule to those who asked for them.

The Second Coming

"You spoke very well," Gert said to Emma. "I was a little nervous for you at first, but once you got going you seemed very natural up there. I was beginning to feel jealous."

"I was scared to death in the beginning, but then I began to hear the colonel's voice in the words, and I recognized some old friends, and it just seemed silly to be nervous in front of them."

"I thought you did fine, Em," Ben said, and then he swung around as the dining room door opened behind him. A pretty young girl came in and walked up to the easel and began talking to Mr. Richardson. "Wasn't Miriam supposed to be here this morning?" he asked.

"She was. I wonder if her not being here has something to do with the colonel. I hope it isn't so serious that she's afraid to leave him. I'll call her after we get a look at the schedule."

They waited a few more minutes until the crowd thinned out, and then rose together and moved to the front of the room. Mr. Richardson smiled as they approached and held out his hand to Ben. The pretty girl stood behind him, smiling weakly and looking a little flushed.

"Mrs. Corcoran, thank you for reading the letter," he said, and Emma smiled. "You handled the pressure very well."

"And you also spoke well, Mr. Richardson," Gert said. "You seem to have things well in hand."

"Well, thank you, but everything is not quite as smooth as it could be. This is Mary Weaver," he said, reaching back and putting his hand behind the girl's elbow. "She's the one student I talked into making the trip, and now it appears that the motel has lost her reservation and given her room to someone else. We're going to see if we can't talk to the manager and get everything straightened out."

"Hello, Mary, I'm Gert."

"You're Gert Frost?" Mr. Richardson asked, turning

to the schedule. "You and I are up first thing tomorrow morning. It's up to us to get this thing off on the right foot. And you and Mary are together Tuesday afternoon," he said, tapping the box on the schedule with their names in it.

"Are you ordinarily a birder?" Emma asked.

"Please call me JP, and no, I'm not. To tell the truth, the reason I'm here is because I have the least seniority at school and they volunteered me. Anything for tenure. I wasn't too keen on the idea at first, but now that I've seen all the excitement the observations have generated, I'm beginning to look forward to it. I'm especially looking forward to meeting Colonel Wheeling. He sounds like a real character."

"He is," Emma said. "And he's also one of the most astute bird watchers I have ever known. He rarely uses field glasses, but he is still usually quicker than anyone else to make an identification, and he rarely makes a mistake."

"Let's hope he gets over the flu or whatever it is he has," JP said. "Shall we ride together tomorrow, Gert?"

"If you have a car. My husband and I drove down with Emma and Ben."

"I rode with someone too, but I think I can borrow a car. What if I meet you at the office tomorrow morning at five thirty? God, that sounds early."

They all nodded politely to each other, and JP and the young woman excused themselves and exited through the dining room's broad double doors.

"I think I'll walk down to the beach and see how James is doing," Gert said.

"Do you need anything from the store?" Emma asked. "Ben and I need a few things, and I want to find out what time the masses are tomorrow. It's Palm Sunday already."

Gert couldn't think of anything she needed. Emma and Ben left, and Gert went the other way. She went out to the path that led over the dunes to the beach. Something irked her about Emma's need to rush off and find out when

The Second Coming

the church services were in the morning. But then she realized what was really bothering her was the almost religious thrill she got at the meeting when Emma was reading the colonel's letter. She knew it had something to do with William James' conversion mystique, which he had pointed out was usually an adolescent phenomenon. She could see that she was at that stage in the development of her interest in the birds. She had passed from the ego-less wonder she felt at the beginning to a painful, subjective, emotional scrutiny of the evidence, laced with an adolescent preconception of where she wanted the evidence to lead her. At the point where she found herself she felt like she should be preparing for the next progressive step, which was initiation, but she didn't know quite how to begin. There was something though in the overall scenario that she found exhilarating. Though she hadn't grasped what it was, she sensed there was something running just under the surface of events that held a key for her.

She slipped off her sandals and let her feet pat on the warm sand. From somewhere in her mind she began to hear the echoed memory of strains of music. She finally recognized that it was Miles Davis' "Nightbird Suite." She listened carefully for the phrases to return. When they did she heard the beauty in the way he could play against the nature of the phrase and still fill it with all the meaning that was ever intended.

Emma was Emma. She could wish like St. Teresa to walk with Jesus under the moonlight in Gethsemane. Gert would have preferred one of the Beats, Gregory Corso or Jack Kerouac, or a musician like Chet Baker, on a bare mattress in the Village. She would have even taken Ginsberg, although she didn't like his beard, and when she had heard him give a reading of his poetry at a humid coffeehouse in Philadelphia she was left with the impression that he must smell bad by the way his clothes hung from his frame.

Doyle Thomas

She guessed she had settled for even less than that. She thought about the boy with the heavy black glasses and the tentative scowl. She had long ago forgotten how she had met him because it hurt to think how she was then, the stereotypical bored housewife escaping the brightness of suburbia for the close darkness of the beat pubs and tea rooms where she could watch as theosophy rubbed elbows with astrology and pointed a finger at nihilism, and minimalism sat quietly stoned in the darkest corner twirling the fuzz on his sweater.

She wanted to think she had met him at the same coffee house where she had heard Ginsberg. It had taken her a while, but once she drew him out it became clear that he had opinions on everything. He loved to talk about music, and he spoke with intensity about his records and the artists who played on them. Finally she got him to invite her to his apartment to listen to his music. While the records played he lectured her about Miles and Charlie Parker and Dizzy Gillespie and some of the newer artists he had heard, John Coltrane, and a piano player who lived in Philadelphia named Thelonius Monk.

When she realized that all he might do was talk, Gert took things in hand and they ended up on his ratty couch for the rest of the afternoon. The one clear memory she still had of him was watching him hop gingerly back to the couch from the bathroom, and the appellation which now stuck in her mind was something she had not read until much later. It was Sylvia Plath's description of "turkey neck and turkey gizzards."

The ocean was smooth with a glassy brilliance in the way it caught the diamonds of the sunlight, and the swell was larger than it had been the evening before. The waves were folding over themselves into white green mounds of froth and foam a hundred feet from the edge of the shore. Down the beach she caught sight of some large black objects in the water on the outer edge of the sand bar where the

The Second Coming

waves started to break. At first she excitedly thought they were porpoises, or perhaps seals. But after a moment she realized they were human forms apparently floating on some plane which made them appear to move magically just above the surface of the water. They were surfers. The shining black outfits were the wet suits they wore as protection against the cold water. She saw one, farther out than the rest, wheel his board toward shore, and with a few strokes he was lifted on the crest of a wave. Immediately, and in one fluid motion, he stood and descended into the trough in front of it where he somehow bent his knees and rotated his arms and the slung his surfboard and himself down the line of the wave, barely outrunning the white water which spun over itself behind him. He drifted laterally back down into the trough of the swell again and made another turn that generated more speed, and this time as he unwound from the turn and hurled back up the face of the wave he tucked himself into a ball just as the lip of the wave threw itself over him. He disappeared behind the glassy scrim created by its fall. She knew he was there, crouching, and she thought he might re-emerge. But instead, after a few seconds, she saw his surfboard pop out through the back of the swell.

    James was on the beach down from the motel. He was sitting on a faded piece of driftwood with his reel cradled in his lap, working to untangle a large and convoluted knot of fishing line that had fallen out of the innards of his reel. She would have simply cut the knot and gone on from there. There was a precedent after all. But James sat, patiently trying to backtrack through the loops, hoping to find the path that would unloose it. Gert tilted back her head, and when she felt the sun's heat tightening her skin, she decided she had better buy herself a hat.

VII

The lounge was named Lita's, and it was one of the few bars in Nags Head that was open year-round. Almost everyone had a theory about where the name came from, but only a few old-timers really knew. The building had originally housed a dress shop when it was built in the fifties, and the first owner was named Lita. It was one of the first shops in the area to sell vacation wear and bathing suits, but it had come a few years before the tourists did, and Lita quickly went out of business and moved from the area. The name stuck. In different incarnations it had been a mom-and-pop grocery store, a souvenir shop, and one season someone had even tried opening it as a bakery selling doughnuts, but no one had ever tried to change the name. It had been a bar for ten years, although the new owners had only had it for three. When they first opened it they thought about changing the name to something nautical, but they never did.

During the previous winter someone had started calling it Lita's Hard Dick Café because there were so few available women during that time of year, and most nights it was filled with a bunch of blades bumping dick heads. Now that the new season was coming and more bars were opening back up it only jumped on one night, Saturday, and most of the regulars just called it Leaners.

It was just after ten o'clock when Rob and JP pushed their way in. Rob had finally gotten Chick on the phone after trying most of the afternoon and told him they needed to talk. Chick suggested Lita's.

Rob felt rested, and although he and JP had done some lines after dinner, he was calm. He was developing a rapport with the coke. He was still getting a good buzz initially, but it wasn't being as physical with him.

He had fallen asleep around nine o'clock Friday

The Second Coming

evening and hadn't stirred until almost two on Saturday afternoon. Before he had gone to bed JP told him he was going out and Rob asked him to keep an eye out for Chick. While JP was in the shower Rob had gone back into the little bag of coke. He made a bindle for JP from a page of one of the magazines in the room and told him to turn on Chick if he saw him, and to be cool and have a good time if he didn't.

When Rob awoke Saturday he remembered immediately that he was broke. He realized that the easiest way to get money was to eyeball some grams to give to Chick as soon as he saw him. He sat on the bed with the satchel in his lap and pulled out the blade and baggies. When he finished he had six little teardrop bags of powder secured with plastic-coated metal ties. He had purposely made them big so Chick wouldn't have any trouble unloading them. He felt the spur of a thought urging him to stop doing any more himself, but it was faint and he knew he would ignore it. Finally, he made another approximated ounce. Then he sealed the big bag again, and realized he needed to think of a safe place to hide it.

Now that they were in the bar, Rob scanned the room to see if there was anyone he recognized. He began to get nervous because he realized he might run into Jane, and he wasn't sure if he was ready to talk to her. He at least wanted to be able to give her some money if he did see her.

The band had just finished its first set and the early crowd was lazily milling around. There was reggae music pulsing through the sound system, churning with its syncopated, Coptic, ganja-induced rhythms. Rob smiled when he thought about the "I and I" vibrations, because he knew that for most of the people in the room they meant nothing more than a good reason to light up another joint and double down on their subjectivity. Most had no idea who the Lion of Judah was.

Rob finally saw someone he knew, a guy he had surfed with years ago. They talked for a few minutes. Rob told him about the last times he had been to Mexico and Aleuthra, and the other guy told him about a mutual friend who had taken Rob's advice and gone to the Indian Ocean and come back with tales of how good the waves were in Sri Lanka and the Maldives. After a few hollow "good to see yous," Rob left him and made his way back to the bar. When he got there JP handed him a beer.

"Have you seen Chick?" Rob asked him.

"No, I don't think he's here yet, but there sure are a lot of girls."

JP had drunk a lot at dinner. He was already looking a bit glazed, and Rob was beginning to worry about trusting him. There were times when he could get to a point where he was beyond anyone's control. On a few of those occasions Rob had thought about punching him just to do it before someone else did.

Rob spotted Chick's reflection in the mirror behind the bar as soon as he came through the doors. He leaned back against the bar and watched him as he stopped to speak to a few people at the small tables that dotted the floor on his way across. His smile was wide open when he reached them. You could tell he was in his environment. He had the look of a benevolent monarch.

"Rob, remember when your mom came home from work early and found us doing those girls on her bed?"

"No, but I remember when you thought you had a brain tumor."

"God, I remember that too. I did have all the symptoms. I still wonder sometimes if it's not up there waiting to burst and send poisonous spooge through my cranial cavity."

"I thought they decided it was hypoglycemia."

"Yes, but you can never be sure. How are you, Bro?"

"Good, how are you?"

"I'm fine. I'm still in the school of 'it's better to burn out than it is to rust,' but I'm realizing I might have to make

The Second Coming

it a controlled burn. JP, how are you? Do you remember seeing me last night? You were wasted."

"Chick," Rob said. "I need to talk to you somewhere in private."

"Well, you picked the wrong place."

"No, you picked the wrong place. I told you on the phone I needed to talk."

"Alright, Rob," he said. "We'll go someplace else. Oh, shit."

A girl who had been sitting at the end of the bar walked up while they were talking, and when she reached Chick she took a big wind-up and slapped him. She was drunk, and when she heard the sound of the blow she pulled back her arm and prepared to hit him again. JP stood quickly and stepped between them, put his hands on her shoulders, and gently eased her away from Chick. He started saying something to her, but his voice was so quiet Rob couldn't hear what it was. Chick backed off a few steps with his hand held up to his mouth where she had hit him. He had a playful hurt look in his eyes. No one else paid any attention.

"Let's go," Rob said. He and Chick walked through the crowd and out the door, leaving JP to calm the girl. "Who was that?" he asked when they got outside.

"That was Paula, the girl I've been living with this winter. We've had a misunderstanding."

"No kidding."

"I really like her, but she started escalating things, so a couple of nights ago I told her maybe it was time we separated our socks, if you know what I mean. I guess she didn't take it too well."

"Do you have a car?" Rob asked.

Chick led the way to it. After they got in, he asked, "Where do you want to go?"

Rob pulled one of the fat grams from his pocket and laid it on the dashboard in front of Chick.

"Is this a present?"

"No, I want you to look at it and tell me what you think. I want your professional opinion."

Chick shrugged and opened the bag. He retrieved a small mirror from under his seat and scooped some of the powder on to it with the coke spoon he had stashed in the lining of the visor above his head. He held the mirror close to his face and turned the mound of coke with the spoon so he could catch the refractions from the lights above the parking lot.

"It looks great. But if you expect me to tell you if it's Peruvian Blue or Bolivian pink flake in this light you're out of luck. This is a test, right? A taste test?"

Rob nodded. Chick pulled his driver's license and a bill from his wallet and divided the mound into a couple of rough thick lines. He rolled the bill, leaned over the mirror, and drew noisily.

"Alright, Rob, it's good. It's great. But you're not just turning me on for old times' sake. What's the point?" He had very white teeth that looked even whiter in the stingy night light. They were one reason girls were so attracted to him. They looked like marble in the moonlight.

"I have some I need to get rid of," he said.

"How much? An ounce, a quarter pound?"

"A kilo."

"You have a kilo of this?" Rob nodded. "From where?"

"Florida," Rob answered. "I was hoping to catch you in Baltimore. I figured that would be the easiest place to unload it."

"A kilo, really?" He held the remaining line up to the light and squinted at it more strenuously. Then he set the mirror down on his lap. "Look, Rob, I know god-damned well you didn't have the money to buy a kilo of this. So how did you get it? Am I supposed to believe no one is going to come looking for it?"

The Second Coming

"They won't know where to look," he answered simply.

"Bullshit. You need to give it to me straight. Whose stuff is this?"

Rob looked at Chick and knew he didn't have any choice. He shifted his position and began to tell him the story of jail and Rios and his cousins, and how he had first gotten an inkling of the quantities that might be involved.

"Rios was obviously a bullshitter about a lot of things, so at first I didn't pay much attention. He kept talking about this courier thing, and how much money I could make doing it. But even those times I thought he might be on the level, he was such an asshole I didn't want to have anything to do with him.

"When I got out of jail I should have gone and spent a night or two with Rory to try to get myself together, but I didn't. I checked into a motel in Orlando instead. I had Rios' address, but I wasn't thinking about using it. I wasn't thinking about anything. I went out and got drunk the first night and spent too much money. The next day I stayed in the room and nursed a pint of George Dickel. I knew I didn't have enough money to last for more than a few days, but I wasn't ready to go looking for a job.

"That second night, at ten or so, I got dressed and went out for some fresh air. I ended up it a phone booth calling for a taxi. When he got there I gave him Rios' address, adding a hundred to the street number figuring that would put me within a couple of blocks. He drove me to the neighborhood. It was just a lot of low cinder block cottages with awnings painted all different pastel colors. It had only taken ten minutes to get there. Once we were on the street I started checking numbers.

"Rios' house was set back behind a clump of palmettos. There were three cars in the driveway and most of the lights were on inside. I could hear strains of salsa music and laughter.

"The taxi driver dropped me two blocks farther down. There wasn't a house with the number I gave him, but I told him I recognized the one I was looking for. I paid him and got out.

"I waited until he was gone and then walked across the street and back down the block toward Rios' house. The only streetlights were on the corners, and his house was in the middle of the block, so I knew it would be too dark to recognize me. The house to the right of Rios' was dark already. There were bikes and toys in the front yard so I guessed that a family lived there. The house on the other side had a 'for sale' sign in the front yard, and the grass was grown up and it looked like it hadn't been lived in for a while.

"I stood for a minute across the street in the shadows, watching and listening. I couldn't see Rios in the house, but I thought I recognized his voice.

"I walked past the house a few more times and then walked back to the motel. I didn't understand why I had gone there, and it bothered me the whole way back. I thought about calling Rory about a job the next day, but I didn't. I just laid around watching TV again.

"That evening I went out thinking I'd find a quiet bar. Then I started thinking that maybe I would talk to Rios. I didn't want to, but money was getting tight, and it couldn't hurt to just talk. It took me a half an hour to get there on foot because I was still balking at the idea and didn't take the most direct route. When I got there, there weren't any cars in the driveway, and there weren't any lights on inside.

"I didn't hesitate. I walked up to the front door. I knew I was pretty well hidden by the shrubs and palmettos, and I'd gotten the impression that no one in the neighborhood paid much attention anyway.

"There were louvered windows running up both sides of the door. I broke two out even with the doorknob and laid the pieces out of sight under the bushes, and then ripped the

The Second Coming

screen enough to get my hand through. I unlocked the door and stepped inside. I don't know why I did it. I guess I was looking for money. I stood for a few minutes with my back against the door, waiting for my eyes to adjust to the darkness.

"It was nice inside, nice furniture, big TV and sound system. I went to the kitchen in the back and saw there was a door, so I knew I could get out quickly that way if I needed to. Before the kitchen to the right was a hall that led past a bathroom to two bedrooms. I followed it to one of the bedroom doors. In that instant I was struck with the idea that there could be someone in the house, sleeping, or maybe hiding if they had heard me, but just as quickly I knew there wasn't. I went to the dresser. There were some framed photos on top, and little boxes, and change, the usual stuff. I opened the boxes and went through the drawers, but there wasn't any money. I was about to check the other room when I saw what looked like a little pillow lying in the middle of the bed. I knew it wasn't a pillow though as soon as I picked it up. Rios hadn't been bullshitting me after all.

"I was standing in the bedroom with the package in my hand amazed first of all that someone would trust Rios with it, and then that he would just leave it lying around, when I looked up and saw headlights outside the curtain in the driveway. I hopped out of the room and down the hall, heading for the kitchen door. It wouldn't open. I fumbled with the lock and it still wouldn't budge. I think the god-damned thing was nailed shut.

"I ran back into the living room. There was a statuette on the coffee table. I picked it up and stood behind the door. I could see a silhouette moving up the walk and I knew it was Rios, and I prayed he was alone. I heard his key go into the lock and the door opened. As soon as his head came around the corner of the door I hit him as hard as I could. The blow made a terrible hollow noise and he fell in a heap. I was sure I had killed him. I bent down and turned him over and he looked right at me. I thought he must recognize me, but his eyes never focused and after a few seconds they rolled back in his head."

"What did you do?"

"I rolled him back over on his face and sat on the couch and tried to figure things out. He twitched a few times and I couldn't tell if he was dying or coming to. Finally I got up and took the car keys and his wallet out of his pocket. I grabbed the bag and went out and got in his car and drove away."

"What did you do with the car?"

"I drove it to Jacksonville and left it there."

"Won't he find it there?"

"Maybe, probably. I don't know. It will take him a while, and he still doesn't know where to look for me."

"Yeah, but a kilo. He might think it's worth his while. His friends might."

"If you can help me out, I'll be long gone. How about it?"

"I can get rid of it, but it might take a while. Some of the boat captains are high rollers, but they're here at different times."

"I don't want to do it here. Too many people know me, and it's too hard to keep things quiet. Someone will end up saying something. What about Baltimore?"

"I don't know. I had some trouble up there. We might pull it off, but we'd have to be careful and talk to just the right people."

"That's the way I want it. You get a third if you can pull it off. Don't give me an answer yet. Think it over carefully."

"How about a few more lines?" Chick asked, leaning back and smiling. "Are you sure we're not too old for this?"

"No, I'm not sure at all. Look, Chick, remember in high school when I bought that pound of pot and fronted you a quarter, and you came back a week later and said it was

The Second Coming

gone and you couldn't get the money? Well, this is different. This might be my last chance to change the way I live. I'll have enough money to take care of Jane and Kelly, and be able to go somewhere where no one knows me and make a fresh start. If I fuck it up, or if you fuck it up, I have to start at zero or worse, and I don't think I can do it any more. Understand?"

"Yeah, Rob, I understand."

He handed Chick the other five eye-balled grams. "Can you get rid of these for me? I'm broke."

"Are these supposed to be grams?" he asked, and when Rob nodded, he smiled and said, "Sure."

There were many more people in the bar and everything was louder when they returned. The blenders whirred steadily and the beer taps gurgled, and everywhere was the steady buzz of conversation. Above it all hung lazy wreaths of pale smoke.

Rob was surprised at himself that he had told Chick so much. Something from JP must have rubbed off on him. He trusted JP much more that he would ever trust Chick, but he would never have told JP the whole story about Rios, and he wasn't sure why.

While they were outside JP had gotten rid of the girl, Paula, and had found a seat at the bar where he had struck up a conversation with two girls on the stools next to him. It always took a few drinks for JP to come out of himself. His face would loosen and so would his tongue, and he would be ready to give his opinions on anything. Chick disappeared into the crowd, and Rob sidled through the throng and stood behind JP so he could hear what he was saying.

"I try to write. For a long time I've been thinking of writing a piece called 'The Issue of Great Men.' It would be a serial, a dramatized account of the accomplishments of the offspring of some of the great figures of history. For instance, you could take Ashurbanipal or Alexander the Great. What did their children do with the great empires they had built up? We know of Alexander's father, but what of his sons? Charlemagne's most famous son was, arguably, Charles the Fat. I guess we shouldn't be allowed to forget Pepin, though most of us have." He was looking from one girl to the other as he spoke. They couldn't tell if he was serious and knew what he was talking about, or if he was just making fun of them. They looked confused, and a little intimidated. "And what about the daughters of great men? How must they have felt? They had to have seen...fatherhood is a great responsibility. One more please," he said to the bartender, who nodded with crisp, grim dissatisfaction. "And what about artists, Goethe or Gauguin? Or philosophers? Or scientists?"

"So what's the point, JP?" Rob asked, stepping up to them.

"Rob, where have you been? This is my oldest friend, Rob Wheat," he said, putting his hand on Rob's arm. "These girls are from the University of North Carolina at Chapel Hill, and I don't quite remember their names. They are more serious about their education than we are at State, I think...or they think. Their school has a great tradition. Thomas Wolfe attended, although I think as tall as he was if he went there now Dean Smith would probably snatch him from the English Department, provide him with a pretty tutor, and try to work him into the line-up at small forward. Anyway, the point I was trying to make is this. Does genius, whether introverted or extroverted, dry up in the loins? Is there some biological set of checks and balances at work? It is obvious that over the generations our physical attributes have improved dramatically. We are taller and stronger and faster over the course of a few generations. But genius, on the other hand, doesn't appear to be lineal." He was squinting and his head bobbed slowly like a snake. "Look at us. As Americans we are the sons and daughter of Aaron Burr and Thomas Jefferson and Walt Whitman, and where the hell are we going? Can I have another drink over here!"

The Second Coming

he shouted, looking up suddenly, extending his arm and twirling the ice in the bottom of his glass. The crowd milled around behind them throwing off incongruous patches of Doppler-affected conversation and laughter.

"Do you live here?" one of the girls asked Rob.

"He used to live here. We both did, but we don't live here anymore. You don't mind if I answer, do you, Rob? Rob's been living in Florida. But people who live at the beach are different. You know why? People come here to get away. Am I right? Isn't that why you came, to get away from things, to escape for a little while? Well, the people who live here have decided to make their escapes permanent. Of course, there are all sorts of things to stay away from, and a lot of people here have forgotten why they had to escape to begin with, but I'd say just about all of them are staying away from something."

"Real deep, JP," Rob said, patting him on the back and retreating into the crowd. The girls would tire of him soon. It didn't take long listening to him to know he didn't care. It was all just an exercise. The clincher would be when he told them what he thought about love. When he drank to a certain point he almost always did. "Love is like a neutrino," he would say. "I'm talking about true love now. A neutrino is an elementary particle with no mass, no electrical charge, no magnetic field. It is not attracted to or repelled by other particles. Neutrinos can pass through us, the earth, anything...as if they weren't there. The only way it can be stopped is by direct collision with another elementary particle, and the odds against that happening are something like one in a trillion. But collisions do happen, even at those odds. But I guess what I'm trying to say is that it isn't something you would bet on." After they heard that they would try to get away, and he would pretend he didn't care.

They had all changed, but JP had changed most of all. Maybe that wasn't it. Maybe a person couldn't change.

Maybe he could only heighten certain of his potentials by cannibalizing some of the other. "The Murdered Self." Where had he read that? Jesus Christ, I'm starting to sound like him. He put his empty beer bottle on the ledge and made his way to the other side of the bar to order another.

An hour later Chick came up and gave him three hundred dollars. "I should have the other three hundred by tomorrow," he said. But Rob knew he wouldn't.

He was ready to leave so he looked around for JP to tell him so. JP said he wanted to stay and would get a ride with Chick. Then he asked if he could use the car in the morning. Rob told him he could and said he'd leave the keys on the dresser.

He went outside. He knew there weren't any clouds, but he could see only a few stars, and those just because they were twinkling very stubbornly. Then he remembered the fire and the smoke. He couldn't smell it, but he guessed it must be hanging up there above him.

He didn't hear JP come in, but when he awoke in the morning he found a note from him.

"Rob,
Chick kept me out and I just came in to get the keys and change my clothes. It was too early to wake you. Jane came in after you left with her new boyfriend. What a maroon! She sounded surprised that you were here. I did my best to smooth things out. I told her you just got in town and would probably call her in the morning. Here's the number, 442-8301. Good luck. I should be back by one. See you then.

JP."

VIII

Jane hurried to get ready. She and Kevin hadn't known each other very long, and because he was so busy they usually had just one date a week, most often on a Friday or Saturday night. They had gone out the past Saturday and everything had gone smoothly until they ran into JP and he told her Rob was in town. She knew she hadn't done a good job of keeping the emotion from her face, although she wasn't exactly sure what the emotion was. Kevin hadn't said anything, but a few times during the course of the rest of the evening she noticed him looking sideways at her.

Now after all their weekend dates, why did he suddenly want to go out on a Monday night when he knew they both had to work the next day? Maybe he was just horny. He had wanted to take her home with him on Saturday night, and she had wanted to go, but she had said no because she didn't want to leave Kelly alone over night. She had done it in the past, either left after Kelly had fallen asleep, and snuck out, and then rushed in the washed colors before dawn to get home before the sun came up. Or she had called around to friends until she found one who was willing to come over and sleep in the house with her. She never had to worry that Kelly would be frightened to wake up in the house alone. Kelly was a calm child and not likely to panic. On a few occasions Jane had even brought a man home with her. But she found you could never trust them to behave the next morning. Until recently she hadn't felt too much guilt or concern. But now she was worried because she realized that Kelly knew exactly what was going on.

Things were getting too complicated. She tried to remember what she had been like when she was eleven and twelve. It may have been a trick, but the memories were almost all uniformly and benignly pleasant. And if they weren't, they had mostly to do with arguments with her sisters about which clothes belonged on whose doll. There wasn't anything in her memories of her mother to suggest a clue to the strife that she and Kelly had experienced over the last year and a half. They were continually at each other's throats, and it seemed to Jane it was because Kelly was always, always pushing her. From what she could remember about her first challenges to authority, they hadn't started until she felt the first mysterious roilings of her dawning sexuality, and she hated the memory of those inchoate urges when she recognized the ghosts of their forms in the face of her daughter.

Lately Kelly had taken a new tack and become quiet and withdrawn. Although Jane knew there was much left unresolved in that silence she was still glad for the respite. It was hard enough when she just had to divide her time between work and Kelly. But now there was also Kevin, and she had to have Kevin.

Kevin was her chance to secure their future. He was their ticket to some ease and prosperity. Jane was sick of having jobs that didn't pay well and weren't leading anywhere. She was tired of the endless monthly struggle to keep up with the finances, budgeting her anemic paychecks and dumbly hoping for the support check that now rarely came. She was thirty two years old and she was running out of options. She could see how things might be different if she had made other decisions in the past. She knew she hadn't always been as responsible as she should have been, but what she had accomplished she had done all by herself. Kevin could change things for them. He was different from the other men she had known at the beach in the years she had lived there. He was educated and refined. He was polite. And he had money.

They had met at Lita's one evening in the middle of winter. She had gone there after work with a friend to wind down and warm her insides before going home to face Kelly and the cold house. Kevin came in and sat next to them at the bar just as they were finishing their second drink and preparing to leave. He didn't say anything to them, but Jane caught him looking at her in the reflection in the mirror behind the bar. When she caught his eye and smiled slightly he didn't acknowledge it or change his expression, but as she stood and reached for her coat he cleared his throat and asked if he could buy them a drink. His offer was to both of them, but he never took his eyes off Jane. Her friend took the hint and said she would like to stay, but she had to get home. Jane knew she should go too. Kelly would be surly if she came in tipsy, which she would if she had another drink. But she hadn't been ready to go, and his offer and the faint smile in his eyes cemented her decision to stay.

  He came on to her quietly and with an oddly apologetic sense of humor. She could tell he was shy around women. But like a lot of shy people he was interesting because he took so much care with what he was saying. She drank slowly to prolong the conversation and to give him a chance to ask her out.

  He spoke mostly about his work. He represented a group of investors from Virginia and he was in town checking out the development potential because they believed that the northern Outer Banks represented the next point on the coastal line targeted for big development. Most of the work was boring, he admitted. He spent a lot of time at the county records office doing population graphs and maps of flood zones and studying building permit trends. But if they decided to move into the area, and he thought they would, he was the lead man and would probably be there for at least a year, maybe two. He liked the area. He apologized if she was one of the people who had come to the Outer Banks to escape the kind of development he represented. But he was straightforward in saying that if it wasn't him there would be someone else to step in his place.

  Finally she had to tell him that it was time for her to go. She rose slowly and collected her things and was about to turn and leave when he put his hand on her arm and asked if he could see her again.

So they began to go out. For a while she had been confused when she tried to figure out what he saw in her. She was secure enough to know her qualities as well as her faults, and somehow it didn't all add up. There were many more women around, younger, more attractive, freer. Jane had been terrified to tell him about Kelly, and she was a wreck before the first time the two of them met. But Kelly had not only agreed to be presentable, but she had actually been polite in her left-handed way. Still Jane had waited for him to cool toward her after that. But he hadn't. After another month of seeing each other she knew she had to have him.

He wasn't perfect. Once he knew her better, a lot of his initial reserve disappeared. She found that he could be blustering and officious sometimes, and imperious and withdrawn at others. But even with the new emotional displays she sensed an underlying steadiness and honesty.

This might be her last chance. She was just at the point when time was not still building her as a woman, nor had it begun to tear her down. It was also a point of a peculiar confluence of her feminine powers, and it was a terrible time to be alone. She had finally settled on whom she was inside and out, what she needed, and what she had to give in return. She no longer gave too much or too indiscriminately. She had learned the art of pleasing a man and still being able to get her pleasure from him. And she wasn't guilty if there was a degree of calculation to it, because maybe there had to be.

Rob had been over that afternoon. He had called Sunday and said that things were too complicated and drawn out to get into over the phone. He wanted to see Kelly and her. She had put him off until Monday. She did it to punish him. But as soon as she hung up the phone she realized she could never hurt Rob with something as subtle as that. She had sat in the kitchen by the phone and the hollow little lie she had told him about Kelly not being home hung in the dead air around her. Though JP had told her Rob was in town, it wasn't until she heard his voice that the bald reality of it finally struck her. She spent the rest of the evening trying to figure out how to approach him. She wanted to be civil. She still cared about him, but she needed to straighten him out.

"I'm sorry, Jane," he said after they'd made their greetings and both stood hesitantly at the entrance of the small living room. He looked good. His face had become thinner and after the years he had spent in Florida the brown skin around his eyes had tightened and lines were beginning to tail away at the corners. He stood shyly near the door as she examined him, and he held a large stuffed bird in his arms.

"Is that for me?" she asked.

"No, it's for Kelly...for Easter. But I have something for you too." After putting the bird on the sofa and fumbling through his pockets, he gave her two hundred dollar bills.

"What's this?" she asked, her face flushing with anger.

"I know it's not much, and it's long overdue, but I promise I'll do better. I've had some trouble lately. I know it's not your problem."

"When this is just about all the child support I've gotten in the last year, then it is my problem. You couldn't call and tell us what was happening?"

"I should have, but I didn't."

"What kind of trouble were you having, Rob? When it seemed like you had dropped off the edge of the world and I called your friends in Florida looking for you, they were pretty evenly divided about whether you were in the Caribbean or Central America. Is that what your trouble was, trying to figure out which trip came next?"

"That's not all there was to it, Jane. I told you I was

sorry."

"And how did we get so lucky as to be on your itinerary? Do you know how many times I've been off the beach in the last year? Three times." She went over to the counter and shook a cigarette out of her pack. "Two hundred fucking dollars. Is this to buy a peek at Kelly and then disappear for two more years? I never get to see her, why should you?"

He didn't say anything, and he was right not to. Jane was determined to have her say, and he'd better be ready to listen. She had to let him know that she had changed since their time together.

"Kelly is different now. She is not an easy child. Sometimes I want to blame it on you when I don't have enough time to spend with her. She ends up learning things and getting all these off the wall ideas from other people. Now she wants a tattoo, for christsake. We end up fighting a lot when we see each other. But we never seem to finish our arguments before I have to go to work, or she has to go to school, or something else interrupts us."

"Maybe I can talk to her?"

"What are you going to say to her, Rob? Are you going to give her some fatherly advice?"

"We used to get along fine. She could always talk to me."

"She's not the same person, Rob. I'm not the same person, and neither are you. We've all changed. We're all different, and the world is different too. All you have in common with her any more is your blood and your blond hair."

Again he didn't say anything and she calmed down. Aside from wanting to punish him, another reason she had put him off for a day was so she could be sure of herself to make her points without getting too emotional. She had expected the emotion to be anger, and it bothered her that as soon as she saw him, along with the anger, there were also

The Second Coming

more of the old feelings of tenderness than she wanted to allow herself. It still puzzled her sometimes that they had not lasted together. What was so sad was that they both knew there was something they could have done, but neither of them had ever been able to figure out what it was.

Everything had been quietly amicable between them when they split except when they discussed how they would divide their time with Kelly. What was between them may have wilted, but while it had their daughter had bloomed. Jane knew it bothered Rob when he realized she would have primary custody. But he was honest enough to admit to himself that it wouldn't really work any other way. As soon as he realized it though, he seemed to lose interest. She guessed it was a defense, but there was something eerie in the suddenness of it. The only thing they wrote up legally was that he would be responsible for some child support. Jane had been proud and insisted she didn't expect anything for herself. Sometimes now though she wished she hadn't been so proud. She never felt that he should support her, but she did have the vague feeling that he owed her something more than she had gotten.

Two years after they split, she filed for divorce. It was a simple case. Rob had moved to Florida and her attorney had taken care of it all through the mail. One day she received a package of notarized paper with Rob's signature on them. A week later she sat meekly in court. The judge called her to the witness stand, asked her a few questions, nodded solemnly at the answers, rapped the block with his gavel, and it was over. She cried quietly on the drive home.

Rob had been good about the support payments at first. The checks arrived promptly within the first few days of the month, usually with a note asking after them and telling them a little of what he was doing. Then two years ago, just after the last time he saw them, the checks began coming later and later, and then one month nothing came at all. She assumed he was having some bad luck and didn't press it. A check did come the next month, but it was alone in the envelope. She tried to call him and found out that he had moved from Jacksonville to Cocoa Beach. Three or four more scattered checks came after that, but none with a note or a return address. There had been only one check in the last year, and it had come eight months ago. It was hard for her, and money was tight, but she thought she knew him well enough that he would catch up when he could. Then one night when she was out, just before she met Kevin, someone had casually mentioned that a mutual friend had seen Rob in Aleuthra a few weeks before, surfing. It was then that she started to get angry. She began calling his friends trying to find him. She never meant to, but she always managed to let it slip that he owed her money. She almost got to the point where she was ready to swear out a warrant against him, but JP talked her out of it. Now he showed up with a couple of hundred dollars and a stuffed animal. She would have been less angry if he had come empty-handed.

"I will make it up to you. I'm working on something now, and if it all pans out I'll be able to make up all I owe you, and even pay some in advance if you want."

"Now you're starting to sound like Chick. Something is always just about to happen. But for one reason or another it never does."

It was then that Kelly came in. Jane saw the change in Rob's expression and knew immediately that he was afraid of his daughter. Something in her breast started when she realized it, and something intrinsically feminine and conspiratorial thrilled at his discomfort. He had to be able to recognize what she was up against. He retrieved the present from the sofa and held it out to her, mumbling an awkward hello as she took it. Kelly took the gift without smiling or saying anything, and when Jane saw the looks on their faces she knew she was shut out from them. They were at opposite ends of an adolescent vacuum, and for the first time in her life Jane couldn't join them because she didn't belong. Rob and Kelly didn't know what to say to each other. And since neither of them had ever been very affectionate, the three of them stood in silence for a long moment.

"Your father is here to visit for a few days," Jane said, and when neither of them showed any signs of saying anything, she added, "Why don't you go straighten your room? We have some things we need to talk about." Kelly turned and walked mechanically down the hallway toward her bedroom, carrying the stuffed animal rigidly in front of her. "I told you she had changed."

"Yes."

"And she changes more every day. I try to remember what I was like when I was her age, and it's just not the same thing. They grow up too fast now," she said. She felt like crying. "Rob, I don't want to threaten you, but things have got to change. I can't do it all by myself. I need that money, and I need it regularly, every month. Kelly needs it. Do you know how much it costs to buy clothes for a girl her age? And maybe you can't visit very often, but at least you could write. She needs to hear from you."

She stopped there. She wanted him to feel her anger, but not to the point where he could use it to alienate himself from them completely. She wouldn't let him do that. She would take him to court if necessary. She had decided that. And she would do it this week if she had to. JP had already promised to let her know if he found out when Rob was planning to leave town. There was a principle involved here. This was one responsibility he couldn't ignore. This one lived and breathed.

Now she turned away from the make-up table and looked at the clock next to the bed. She knew she had to hurry. Kevin was maddeningly punctual and though she endlessly tried, Jane had never learned the art of budgeting her time. She could start getting ready three hours early, or thirty minutes. It didn't matter. She would still be fifteen minutes late. It was only by monumental efforts that she could manage to be ready within five minutes of Kevin's arrival, and then only if she put her make-up on in the car. After he was hers she would wean him of his preoccupation with the clock. It was so infantile.

She was still in her bra and panties when she heard his knock at the door. Kelly had left an hour before to spend the night with a friend. Jane had thought that would give her plenty of time with no distractions, but it still hadn't helped matters. Kevin came in and called down the hall to her, and she decided she would begin to train him right then and there.

"Would you come here for a minute?" she called back. When he pushed open the door she walked up to him and said, "I'm running a little late, but I'll make it up to you."

She put one hand between his legs and with the other she began to pull at his belt tab. She could tell he thought she just wanted to get laid, so before he could protest she looked steadily in his eyes and went down to her knees. By then she had undone his belt and separated his pants hook and begun pulling at his zipper. With a little help his pants fell easily to his ankles. She then hooked her fingers around the elastic of his briefs and pulled them down.

It was the oldest trade in the world. Love you could give and receive freely, but security you bought no matter who you were. It was nice if you could get them to go hand in hand, but sometimes they didn't. The difference was that if you lived without love you only suffered emotionally, and she didn't deny that could be bad. But if you lived too long without security your whole world began to rot. She was still looking in his eyes when she realized there was a time she would have hated herself for thinking like that.

She never liked the idea of giving head, but once she was actually doing it, it was never as bad as she thought it would be, and the feelings of control were terrific. She took

The Second Coming

his penis in her hand and stroked it. It was still spongy, but the blood was rushing to it steadily and the mantled head was purple and shining. She slowly put her lips around it and drew it into her mouth until she felt the tickling spiciness of his pubic hair. It grew quickly after that and he was hers until she finally felt the first warm spurts of his semen inside her. More and more of it came and she swallowed it all though it sickened her a little. As he finished she slowed her strokes gradually and when it became smaller she let it slip from her mouth. Her jaw ached and her lips were bruised, but she looked up at his flushed face with her sweetest smile and sent him back down the hall telling him she would be ready in a few minutes.

She wasn't hesitant about keeping him waiting after that. She took all the time she needed to finish her makeup and laid three outfits on the bed and tried them all on before she decided which she would wear. It was a half an hour later when she came out to the living room and picked up her bag and coat.

He talked about art on the way to the restaurant. She had grown accustomed to the fact that he knew a lot more about cultural things than she did. When he spoke of them he wasn't trying to be condescending, but something like condescension always crept into his voice. Rob had known some of the same things when he was younger, but he was different talking about them. Rob might bring something up if it struck him, but if she wasn't interested he wouldn't press it. If she did show any interest he would speak more and more enthusiastically about whatever it was and sometimes she would end up not even listening to the words, but just looking at him and listening to the sound of his voice as he spoke.

Kevin lectured, and he was a good lecturer, interesting and precise, but she could never have remembered all of what he said in one of his monologues unless she took notes. One night he had gone off on a tangent about "Guernica." She knew little enough about Picasso and absolutely nothing about the Spanish Civil War. When he jumped to Hemingway, and then to fascism and Franco and Hitler, with little asides about Mussolini and Abyssinia, she ended up totally muddled. The worst part though was that she could not get him to understand that it was not just one part that she was shaky on, but the whole structure of his conversation.

"You're not going to make me drink red wine again?" she asked when they were seated in the restaurant and he was poring over the wine list.

"Jane, as I've said before, it's an acquired taste. But I think if you're persistent you'll find it well worth the effort."

"But as I've said before, I don't think I want to like red wine."

At first she had been amused when he talked about a big cabernet, or remarked on the underlying hints of currant or chocolate in the bouquet of some unpronounceable Pauillac. But then she realized he expected her to drink them with him. Her experiences with wine had never gone much beyond white zinfandel, and she had no desire to go further. She had begun to order fish so at least she could have white wine, which wasn't quite as bad. But tonight she didn't want fish, she wanted beef. And because he decided on duck, he ordered a Chateau Neuf du Pape.

"Do you know what it means?" he asked after he had gone through the ritual of tasting the wine and the waiter had poured them each a glass.

"Do I know what what means?"

"Chateau Neuf du Pape," he said, putting his finger against the inside of his mouth and popping it out at the last syllable.

"No."

"Well, roughly it means 'The new house of the Pope,' and there is an interesting story attached to the name."

With that introduction he told her the story of the

The Second Coming

Babylonian Captivity and Popes Boniface and Clement and how their struggle began and progressed, and of Clement's eventual move to a place near Avignon on the Rhone River in France. He drew a startling picture of the two popes excommunicating the followers of the other and hurling papal edicts at each other, and how more than a religious struggle, it was really a secular struggle against the power and influence of the Roman church over European political affairs. As he spoke, she noticed that the wine became less chalky and astringent, which was not unusual. But what was unusual was that the taste became more pleasant, and when her entrée came she found that it went wonderfully with her beef. Perhaps she was acquiring the taste after all.

She had to hand it to Kevin. She had been preoccupied and a little sullen before dinner. But after the meal and the protracted anecdotes about the feuding popes, and his explanations of the contributions of the Syrah and Grenache grapes to the wine's body and taste and aging potential, she felt marvelously relaxed and was looking forward to spending the night with him. It was true he wasn't the most exciting or creative lover she had ever had. But he made up for his predictability with tenderness. She knew that at the moment she wanted and needed to be held, he would be there to hold her. He was a good soul and he had a good heart. How could she expect more?

Neither cared for dessert, and so after coffee they left the restaurant arm in arm. They walked across the parking lot with promising whispers to each other.

IX

JP was still buzzed after he showered and changed. He stood next to Rob's car in the parking lot, feeling a few fingers of paranoia as he waited in the semi-darkness. But as he saw the older woman approaching, his ingrained social habits took over and he calmed himself enough to make the necessary small talk on the short drive to the colonel's house. When they pulled up in front of the house, it seemed very quiet and still until they realized how many birds were up and singing.

A small round woman wearing a robe and a tight smile met them at the door. After a few perfunctory hellos she put her finger to her lips and led them upstairs to the room the colonel had set up for the observations. Everything was carefully planned and laid out. The room was at the southwest corner of the house on the second floor, with large windows set in each wall providing a panoramic view in both directions. There were desks in front of each window, and each desk was provided with two chairs and a pair of field glasses, along with a bird guide, pencils, pens, and drawing and writing paper. A small refrigerator and coffee maker were set on a table on one wall, and a couch with a quilted comforter draped over one arm was set against the other.

"The colonel wanted to greet you himself, and I'm afraid he will be angry with me, but he hasn't been sleeping well, and I hated to disturb him. Mr. Richardson, I'm sure you understand what the observations require, so I'll leave you to make yourselves at home. You should have everything you need, but don't hesitate to call me if you don't."

"I'm sure we'll be fine," Gert said, and the woman smiled and closed the door. They heard her retreat quietly down the hall. "There is an almost oriental quality to her

The Second Coming

politeness, isn't there?"

"I guess there is, now that you mention it," JP said, and felt a rising, light-headed wave of nausea. He walked the few steps to the west window and looked at the large bare tree that dominated the view in front of him. Two silhouetted forms perched silently in the uppermost branches. "There they are," he said. "What an ideal set-up. The colonel hasn't missed a trick, although with the quality of their eyesight I wonder who will be doing the more effective observing, them or us?"

"This is all very exciting for me," Gert said, moving closer to him and placing her thin arms on the desk. "I hope my enthusiasm is not going to bother you, but I can't help it. I've been looking forward to this for weeks. I just have the feeling that there is more to it than we may suspect, a potential for extra understanding, something. Would you like some coffee, JP? You look as though you could use it."

"I guess I haven't hidden it very well. I went out last night and ran into every old friend I ever had. Sometimes I think they do it on purpose. You know, toast you 'til you tumble." He smiled at her and nodded toward the tree. "There is one thing I've never been able to understand," he said. "I've always had a great admiration for ospreys, their range, their hunting skills, even their monogamy. But I could never understand why they choose to live so close to man. We destroy their hunting grounds, we poison and run off their prey, and when you look at something like DDT, it's almost like a planned attack at their very basic structure, the nest. It's not as if it's symbiotic. We admire their grace and beauty, but we'll bulldoze them in a second if their presence impedes our progress. So what do they see in us?"

"I don't know, JP. Perhaps they don't notice us at all. But I can see that besides making you wound up a taut, hangovers also seem to make you conundramatic, if that's a word, and it's too early in the morning for me. How about that coffee?"

Doyle Thomas

"No, thank you," he said, and turned back to the window. At another time he would have enjoyed a little playful repartee, but not this morning. He looked again at the tree and the chameleon brown and green background of loblolly pines and squat water oaks rising up the hill behind it. To the south was a broad, bulk-headed canal. Across it JP saw other houses, usually with intervals of wooded undeveloped lots between them. In front of most of the houses, along the canal, were small docks. Most had motor launches or day sailors or john-boats moored to them. The colonel's house stood at one of the canal's broadest points, before it narrowed and fingered out into smaller canals and forks. The ospreys nested there knowing they could always pick up an eel or bream a few feet away, though they usually flew the extra quarter-mile to the sound to do their serious hunting. The surface of the water in the canal was as still and flat as a piece of glass, and it was just beginning to reflect the pink that was slipping in beneath the mist.

"That must be what's left of the branch that broke off," Gert said, returning from the chuckling coffee pot and pointing to the awkward stump that stood on a level with the other two limbs ten feet below the smaller limb the ospreys were perched on. As the colonel had pointed out, the two limbs that remained grew on opposite sides of the trunk. The missing limb in the middle looked like it had been the heaviest of the three and had probably served as the anchoring base for the structure of the nest. With it gone, JP could see that there was little possibility that the birds could engineer a new nest of any size or stability at the same site, though he was amazed at the size of some of the sticks they had already managed to get to that eighty foot height.

It was as they were beginning to be absorbed by the ospreys' dilemma that they began to hear it. At first it was small and percussively sonorous. It was like a large animal's growl softened by strangling jungle foliage. But gradually it became louder and more obviously painful until it finally

The Second Coming

stood unhidden as a large, awful beast.

"Are we supposed to pretend we don't hear that?" JP asked after several moments. Finally they heard the muffled treads of the colonel's wife passing their door on her way to him. "That sounds terrible."

"And not quite human. I know Emma was worried about him, but I wasn't quite prepared for that. Do you think they need any help?" she asked, taking a few steps toward the door. But then she stopped and shook her head. "Perhaps if we concentrate on the birds we'll be able to block it out."

"I'll try anything. I've never been much good as a witness to the suffering of others. I either feel inadequate if I can't do anything, or else I'm resentful that it's being inflicted on me. God, I know that sounds terrible, and I'm sorry. Look, you've caught me at my worst, and I'm not going to make any more excuses. Let's change the subject. Tell me, what do you know about these birds?"

"Not very much, I'm afraid. I haven't been a bird-watcher long, and all I know of ospreys is what I've read over the last couple of weeks. It's all a lot of fragments really. I know they are raptors in a family of their own who catch their prey in their claws, and because their main prey is fish, they are sometimes called fish eagles. They have developed bony spurs on the insides of their claws so they can steady their slippery prey after they have grasped them. The large of the two is probably the female, although I guess that is the case with most birds. I read somewhere that they have overlarge uropygial glands that allow them to repeatedly preen themselves so they can keep their feathers resilient and water-proof even after repeated dives. They don't have much fear of humans and live close to them in many areas, although the relationship had not been trouble-free. In the fifties and sixties, the uncontrolled use of DDT created problems because rain caused the chemical to run off into marsh and tidal areas where it traveled up the food chain. When it reached the ospreys it weakened the shells of their eggs to the point where few of them survived long enough to hatch. Since DDT has been banned they've made a remarkable recovery, although they're still not up to their previous population levels. They are famous for their large and sprawling nests, although this pair seems to be the exception that proves the rule."

"They aren't having much luck, are they? I can see how it worked before, but now that stump seems too short to allow them to form any base. It's a shame. I wonder if the colonel was able to salvage anything of the nest that was destroyed by the storm. It must have been quite a large structure. I'll have to remember to ask him."

His remarks were punctuated by the birds' first morning cries. Coming from such large birds, the high-pitched calls seemed incongruous and irritating. The male began first and then the female answered. After a few minutes pursuing their conversation, the male alighted and flew away.

By then the coughing had subsided to a few infrequent hoarse cackles. But JP and Gert were still both uncomfortable because the initial attack had been so violent, and they were apprehensive that it might return. They could barely hear Mrs. Wheeling's voice through the wall, and then another voice, commanding, but very weak. JP was starting to feel like hell. He wished he had saved some of Rob's coke so he could go into the bathroom and give himself a bump. His head had begun to throb somewhere vaguely behind his eyes, and his stomach was beginning to knot up. After some of the things he had said to Gert, he was afraid he might start getting nasty. He felt more and more uncomfortable and confined.

The male returned over the trees from the direction of the sound to the southwest with long even wing strokes. As it got closer they saw that it held a small fish, JP thought it was a mullet, firmly in its claws, carefully aligned with its

The Second Coming

head forward to break the wind resistance. The bird landed next to its mate and offered her the fish with loud, excited cries. She took it and began to devour it with her sharp hooked beak.

"A tender gesture, I suppose," Gert said.

"It is a thing of most basic beauty," said a voice behind them.

They turned and saw a short man in a robe leaning his slight frame against the door jamb. They knew it must be the colonel, but they were both shocked by what they saw. JP knew the man had been sick, but he wasn't prepared for the lusterless look he saw in his eyes. He thought the colonel must have recognized what was on their faces because for a moment he seemed a little flustered.

"I'm sorry if I disturbed you before. I had asked Miriam to wake me. I've had a cold. And combined with this damned pine pollen, and now this confounded smoke, it's been making me quite miserable in the mornings." He walked across the room as he spoke, and although they were both nervous as he took his first steps, he moved surely and compactly toward them. "Albert Wheeling," he said, holding out his hand to JP.

"JP Richardson."

"JP, I'm glad to finally meet you," he said. He spoke carefully, as if he were afraid his words might trigger another coughing attack.

"And this is Gert Frost."

"Yes, Emma's friend. I'm happy to meet you as well, ma'am," he said, bowing slightly. "Well, JP, I guess you've been here long enough this morning to see the problem we have. They've been trying for four days to get something going on that nest, and they haven't been able to make any progress. I'm beginning to think from an engineering standpoint, they're not going to. They should begin collecting material again soon, and you'll see what I mean. They usually start a little after breakfast. If they don't accomplish anything today, I think we should begin seriously looking at some alternatives."

"I don't know anything about these things," Gert said, "but I'm very impressed by your set-up here."

"Thank you, and don't hesitate to call Miriam if there is anything you need. We tried to anticipate everything, but you can't really tell about these things until you actually begin working with them. Let me let you get back to it. It was nice meeting you, JP. I hope we can talk later. Mrs. Frost." He bowed, and gave them a smile which, if not blurred by some residual pain, was at least marked by some discomfort. Then he retreated slowly, pulling the door closed behind him.

JP and Gert sat in silence with their respective impressions, and only slowly returned their attention to the birds outside the window. The sun had risen quickly and everything was bathed in a fresh yellow light. The ospreys called periodically, but whether to each other, or for some other reason, JP couldn't tell. There were other ospreys in the area, a few on the wing to the south, and one pair which occasionally rose above the line of the woods to the northwest. The birds across the way did not move from their perches. They remained on their branch for an hour after they had dropped the mullet's carcass to the ground below.

Finally, after making a great show of spreading and flapping her wings, the female took off. She swooped down first and then banked up in a long wide arc toward the crown of the tree. As she rose past her mate he followed her example, matching her flight pattern and following her into the air above the tree, where they chased each other, calling excitedly. After a few minutes the male broke off his chase and veered toward the woods that stood fifty feet beyond their home. He glided over the treetops, circled back over the bare ground, and then back toward the trees where on his second pass over them, he suddenly dipped his wings, dropped his talons, and snatched a large branch from the

The Second Coming

crown of one of the taller trees. JP had been watching rather indolently, but the sudden movement and the resounding crack rushing over the ground to them brought him to the edge of his chair.

"Did you see that?" he asked, moving closer to the window so he could watch as the bird climbed higher above the trees. "That's a live branch! Just look at the size of it!"

"I thought they just picked up dead branches from the ground."

"So did I. My God, can you imagine how powerful they must be in order to do that."

The bird returned to the tree with the branch clutched in its talons. He adjusted his grip as he perched, finally turning the branch so it rested atop the limb he stood on. He almost seemed to be examining the possibilities of how to place it. After a few minutes, he took it again and hovering between the limb he had perched on and the stub of the limb the storm had blown away, he tried to wedge it as close to the trunk as he could. When he was satisfied he released his grip and flew easily upward. The branch hung in the crook momentarily, but the hold was too precarious and after ten long seconds it fell, turning slowly end over end until it struck the sandy earth below.

"I'm beginning to see what the colonel meant," Gert said. "It's a shame that had to be the result of something that started with such power and grace."

"I had no idea."

The female returned ten minutes later with a branch and made her own attempt, but it met with the same result. They didn't give up. They continued their flights, periodically returning with branches of differing lengths and curves, but none would hold. All fell eventually in the same lazy manner and kicked up the sand when they struck the ground and the bayberry thicket below. The birds had an obvious, basic, ingrained determination to rebuild their nest in the old tree. But after two hours watching them try JP and

Gert could both see that their attempts would ultimately be fruitless. JP began to become impatient with their resolve. The muscles in his jaw became tighter, and along with the pain behind his eyes, his head also began to throb above his temples.

"It's obviously not going to work," he said, "no matter how hard they try, and I'm going to be disappointed if they don't realize it soon."

"That would be giving them too much credit for intelligence, wouldn't it?" Gert asked. "I can see they're beautiful and powerful, and they seem to be resolved. But you yourself made the point the other morning of saying that their intelligence was mostly instinctual, didn't you?"

"Yes, of course you're right," he said, but something about the way she made him realize it irked him. He was coming down hard, struggling to make sense out of the weird filament of images that ran somehow from Rob to Chick to the colonel and then to the birds. He couldn't get a handle on what the connections were, and he couldn't concentrate enough to trace them back to their sources.

They continued to observe, and made their separate notes in silence. It was almost nine thirty when Mrs. Wheeling came in and excused herself, and told JP that the colonel would like to talk to him. She led him down the dark hallway to the room and held the door for him as he entered. The colonel was in bed amid a clutter of books and papers. As JP came into the room he recognized something, a smell he thought, that reminded him of his father's hospital room. He immediately put on the same smile he had worn there.

"What do you think, JP?" the colonel asked hoarsely. "They don't stand a chance in that tree, do they?"

"No, it doesn't look like it."

"And if I'm not mistaken, they're going to realize it shortly. If we don't do something, our little experiment is going to be without a subject."

The Second Coming

"I'm afraid you're right, but what can we do about it?"

"I propose this," the colonel said, unrolling a large blueprint and spreading it on the bed in front of him. "An artificial nest. I've read they've had luck with these up north, luring birds back after the DDT debacle. As you can see, it's basically a long pole topped with a wooden crown held together with chicken wire. I thought we could erect it, hopefully in one day, and seed it with a few of the branches the birds have tried to start their old nest with to give them the idea, and see what happens. We won't be able to get it as high as the nest they're used to, but we should be able to get up thirty or forty feet with it."

"Where would you put it?"

"I thought fifteen or twenty feet in front of their tree but a bit closer to the canal to give them the same basic view. After looking over our list of volunteers I think we have enough manpower for the job, but we'll need a carpenter."

"I have a friend who might be able to help us. I'll talk to him this afternoon. I'm sure he could do it, but I don't think he has any tools."

"That won't be a problem. I have a garage full. Do what you can on your end and call me this evening to let me know what your progress is. I'll get a materials list together, and see if I can arrange to have everything delivered tomorrow. If we get an early start, we should be able to complete it by evening. I don't think we have much time."

"We should probably work on some back-up plans too, in case they don't go for it."

"JP, if this doesn't work, I'm afraid I may be too discouraged to worry about developing any more plans. I've spent so much damn time on this, and fate just doesn't seem willing to cooperate. It all seemed so easy when I first got the idea. The birds have been here so long they seemed like part of the family. I know their habits, their likes and dislikes. I can predict to within a couple of days when they will arrive from South America, and I can tell when they're ready to leave. I know where they like to hunt in the mornings, and where they go to bathe in the evenings. I've watched them raise four broods and seen them teach their young to fly and hunt. I just wanted to share them with people. Maybe that's the problem. Maybe they're not mine to share."

"I'm sure it will all work out. The important thing is for you to take care of yourself. Have you seen a doctor?"

"I'm fine," the colonel snapped. "I'm taking care of myself. It's just a bad cough. Talk to your friend and get back to me this evening."

JP left the colonel's bedroom and made his way back to the observatory. Another couple waited there to relieve them. The man was balding and owlish behind his glasses. JP recognized him from the meeting. The man's wife looked like some kind of bird too, although he couldn't think exactly what bird it was. He was amazed at how many of these people looked or acted like one bird or another, but he didn't want to think about it. The possibility of relief brought an overwhelming fatigue that he had been struggling all morning to ignore. He heard Gert explaining where everything was and describing what they had seen since dawn. After greeting them, JP left the room and went outside. He leaned against the car and tilted back his head, hoping the heat of the sun would make him feel better. But when he closed his eyes behind the redness of the lids were images of his father.

He could usually handle the images and control the memories. It was never any trouble with the most conscious and forthright of them, even if they were unpleasant, because the obvious ones were attached to the steady light of his acceptance of the world as it was. But then there were other memories, the ones hidden behind the congeries of everyday events, not memories of what had happened, but awkwardly

The Second Coming

phrased questions of why certain things did happen.

His father had been two men. The first was the one who was stronger and smarter than anyone. JP always remembered the same apocryphal thing about him. They were walking in the evening after dinner through the darkening neighborhood. His father was telling him about something, he couldn't remember what. But he could remember the clear voice rising with enthusiasm, ringing beneath the canopy of trees that lined their street. Suddenly his father had stopped and put a hand on JP's shoulder and squeezed. Everything he had, everything he was, he transmitted in that pressure. JP knew even then that he sensed he didn't have long to give it.

That version disappeared soon after, unable to survive in a medium with so much alcohol. JP thought later that if they had done an autopsy on the rotting shell the second version left, they would have found some hint of the evanescent earlier version floating like a fetus within.

The second version arrived when JP was ten, although there wasn't an actual arrival, or a real transition from one to the other. The second version was just suddenly there. And while JP never mistook him for whom he had replaced, he still had the feeling he had been there the whole time. The earlier version left with only that squeeze of his shoulder as a goodbye.

The change terrified JP because everything was suddenly so unpredictable and JP was a sensitive child who saw living forms in the shadows, and even then could recognize how essential and exquisite certain moments could be. The second version of his father never lived an exquisite moment. He would lumber around at night bumping into things, sometimes mumbling to himself, sometimes sobbing. Then there would be the times he would get like Huck Finn's "Pap" and sit in his chair with tightened eyebrows waiting for someone to get close enough to strike at. JP had sometimes heard him struggling with his mother through the walls at night. But for a long time he was never sure if he was striking her because the tone and volume of her voice would never change. On the nights it really got bad, she would come into their room and wrap him and his brother in blankets and take them to her sister's house across town. JP would never forget those late-night drives, lying on the back seat, hovering a little above sleep and the road that rushed by hissing a few feet below him, looking up at the startling lights that shot through him for an instant and then were gone. Those lights were like shooting stars. Better.

As soon as he could, JP removed himself. He spent less and less time at home and insulated himself with books and music when he was there. By the time he was fifteen, he and his brother and mother had moved out and were living on their own. Occasionally his father would pay an apologetic visit. JP hated those visits because he had to look into those defeated milky eyes, and know they were where he came from.

At the time of his last stay in the hospital JP had not seen him for more than three years. His mother had to beg him to come. They went together to the hospital and were led to the intensive care unit where they found him cowering shrunken beneath the blankets, trussed by tubes and guarded by blinking lights. They sat with him for a while and he never woke up, but JP could see his eyes beating ferociously beneath the lids.

Gert came out of the house and he felt a wave of embarrassment about what he had been thinking and feeling. They got into the car. He was glad when she asked what the colonel had said, and he used the drive back to the motel to explain it to her.

Rob wasn't in the room when he got back. JP stripped and climbed under the covers on one of the double beds and tried to sleep.

John Phillips Richardson, Sr. officially died the day after JP and his mother visited him in the hospital. He left

The Second Coming

little behind. JP was never really sorry about it, and it didn't seem anyone else was either. They were sorry for what he might have been, and that led them to be sorry for what they themselves might have been, and there is a real sadness to that. That was why so many of them were able to cry real and convincing tears the day he was laid to rest. JP felt a nettling anger at the funeral and at odd times afterward because he knew that somewhere along the line he had been cheated of his opportunity for grief. But he didn't think it all that clearly because he was falling asleep.

X

It suddenly struck Mary that she hadn't seen the moon in weeks. And now there it was above her, yellowish, almost brown, and almost full. The night air felt wonderful to her skin, and it was good to escape. She was almost sure he would follow her so she waited just half in the moonlight. There was a hesitating crack of light in the doorway and then it opened fully and a young couple rushed past her on their way to the parking lot. She returned her attention to the sky, and then realized he had somehow slipped out behind them without her noticing. He stood very close to her.

"Where are you staying?" he asked.

All her predispositions to be coy or mysterious disappeared, and she found herself giving him directions and trying to recall landmarks around the cottage. She explained how she ended up staying there though she was part of the bird observations, but she quickly sensed he wasn't interested and let her eyes and voice drop.

"Are you leaving now?" he asked.

"Yes, I'm tired."

"Then maybe I'll see you tomorrow," he said as another group swept past them.

"I hope so," she said, but she didn't know if he heard her because he was already reentering the bar.

Mary had seen Tony briefly before she left, but she had not gotten the reaction she wanted. She was miffed when he didn't show any disappointment. He didn't seem to care at all that she didn't want to go to the mountains. He was more interested in knowing if she'd seen his running shoes, and when she became testy, it didn't cost him a rapid step. He told her to have a good time, gave her a peck on the cheek, and disappeared behind the hollow, echoing sound of the apartment's closing door.

She had packed slowly and carefully, left a note for

The Second Coming

Dianne and Cindy, and then climbed into her little car a few minutes after five. It took her a while to pick her way through the rush hour traffic, but within an hour she had left Raleigh far behind. She decided to use the driving time constructively, and she spent the next two hours pondering where she was in her life, how she had gotten there, and where she wanted to go. She was pretty sure where she was, and she could in general trace how she had gotten there. But as for where she was going, that spread out mysteriously before her like the flat gloaming road she drove on.

Night fell haphazardly behind her and she made good time, even through the small towns with their arbitrarily reduced speed limits that dotted her route. It was dark by the time she passed through the last town and entered the long stretch of empty road running through the marshes and cultivated forest land. After she had driven a half an hour into it, she saw the red brake lights of a line of traffic stopped in front of her. There was a strong smoky smell in the air and an eerie pink and orange glow above the trees in front and to the right of her. She pulled up to the line and sat for a few minutes wondering what was going on. Finally a man from the car in front of her got out and began talking to someone who had walked back from farther up in line. They stood for a while, alternately gesticulating down the straight road in front of them, and standing with their hands on their hips shaking their heads. They looked fluid and illusory silhouetted in her headlights, with shifting, soft boundaries. When they ended their conversation one of the men walked back toward her car. In her mirror she saw two cars pulling up behind her. The man hesitated as he put his hands on her door and smiled blindly at the approaching headlights.

"The State Police have closed the road up ahead," he said. "There's a fire up there and they say it's gotten too close to the road." He looked at her, and then past her at the bags and pillow on the front seat beside her. "Thirty minutes earlier and we would have made it. You going to the beach?"

"Did they say how long it would be?"

The man was about to answer, but then he hesitated because someone from the first car behind Mary had gotten out and was walking toward them.

"There's a fire up ahead," the man said to the approaching figure.

"I know. We heard it on the radio."

"Did they say how long it would be?" Mary asked again.

"No," the man from the car behind her said. "They just said they were afraid the fire was going to jump across the road. They've had forestry crews watching it all day."

"The wind doesn't seem strong enough to blow a fire across the road," Mary said.

"If a fire is big enough it can make its own wind, can't it?" the first man asked. "Because of changes in the surrounding air temperature or something?"

"If it was that big, wouldn't we see it from here?" Mary asked.

"You can sort of see it glowing over there," the first man said, pointing.

Another person, a woman, approached from behind them and began asking the same question. The two men quietly vied with each other as to whether the information from the radio or from farther up in line was more accurate. Mary began to feel small and insecure looking up at faces she didn't recognize. Why had they chosen to stand around her car, she wondered? She looked up again and caught both men staring at her bare legs below the hem of her short denim skirt. Jesus, she thought. She grabbed her steering wheel and squeezed it, wishing they would go someplace else to speculate. They spoke for a few more minutes above her, and then gradually drifted back to their own cars.

Mary couldn't guess how many cars were in front of her because of the distortion in the way their red brake lights

The Second Coming

seemed to disappear into the earth. For a while she tried to count the vehicles that lined up behind her. But eventually she gave up because the new headlights, refracted through so many windshields, began to multiply and warp their beams, or the points of light formed into lines and arcs until finally she wasn't sure what the lights behind her meant. Gradually people in line turned off their motors and lights and then, except for someone accidentally stepping on a brake pedal or opening a door to get out and stretch, the only lights she saw were far in front of her. At one point she got out of her car to get a better view of the fire. She almost imagined she saw the tips of yellow flames licking up above the trees toward the sky.

It was more than an hour before she heard the hoarse, chattering coughs of motors starting in front of her. Slowly the line began to move. It took ten minutes to get to the point where she could make out the flames in the trees to the right of her. They seemed subdued and harmless and had a weak orange, almost blue, color to them. They burned low, well within the border of the trees. A line of hooded firemen was posted on the near side of a large dry drainage ditch that ran along side of the road. They leaned on their axes and shovels, smoking and talking to each other. Occasionally they would turn and watch a few cars pass. Beyond them were three trucks pulled on to the shoulder of the road, dark under the great red lights spinning eerily on the roofs of their cabs. As she passed the last one it suddenly rained a great ineffectual blast of water in the direction of the fire, and the people in the car behind her let out a lusty cheer at the demonstration. The speed of the line of cars gradually increased and the evidence of fire and firemen fell further behind them. Finally the line spread out to the east like a newly slipped strand of pearls.

Because of the delay it was almost midnight when she pulled up in front of the motel. The office was dark and no one came when she pressed the service bell. She was tired and cranky. There were sounds of music and conversation coming from the bar around the corner of the building and up the stairs. After a few indecisive moments she forced herself to go up. Once she was upstairs there was a hallway leading to the short leg of an L-shaped bar. The room beyond was about three quarters full. There were a lot of college kids like her and also some older, bored-looking locals. She got the bartender's attention and he informed her that he only leased the bar from the motel owners and didn't know what their schedules were, but he had rarely seen anyone around the office past eleven.

Mary didn't know what to do. For an instant she hoped she would see Mr. Richardson. But then she realized she didn't want to see him at all under the circumstances, and she was frightened by the possibility that he could be in the bar.

"Mary," someone behind her said, "what are you doing here? We thought you were in the mountains with Tony." It was Pam, a girl she had met at school who was tight with some of Tony's friends. They had only spoken a few times at parties and Mary had wanted to get to know her better, but it had been a month since the last time they had seen each other. Pam was cocky and blunt in a benign way, but the most obvious thing about her was her height. She was very tall, taller than any woman Mary knew, and most of the men. But she was built with beautiful proportions, and she carried herself with a captivating, coltish grace. She was one of those tall people who never seemed to have gone through an awkward phase. But now she was drunk and swaying and it was awkward for Mary to look up at her because it took so long to get from one side of her sway to the other.

"I was going to, but I decided to come to the beach instead."

"Where are you staying?" Pam asked. There was a boy behind her, shorter and drunker than she was. Mary saw

The Second Coming

his slitty eyes and sloping grin each time Pam rocked to the left.

"I'm supposed to stay here, but there isn't anyone in the office, and I'm not sure what I should do."

"Have you tried to call the motel phone number?"

"No."

"See if you can get the bartender to dial it for you."

They all turned back to the bar and waited for a lull in the bartender's activity. Mary raised her hand and asked if he would dial the number. She waited as he scanned the drink-spattered list of numbers on the wall next to the phone. He dialed and held the receiver to his ear, pointedly ignoring the customers who were queuing up for another round. He looked her up and down as he let it ring. Finally he shrugged his shoulder and replaced the receiver on its hook.

"You can spend the night with us," Pam said. "Don't worry. We can take care of everything in the morning. In the meantime, let's have some fun. Do you know Bobby? He's been following me around like a puppy all night. Come on. You know Ken and his friend, Jean, don't you? They know Tony. They're out on the deck. Doesn't this place remind you of the Ace Café? The locals all look so tough. But I bet if I went 'boo,' half of them would pee in their pants."

She led Mary and the drunk boy out to the terrace at the side of the bar. Ken and Jean were sitting back in deck chairs, under the stars and the heaving moon, sniffing at the salty air. Everyone was introduced. Jean, who was French, spoke to Mary in his most blurred accent, but she was too tired to show much interest. An hour later she followed them back to the cottage.

There were eight people staying in the four bedroom rental house. Two couples each had a room, Ken and Jean shared one, and Pam and a friend shared the other. Mary was offered the couch in the living room and a rough wool blanket brought down from one of the closets. She was glad she had brought her own pillow. People roamed around for a while, not quite ready for the party to end, but Mary was so tired that she lay down on the couch anyway, turned her back on them, and quickly went to sleep.

She got up early, wrote Pam a quick thank-you note, and left before the clock above the stove said eight o'clock. It was still cool and crisp outside, but the sun was already strengthening and she could tell it would be another warm and brilliant day. The motel was five miles north of the cottage on the Beach Road. She drove toward it, occasionally passing a puffing jogger or a group of surf fishermen standing with their tackle and pails, waiting to cross the road and walk through the fluttering sea oats to the beach.

There was a large older woman sitting at the motel desk. She looked up at Mary over the rims of her glasses. Her eyes were lazy and myopic, but after their first few sentences together, one eyebrow rose perceptibly.

"But I had a reservation," Mary said.

"Yes, you did. But it was never confirmed, and you weren't here by ten o'clock, and it is our policy not to hold an unconfirmed room after that. We're very sorry, but it's spelled out plainly in our brochure."

"But I didn't make my reservation. It was made through the school, and I assumed they would have confirmed it."

"Mr. Richardson called yesterday morning and confirmed his, but I'm afraid there wasn't any notation that you were part of his group."

"When will you have a room?"

"Not until after Easter. This is our busiest week of the spring and we're booked solid. You can try some of the other motels, but I'm afraid you'll probably get the same answer from them."

"What room is Mr. Richardson in?"

"206," the woman said, and her eyebrow rose again.

The Second Coming

An older couple came in, and by the way the woman looked past her toward them, Mary knew their interview was over.

She went outside and hesitated, wondering if it was too early to knock on his door. She was angry because she knew at least part of the mix-up was his fault. Up on the open breezeway people were coming out of their rooms and heading toward the beach or the old-fashioned dining room. She had a couple of hours until the meeting at eleven so she decided to eat some breakfast and take a walk on the beach and then see if she could catch him before the meeting started.

She was seated in the dining room at a table back near the entrance to the kitchen. The restaurant filled up quickly with people impatient for their coffee and breakfast, and there was soon a steady stream of waitresses passing her on their way to and from the kitchen. She wasn't very interested in her eggs, but she ate them anyway. Instead of walking on the beach, she decided to go back to Pam's cottage to see if there was any possibility of her staying there. Within a few hundred yards of the cottage she almost decided to forget the whole thing and drive back to Raleigh, but she saw Pam in a lounge chair on the deck and she knew she should thank her for her help so she pulled into the driveway.

It turned out that the girl who was sharing the room with Pam was leaving on Monday to go to Pennsylvania for a family reunion. Mary was told she was welcome to crash on the couch until then, and share the room with Pam after that, until Friday anyway, when Pam was hoping her boyfriend could get away from work to spend the weekend with her. Mary explained that she didn't have much money because she expected that a room was going to be provided for her, but Pam told her not to worry and that they could work out the details later. She told her to relax, and tried to talk her into putting on her bathing suit. Mary declined and they talked for a while, gradually letting the gaps in their conversation broaden until Mary fell asleep under the sun.

Her waking was one of those dizzying, falling affairs that meant, she had heard, that her soul was plopping back into her body after some irretrievable out-of-body experience. When she was sufficiently herself again, she checked the clock inside. It read eleven ten so she ran downstairs, hopped into her car and drove to the motel, hoping the breeze coming through her open window would loosen the curling hairs that were plastered to the nape of her neck.

The meeting had already started and the double doors to the room were closed. Rather than disturb the proceedings, Mary hung back in the lobby. She tried to follow what was going on inside. After she got confused trying to do that, she sat down and read one of the brochures that were littered about on the low tables at the entrance foyer.

Mr. Richardson was speaking when she first arrived. When he finished he introduced an older woman who carefully read some message that Mary tried, but couldn't, follow. When she finished Mr. Richardson again took the floor and answered a few questions. Then the meeting began to break up. Mary still hung back because she was suddenly embarrassed about her predicament again. The thought that Mr. Richardson might get the wrong idea embarrassed her even more, but there was a principle involved. She wasn't willing to pay for a place to stay when she had only come down because one had been promised her.

As soon as she could approach him she took him aside and explained what had happened. He listened carefully and had a concerned look on his face, but she could tell that the concern ended very close to the surface. They had to pause a few times while he talked to stragglers, and he introduced her to the older woman who had spoken at the meeting and another woman she would be paired with later in the observations, and then they were finally left alone.

The Second Coming

After he collected his things he returned with her to the office. There was a man behind the desk this time, but the story was the same. He had the confirmation on JP's reservation, but not on Mary's. Even without the confirmation he had held the room for an extra hour and tried to get hold of JP to see if she was with him. When he couldn't be found and she didn't show up, he rented the room. Like the woman earlier, he told them there was little chance a room would come open, and he had also heard that all the other motels on the beach were full.

"I guess I'll have to go back," Mary said once they were outside.

"Nonsense. There has to be a place for you to stay on this beach, and we're going to find it. Did you see the people in that meeting? Three quarters of them must be over sixty. Don't get me wrong. I don't have anything against senior citizens, but we have to keep these things balanced."

"There is a place I can stay, but I can't afford it. The only reason I could afford to come in the first place was because of the free room."

"If there is another room, take it. As long as it's reasonable the university will pay for it. And I'll make up any extra. You don't have to worry about that. Where is it?"

"Just down the beach road. Some friends from school rented it for the week."

"Do you need me to talk to them?"

"No."

There was a new group of people at the cottage when she got back. Most of them already had red faces and arms from the unfamiliar sun. She knew some of them, and some she recognized from around campus. Then there were others wearing the colors and emblems of other schools.

Pam seemed genuinely glad she could stay. They locked themselves in the room together and talked about all sorts of things. Then they put on their bathing suits and spent the afternoon on the beach.

A large group gathered at the cottage that evening and after a spirited and disorganized cook-out they decided to check out some bars. They assaulted each en masse, drank a beer or two, and then moved on to the next. By the fourth or fifth bar they began to lose some of the boys who had started off too quickly, and couples began pairing off, and gradually the group whittled itself down to a manageable core that ended up in a dark booth at the biggest, most popular bar on the beach. After all the casualties and desertions only Mary and Pam and Jill, the girl who was sharing Pam's room, were left. They were still approached by boys who recognized them, boys who would walk up smartly, but within a few minutes discover the collective silent resistance among them. After the creases in their come-ons had withered, they would gradually drift away.

Pam had a sharp comment on everyone in the bar, and they all enjoyed listening to her and adding their own small barbs when they could. There was nothing inherently vicious in it, but none of their comments were kind.

They had heard last call and were about to leave when Mr. Richardson came in with another man. They were both drunk, but Mr. Richardson was much more loaded than his friend. The other man left him as soon as they came in and disappeared among the crowd. Mr. Richardson lurched as he walked and when he fell into an empty table and scattered the empty beer bottles on it, one of the bouncers went over and grabbed him under the arm and began talking to him. She couldn't hear what the bouncer was saying, but he was obviously annoyed and trying to control himself. Mary finally realized he was being so patient because he knew Mr. Richardson, and that was why he wasn't just throwing him out. The man he had come in with returned and took Mr. Richardson under his wing again. They talked to a man at the bar for a while. At one point Mr. Richardson turned around and looked directly at her, but there was no sign of

The Second Coming

recognition in his face. They only stayed a few more minutes and then they reeled back into the night.

Although she had been told that there would be something for her to do every day, her first shift wasn't scheduled until Tuesday, and once her living arrangements were resolved, she relaxed and spent the next two days soaking up the sun. No one could have asked for better weather. The sun was big and warm in the cloudless sky, and the wind blew from the land across the beach and out to the cool green ocean. Jill left on Monday afternoon, and Mary moved her things into Pam's room. She declined an invitation to a beer bash at another cottage that night and went to bed early, falling asleep to the sound of the breeze whispering through the empty house.

Small docks and canals lined the border of the road that led over the low marshland back to the Colington subdivision. The directions were straightforward and she had no trouble finding the house. When she got there she found herself in the middle of quite a bit of activity. A table had been set up in the yard at the side of the house, and Mr. Richardson and five or six other men were alternately leaning over some papers spread on it and pointing to a tree that stood seventy five feet west of the house. She looked up as she got out of the car and was surprised to see the ospreys resting calmly atop it, seemingly oblivious to all that was going on below them.

She was led into the house by a quiet pinched woman who seemed distracted by all the activity, and led her unceremoniously up the stairs to a bright room that faced the ospreys' nest. There were three older people, two women and a man, in the room, and they all turned to her when she came in. She recognized them from the meeting on Saturday morning, and she thought the older looking of the woman was the one who had spoken to the group. The man seemed nervous and made a few jerky movements with his arms as she came in, but he composed himself quickly. No one said anything for a moment and just when it seemed that things were getting a bit awkward, the other woman who had very crisp-looking hair and a relatively unlined face stepped up and held out her hand.

"Mary?" she said. "My name is Gert. JP introduced us at the meeting, remember? And this is Mr. and Mrs. Corcoran."

"Hello," Mary said, a little more brightly than she felt.

"Are you going to fill her in, Gert?" Mrs. Corcoran asked as she and her husband moved toward the door. "I'm going to look in on the colonel."

"Is this your first shift?" Gert asked after the other couple had gone out.

"Yes."

"Well, there's not much to it. Our job is to observe the birds and record their actions in these logs. You can see from Emma's notes that not much has been happening this morning. You've heard about the problems we've been having, haven't you?"

"Yes, sort of."

Gert reiterated what had happened to that point, starting with the storm and the missing branch. "It comes down to the fact that the colonel decided the best course of action would be to construct an artificial nest and hope the ospreys will adopt it as their home. That is what they're doing down there now. They're being held up waiting for the lumber."

"Which one is the colonel?" Mary asked. About ten more people were on the lawn than there had been when she arrived only a few minutes before. They stood in small groups, nodding and talking to each other.

"He's not down there," Gert said. "He's been ill. That's why Emma went to look in on him."

A few minutes later the lumber arrived on a flatbed truck, and there was more activity as it was unloaded. The

The Second Coming

men became excited and there was a lot of arm waving and pointing and movement from the table on which the blueprints lay to a set of sawhorses where the lumber had been dropped off.

"The men are almost more interesting to watch than the birds this morning, pacing off their territories and developing their pecking order."

"Who's in charge?" Mary asked.

"JP, I guess. The other young man is the carpenter. They're friends, I think. At least I've seen them around the motel together."

Mr. Richardson had been conferring with the man over the blueprints and finally he nodded and walked around the house toward the front door.

While he was in the house the carpenter set to work under the eyes and with the suggestions of the rest of the men. He measured boards and cut them with an electric saw and nailed them at angles to the end of one of the long green, salt-treated posts. Mr. Richardson came back into the yard with some shovels and a post hole digger. After examining the carpenter's work, he led some of the men across the yard to a place fifty feet in front of the window but angled off to the left toward the canal. After more discussion they began to dig in the soft, sandy earth. The rest of the men drifted back and forth between the saw horses and the deepening hole, examining progress and offering advice.

After a half hour of digging, Mr. Richardson abruptly turned around and looked up at them. He handed his shovel to one of the other men and headed toward the house. A few minutes later he walked into the room.

"How are you two this morning?" he asked cheerfully.

"We're both fine," Gert said. "And you look much better than the last time I saw you."

"I feel much better, thanks. What do you think? If we go up forty feet from the hole..." he said, extending his arm and sighting down it, trying to triangulate where the nest would sit. "I hope it works."

"Mr. Richardson, will they mind being so close to the house?" Mary asked.

"I don't think so, and please call me JP," he said. "They don't show much fear of humans. Sometimes I think disdain would be a better word."

"Did you ever get a chance to look for the remains of the old nest?"

"No, and I'm glad you reminded me. We've got people bumping into each other down there looking for something to do, and that might just be the thing to get them occupied. The birds usually take a short flight around noon, so maybe we can try then."

"Have you seen the colonel today?" Gert asked.

"Yes," he said, lowering his voice. "I saw him earlier and he didn't look good. Your friend Emma was sitting with him. I think this has all been more of a strain than he was prepared for."

"Oh, there goes one!" Mary said, raising her binoculars.

"Yes, that's the male," Mr. Richardson said. "I've got to be going. The female will probably follow him in a few minutes. Thanks, Gert, for reminding me about the old nest."

Mary watched the flight of the osprey. It banked and stroked to the southwest.

"JP is your teacher?" Gert asked, and when Mary nodded, she asked, "What do you think of him, really?"

"I don't know, as a teacher or as a person?" Mary asked, not taking her eyes from the birds, and not really wanting to discuss it. She remembered him saying that JP didn't stand for anything. "I don't know if I'm qualified to give an answer in either area."

"A person is always qualified to give an opinion. And the interesting thing about them is that they usually tell

The Second Coming

as much about the person giving them as they do about the person they're speaking of."

"Maybe that's what I'm afraid of."

"You needn't be afraid, and what I'm interested in are his teaching abilities."

"He's a good teacher," Mary said, choosing her words carefully. "At least, he has the faculties to be a good teacher. But I don't think he takes things seriously enough. I know when I'm older and look back on my education I'll realize some of the things I've learned aren't important in the grand scheme, but I want to be able to make those determinations myself. Sometimes I think the most important thing I'm getting out of my education is the discipline I've had to develop to carry the work load. And it's hard to have Mr. Richardson, JP, teach you something out of one corner of his mouth, and then be telling you it doesn't matter out of the other. He's good at communicating with us on our level, but he doesn't realize how quickly he can ruin it with a cynical remark or a bored look."

"I noticed the same thing about him Saturday morning. As you said, some of the important things we learn, in life as well as in school, can be exciting and a real adventure. But then there are also some important things we learn that can be frightfully dull if we let them be. One of the great struggles in an individual's education and maturation process is keeping an unjaundiced eye open for the new. It doesn't seem JP has learned that. I read somewhere that most faculties have a member who fits into the category of 'resident adolescent,' and what is a more acute symptom of adolescence than a perpetual, high-strung boredom? I think what happens to them is that their development gets arrested somewhere along the line and they end up in a kind of limbo, strung up between the rest of the teaching establishment whose pedantic ways they resent, and the shifting, amorphous student body in whose faces they see the youth and idealistic innocence that has escaped them. It's sad really, because they often seem to be among those with the most potential. It's never the dull ones who end up that way."

Mr. Richardson again emerged from the side of the house, and as if by some pre-arranged signal the female osprey left the nest with a high piping call and followed her mate. Mr. Richardson, JP, gathered around him the men who seemed to have the least to do, and after a short conference he led them to the ospreys' tree and the tight skirt of bayberry bushes beneath it.

"Do you like school, Mary?"

"It's hard, but I'm enjoying it."

"I can almost resent the opportunities and advantages you have that weren't available to me when I was your age. It's a different world now."

Mary nodded, but she wasn't really listening. The man working on the artificial nest had been left alone when JP organized the posse to search for the remains of the nest. He had taken off his shirt and sweat glistened on his brown skin. When he swung the hammer she saw the muscles jump beneath the skin, up his arm, and through his shoulder toward the middle of his back.

"It was such a struggle when I was young for a woman to get herself educated. Then even if you did, you found yourself faced with a culturally subsidized prejudice against your succeeding in the outside world."

The carpenter began to string wire from a small bale around the artificial branches he had nailed to the end of the post, stapling the strands as he wound them in wider and wider rings around the crown.

"Of course, it was even worse when I graduated because it was right after the war, and it was considered unpatriotic to take a job away from a returning veteran. Other women did it, but when I saw how much I would have to harden myself to get where I wanted to go, something held me back. And I've resented myself for that weakness

The Second Coming

ever since."

The man finished. Mary saw him look around for someone to help him carry the heavy post to the hole the other men were digging. He looked toward the group rooting around in the underbrush, and then toward the men who stood leaning on their shovels above the hole. She could see he was about to call them when a cry came up from the underbrush. Everyone turned, and after a moment's hesitation, they all rushed toward the ospreys' tree.

The carpenter watched the old men shuffling across the bare ground and for a moment Mary thought he would follow them, but he didn't. Instead he crouched under the heavy piling and slowly rose, lifting the crowned end of it.

"I hope you won't make the same mistakes I did. You're not faced with the restrictions I was faced with, but it's easy sometimes to lose sight of your goals. My advice would be to make your career first, and then worry about a husband and a family, because you can't work it the other way around."

Mary saw how he strained trying to steady himself under the weight of it. Gert noticed her watching him, and she became silent and watched him too. He bent under the weight, and with plodding measured steps he dragged the post across the yard. The men under the nest were so occupied with their find that they were oblivious to his efforts, but Mary knew he wouldn't have done it if he suspected anyone was watching him. He was testing himself. She felt a secret, chilling, voyeuristic thrill as she watched him. It took him a few minutes to cover the distance, and when he arrived at the hole he slowly knelt until the weight came to rest on the ground. He rose and stretched, and then walked toward the huddled group of men under the bare arms of the spreading tree.

The nesting platform was completed and raised later that day, after Mary and Gert had been relieved, and Mary didn't see it until two days later on Thursday afternoon when she arrived for her next shift. She was paired with a quiet man about forty years old who wore tinted glasses and spent the entire shift with his index finger drawn across his lip, scribbling in a spiral notebook. The couple they relieved briefed them by saying that the birds had only budged from their perches sporadically in the time they were there, and hadn't shown any interest in the new nest. Looking over the notes in the log from the past two days, Mary saw that it had been the same story since she initialed the book on Tuesday afternoon. The new nest, with its severe symmetry, rose in front of them, and the crown had been garlanded with some of the remains of the old nest, but its outlines were skeletal and empty.

Mrs. Corcoran arrived by herself a little after four, and JP drove up with the carpenter at about five o'clock. The carpenter stayed in the car as JP got out and ambled toward the house. A few minutes later she heard a murmur of voices coming from the colonel's room.

Because of the inactivity of the birds, speculation about the colonel's health had become the main topic of conversation among the volunteers. There were some who had him on his death bed, with so few breaths left that they imagined you could hear them rattling around within the confines of his fragile, translucent breast. Others thought it was fear of contagion that kept him to his room. Whatever the answer was, it was a mystery, and they all wondered. Almost everyone who had spent a shift in the house had heard voices coming from his room, but no one except his wife and Mrs. Corcoran and JP had seen him since Saturday.

The mystery surrounding his health, combined first with the hesitancy, and then with the inaction, of the birds, had thrown a pall over the observations. No one wanted to say anything, but more and more of them thought they might be wasting their time. Mary noticed that her concentration was suffering. It would dissolve along with her eyesight and random thoughts and fantasies would develop themselves

The Second Coming

according to their own logic and sequence. Then she would come back to herself, and her eyes would re-focus on the shadowy forms of the ospreys perched in the tree in front of her.

A half hour after he entered the house, JP pushed open the door and entered the room. Mary and her partner had already begun straightening up for the morning shift.

"Not much to it, eh?" he asked.

"No," Mary said. Her partner just smiled. "They haven't done more than ruffle their feathers since we got here."

"I know. The colonel told me. He watches from his room."

He looked over the notes in the log while they straightened up, and then walked downstairs with them. Mrs. Wheeling came to the door to say goodbye, and then returned to the kitchen where she had been talking to Mrs. Corcoran. Once they were outside her partner said a quick goodbye, and as he walked to his car Mary realized that it was almost all he had said through the whole afternoon. She was about to go to her own car when JP stepped up and took her by the arm.

"Some of us are having dinner tonight and I wanted to invite you to join us. I know it's short notice, but I hoped it might help to make up for my botching your reservations. It will just be Rob and me and a few old friends. Nothing very formal, but it should be fun. What do you say?"

She was about to refuse until she heard the name Rob and attached it to the figure leaning against the car at the end of the driveway. She hesitated, and then blushed.

"It will be casual," JP said, thinking her embarrassment was because of some attraction she had for him.

"I'd love to go," she said, recovering quickly. "What time?"

"About eight. Would you like me to pick you up, or

would you rather meet us?"

"I think I'll drive."

"Alright, meet us at the motel bar at eight. We'll have a few drinks and go from there."

"Could I bring a friend?" Mary asked, suddenly remembering Pam and thinking she might come in handy. "We were supposed to do something tonight, and I wouldn't feel right standing her up."

JP thought it was a great idea and everything was settled. Pam was all for it too. Her boyfriend was coming the next evening, but she was always glad to have someone buy her a nice dinner. They kidded each other as they dressed, both wondering at how quickly they had fallen into their new friendship.

They arrived at the motel and walked up to the bar a few minutes after eight. JP crossed the room to greet them as soon as they came in and led them to the low table in the corner where the rest of the party sat sipping their drinks. He introduced them to Rob, who smiled bleakly but didn't say anything, and then to a man with large and handsome features named Chick, and a girl their age or a little younger who was with him. Mary thought she recognized Chick as the man who had been with JP the night he was so drunk, but she couldn't be sure.

JP was very much the host. He fetched seats for them and made sure they were comfortable, and all the time kept up an animated monologue. Mary sensed there was something artificial and induced in his enthusiasm, though he was usually full of cynical histrionics. But gradually she began to enjoy it because he didn't try to make it seem genuine, and his expansiveness removed the pressure from the rest of them to keep up their parts of the conversation.

"We're drinking margaritas first because tequila makes strangers just the right amount of crazy," he explained as he poured from the pitcher into their tall stemmed glasses.

They shared a few pitchers and learned enough about

The Second Coming

each other to draw the vague personality sketches that come with first acquaintances. Mary had long ago noticed that she drew the lines of some people with broader, darker strokes and a surer hand, and she trusted that the strength of those strokes was attached to some developed sense of outline that helped her recognize things in the people around her. That was the way it was with Rob. From the first moment she had seen him raising his hammer the day before, she had known she would see him again. It came with the quality or renewing an acquaintance rather than initiating one. There was no mystery for her in his actions. He was quiet not from any latent shyness, but from some preoccupation. He could sit so still because the time was not yet right for action.

Pam soon caught on to JP's game and they did most of the talking, vying with each other in a private contest to see who could be quicker and wittier. Chick and the girl with him mostly ignored the rest of the party and spent their time huddled with their heads close together, whispering to each other. It didn't seem they had known each other very long.

After an hour they left for the restaurant. When Mary insisted that she and Pam would go in her car, JP asked if he and Rob could ride with them. As soon as they were in the car and moving, Rob, who was in the back seat with Pam, pulled out a small bag and handed it to JP. Mary and Pam both knew what it was, and Pam immediately became more keyed up and talkative after she saw it. Mary hadn't had much experience with cocaine, and those experiences had never lived up to the good parts of its reputation. Tony would buy some now and then, and give her shit for as long as it lasted because he could see that she wasn't enjoying it properly. He would end up doing twice as much as she did when they were together, and she knew he was sneaking off by himself to do more when he could.

Mary didn't like the way people, herself included, acted when it was around. The first rush was great, but then an infectious, latent mania followed. The whole scene was set on edge for as long as there was the possibility of doing more. There was a prowling, stealthy quality in the way it made people act. They either didn't look you in the face, or there was an unformed challenge in their eyes if they did.

It wasn't a long drive to the restaurant, but it was long enough for her passengers to do a couple of lines each. Pam hungrily inhaled hers, and in the rear view mirror Mary saw the visible chill that ran through her when she did. JP tried to put the mirror under Mary's nose and offered to hold the wheel for her, but she convinced him that she would enjoy it more if they waited until they got to the restaurant.

She had decided not to do any and was rehearsing her refusal when the mirror was again offered her in the parking lot. When she thought about it later, she realized it was her social instincts that changed her mind. She thought that if she did a little now it would deflect any attempts to get her to do more later. After she had done hers, JP put out more lines for Pam and Rob and himself.

It was then Mary realized that they must have quite a bit. Most of the time with cocaine, there was a definite and rigid etiquette. Great pains were taken to ensure the appearance of equal portions for all present. She had seen how painstaking people could be with a razor blade, trying to draw lines of the same length and width. And she had heard the breathless hush when someone had snorted two lines when simple arithmetic would have told them that only one was their's. "Oh, I was only supposed to do one? Sorry." It was usually a woman. The only time the ritual varied was when there was a lot, and the host was showing his insouciance by his unequal distribution. It was then you would see a large mirror or a glass-top table covered with long sweeping lines like the backbones of mountains with great boulders rolling down their sloping sides, or designs like the double helix of the DNA molecule. JP finally asked her if she would like another line, but she said no, and they

The Second Coming

all went inside.

There was alternately a tension and a sense of collusion among the group as they sat at the table. JP seemed oblivious to it all, or tried to be. He drank quickly, and by degrees became more voluble. What had seemed so mysterious about Rob began to be more clearly a rising sullenness. Mary sensed a growing tension between him and Chick, especially as Chick began to wear a path in the carpet with his frequent trips to bump in the bathroom.

The food was good, but no one was very interested in it. They played with it with their forks and scattered it around their plates, but little of it was actually eaten. They drank expensive champagne and at different times Mary caught people at other tables surreptitiously watching them. She knew part of the reason was because they were high-rolling and obviously spending a lot of money. But another reason, she realized as she looked at the faces around the table, was because they were a very handsome group. They just had a look about them, an offhandedness that she knew she would probably envy if she were not with them. The other diners didn't feel the low-heat tension that shimmered like a desert horizon among them. Part of it was sexual. She had noticed that effect of cocaine before, the confidence of the lower glands, but only under certain conditions and doses. Thinking that she had an immediate wicked fantasy of being with all of them, although she knew she could never do it. And even if she could, it could only be if she were sure she would never see any of them again.

"I think we should go free Harold," JP was saying, leaning forward with the idea, pushing his plate back so he could rest his arm on the table.

"Who's Harold?"

"Harold is a legend of the Outer Banks, like Virginia Dare, or Blackbeard, or Wilbur Wright."

"Harold who?" Pam asked.

"Not Harold who. It's more like Harold 'how

many'."

"I don't get it."

"Harold is royalty. He doesn't have a last name. He has a Roman numeral, although I'm not sure what it is."

"Where do we find this Harold?" Mary asked.

"Where is he imprisoned? At the Marine Resources Center on Roanoke Island. Harold, my friends, is a lobster, a king among lobsters, an emperor of crustaceans. He was kidnapped by the brigands and cutthroats of the Amy L and brought in chains to this place. He was actually held for a few days in the walk-in refrigerator of this very restaurant, surrounded by disemboweled relatives and unrecognizable lumps of his former subjects. He was even paraded out here for the amusement of the guests on a silver salver garnished with chicory and endive. It's been a humbling experience for one of such noble blood. Do they have blood? He weighs in at twenty three pounds and change, and his age is reckoned to be at over one hundred years. Even as we speak, his subjects compose legends of his exploits and pine for his return. His demersal myrmidons plot his escape in cold dark caves on the ocean floor."

"Jesus Christ!" Chick said, rolling his eyes.

"But how could we do it?" Mary asked.

"It could be done. The place is not impregnable, but it would require great stealth and cunning."

He went on like that for a bit longer. But after the champagne on top of the scotch he had before dinner on top of the tequila, even with the relatively steadying effect of the cocaine, he was quickly to the point where he could no longer hold the threads of thought or conversation together. His speech rapidly deteriorated to an embarrassed mumble, and he had to escape to the bathroom to try to recover.

As she watched him stumbling to the bathroom, Mary marveled at how her image of him had transformed in the last few days. She had thought that he didn't care about anything, but now she knew he did. He cared deeply, but he

The Second Coming

couldn't handle it. He had somewhere lost the connection between what mattered and what didn't, and consequently he was a soul becalmed, unable to find a following wind and unwilling to row.

The plan after dinner was to go to Lita's. Rob and JP again rode with Pam and Mary. JP was so reduced that he didn't move or say a word, just jellied along in the back seat. Rob and the girls did more lines before they went in. Once inside, after ten minutes of watching people, Mary was ready to leave. Pam told her she would get a ride. It had only taken one long look to get Rob to come out to her. She thought about getting the blanket out of her trunk and asking him to walk over to the beach with her, but he was too jazzed. She was almost glad when she turned and saw that he had disappeared back into the bar. She stood for a moment under the moon, and then smiled to herself and walked across the parking lot to her car.

XI

Chick wasn't going to Baltimore. He could sneak up there sometimes for a night or two, but he couldn't spend more than a few days, and he definitely couldn't do any business. He had fucked up, which was alright when he didn't think about it, but now Rob had made him think about it. He couldn't have told Rob how bad things had gotten or why. He couldn't have properly diagrammed the circumstances because he was unable to see himself in those circumstances.

He wanted this deal with Rob. First of all, there was the money. More importantly, he wanted it because if he could pull it off it would put him back where he needed to be. He had wracked his brain trying to figure out a plan, and had finally decided that the best way to handle it would be to stall Rob, stonewall him, and talk him into going to Ocean City the week after Easter. It would be quiet then, and they could probably unload it all on that crazy motherfucker who owned the surf shop. Also, if anyone from Baltimore had gone to Ocean City for the weekend, they would have returned to town by Monday.

He wished Rob had gotten there a week earlier. It had been a long winter and Chick had struggled through, bleeding his little bankroll until now, when it was just turning spring, he had pretty much exhausted it. The week before Rob arrived, Chick had run into Harvey Smollett, and Harvey had offered to take him scalloping. Chick had gone out with him on a couple of trips four winters earlier, and the money had been great. But the work was dangerous and it was always bitterly cold, and those were long trips pitching in the gray North Atlantic. Also, when things weren't going his way, Harvey could be a real son of a bitch. Chick hadn't seen Harvey since their last trip together. Everything had gone wrong and Harvey had worked himself into a state.

The Second Coming

When they finally limped into Cape May for an engine part, as soon as the lines were secure and Harvey was looking the other way, Chick jumped ship and thumbed to Baltimore.

When he first saw Harvey again and remembered his temper and the circumstances the last time they had seen each other, he thought there was a good chance he was going to get his lights punched out. After swallowing his nervousness and talking with him for a few minutes though, he knew he was safe. He was safe because he had an oily loquacity and if he got the chance to use it, it worked like the water-proofing from a bird's preening and usually protected him. He had the habit of remembering things about people that they wanted to hear about themselves, and a gift for subtle exaggeration that easily dissolved old grudges. He had been cold-cocked a few times before, but he could never remember being hit if he got the chance to speak first.

Harvey told him that he was having some re-fitting work done, and that he planned to leave with the first tide on Good Friday morning. Chick said he would be there. But then Rob rolled into town, and he quickly changed his mind. Now that he had some time to think about it though, the idea of hanging with Rob was beginning to scare him more than the thought of being on a scallop boat for two weeks with Harvey Smollett. After the story Rob had told him, he didn't think it was safe for him to stay in one place for too long. Rob acted like he didn't think anyone would follow him, or know where to look if they did. But a kilo was a kilo, even if might be only a kilo to these people. And if it didn't belong to Rios, it belonged to someone. And if you had a kilo, especially if it was only a kilo, you couldn't allow yourself to be fucked with.

So now Chick was confronted with more choices than he wanted to deal with. He was never good at decisions because almost every choice had its benefits, and he always wanted every reward, no matter how small. He couldn't tell Rob that he couldn't pull it off in Baltimore. He had to figure out how to stall him until after Easter, and then convince him that Ocean City was the ticket. They had to lay low if they decided to stay in Nags Head. Or else they had to go someplace else, Virginia Beach or Richmond, until the time was right. He knew Rob wanted to move fast, and he didn't think he had much chance of stalling him. His only hope of slowing him down was in being able to convince him how much he needed him. But when he thought about it, he knew Rob must need him, or he wouldn't have searched him out to begin with.

    He finally decided to pretend he had it sold in Ocean City and then rig the timing to coincide with his needs. He didn't know if that approach would work, and he half-expected that Rob would bolt. But when Chick laid out the skeleton of his plan he could see by the look on Rob's face that he would go along, although there was such a marked look of resignation in his eyes that it worried him. Rob had seemed so directed when they first talked, and Chick wondered where the edge had gone.

    His next step was getting Rob to give him an ounce. They needed to sell half of it to bankroll their trip, but Chick wanted the other half for himself. Rob had already shown him that he would turn him on to all he could handle when they were together. But to Chick the high wasn't the point. Cocaine was an attitude drug. It left its own recognizable stigmata on you psyche, and it was the one inanimate thing you definitely had to develop a rapport with. Chick wanted to re-introduce himself to it properly. And there was another reason he wanted it. There were some people around who thought he was sinking down, and he wanted to set them straight.

    Rob agreed to give him the ounce so quickly that Chick wondered if he had been planning to do it all along. He said he'd have it ready for him before they went to dinner the next night. He couldn't vouch for the weight because he was going to have to eyeball it. But he figured that if it was

The Second Coming

short Chick could add something to bring it up to weight, and if it was over he could do whatever he wanted with the extra. Chick offered to get some scales so they could weigh it out properly and also weigh the rest, but Rob didn't want to have anything to do with scales.

"As soon as you get the money, I need five hundred dollars. It's for Jane."

At one time Chick had acted as a go-between for Rob and Jane. When they were married Jane would sometimes come to him with her complaints, and though Chick always acted sympathetic, he almost never was. Her complaints usually had to do with Rob not living up to some expectation that he had never led her to expect he would live up to. Jane had married him with the idea that she could change him, but when she tried she was confronted with a glacial stubbornness she couldn't surmount. It would probably have been the same with anyone. Chick always thought she expected too much from everyone but herself. She was very much his sister.

The thing Chick couldn't understand was how Rob had gotten so far behind on his support payments. He had always severely limited the range of his responsibilities, but Chick respected him because he was so scrupulous with the ones he accepted. He could understand if Rob thought the money wasn't getting past Jane. But for all her faults everyone knew how much Jane loved her child, and anyone close also knew how much Rob loved Kelly. Chick had heard Jane singing her complaints through the winter, and he knew she had complained to other people as well. As soon as they pulled off the deal though it wouldn't matter because he knew Rob would take care of both of them.

Chick didn't want to be the arbitrator, so he kept his mouth shut. If Jane wasn't getting the support she needed from Rob, she should get it from someone else. He was a little encouraged when she started seeing the new guy because everyone knew he had money. He wondered about the guy though. Women Jane's age, especially if they had kids, were easy marks. If a woman that age was alone, there was a reason. Some of them wanted it that way, but Chick was convinced they were a small minority. For others, Jane included, Chick thought it was because they had some special flaw or weakness they couldn't hide. Chick liked them sometimes. They were usually more interesting than their married counterparts. But with all the younger, freer women around, especially in the summer time, they sometimes pressed too hard. They were usually philosophical about settling for less than they wanted though, and they would jump through hoops in bed because they had to and they knew it.

Chick knew a lot about women. When they were younger JP had given him his all men for all women rap, pointing out the need for the elimination of the proprietary aspects of relationships, saying that if you eliminated them you would also eliminate jealousy and narrow-mindedness. It sounded good, but Chick thought he had missed the essence of it. Most women didn't want to broaden but to narrow their emotional possibilities. Chick found that the key to dealing with them was to tell them exactly what you wanted them to do, and then let them know you expected them to do it. It was obvious that women were the more reactive of the sexes. Everything pointed that way, their emotionalism, their intuitive responses to their environment, their sexual receptivity. JP had once told him about something called a doctrine of signatures. He believed it. Just as a physician in the Middle Ages thought a plant with leaves shaped like the five fingers could be used as a curative for injuries of the hand, Chick always looked for similar correspondences. Because women were reactive, he judged that if they were given the proper stimulus their responses would be fairly predictable. Of course, it didn't always work. And he knew his looks gave him an extra edge, but he was convinced it was a valid system. If you

The Second Coming

approached a woman the right way you could get her to do almost anything...like the girl he was taking to dinner, although she was easier than most. Chick didn't respect women, and he didn't think he ever would, but he did love them. His desires were paramount, but once they were satisfied there were moments when he was capable of a numbing, palliative tenderness.

The dinner hadn't gone well. Rob's mood grew darker and more sullen. Chick could sense that most of his anger was directed at him, so he ignored him and huddled up with the little girl. JP got drunker and drunker and went off on one of his patented diarrhea of the mouth benders trying to impress the two girls he had invited.

When they were sitting at the table after dinner sipping what was left of the champagne, Chick thought about how different they had been when they were younger. Only JP clung to some semblance of what had been their predicted paths, and he was the most miserable of the three because he was the one who most obviously should have found and taken his own road. Chick had been jealous of him when they were younger, covetous of his peripatetic ideas and the peculiar turns of his mind. But when he looked at him now he recognized how directionless it all had become, and he had to admit to himself that he was glad.

Rob had a certain soullessness too, but he aspired to it. Those long conversations the three of them had in school didn't amount to anything, and he knew it. But he didn't have Chick's hedonism to fall back on, or JP's ability to drown things. It was funny because everybody always said that what Rob lacked was discipline. He didn't have the discipline to finish college. But it was Rob that fall when he didn't come back who worked two jobs for the next six months so he could go by himself to the Indian Ocean to find surf on islands no one he knew had ever been to before, places with sea snakes and volcanoes and fire coral, and no doctors, and natives who were just one slim generation removed from cannibalism. He came back six months later looking slimmer and older and spoke quietly of where he was going next. He talked about Panama and Peru, but he only got as far as Mexico, and he didn't stay there long. He came back unexpectedly, and within a few months he and Jane were married.

Chick got rid of the quarter ounce after dinner on his way from the restaurant to Lita's. He made the girl wait in the car while his customer tasted it. She was pouting when he came out so he drove to the ocean and gave her a few lines and let her know how glad he was to be with her. By the time they got to the bar she was purring and rubbing against him like a kitten.

It was twelve thirty when Jane came in with her new beau. Anything could have happened if she had been alone. She had always possessed a flair for the dramatic. Most of the people in the bar knew about her situation, even though Rob hadn't been around for a while. If she had come in alone she might have started something for their benefit. Like most astute women she had a good idea about what people would and wouldn't remember in that kind of a confrontation. But she was with this new guy with his money and his little paunch so she knew she had to behave herself. Chick saw her spot Rob right away, but she didn't offer any signs that she saw him. They took a table in the corner and talked quietly while they waited for their drinks.

Rob was babysitting JP and didn't notice them come in. A little while later he got up and half-guided, half-dragged JP toward the door.

"Can you give us a lift?" he asked, pausing at the table. The young girl looked up at the unseeing JP and gave him the same inviting look she had been giving Chick all evening without a shade of incongruity.

"I'll be back in a few minutes," he said to her. He took JP's other arm and together they helped him to the car.

"You know I can't do this without you," Rob said, as

The Second Coming

they drove to the motel. "I don't know anyone and I don't have any connections. By myself, I'll end up doing it all, and wind up either dead or crazy. I want to move fast, but if you say we have to wait until Monday, then we wait until Monday. But I want to do it right."

"Don't worry, Rob," Chick said. "We've got it dicked. Just leave everything to me."

On the way back Chick thought about what Rob was trying to do, and about the five C-notes in his pocket. He wondered why he didn't feel guilty about not giving them to him. When he got back to Lita's the girl was talking to someone at the bar, and he took the opportunity to talk to Jane and her date. As he got to the table Kevin stood up with a solemn smile of recognition and held out his hand.

"How are you two tonight?" Chick asked. "I just had dinner with Rob and JP."

"I know," Jane said. "We saw them leave."

"We went to a movie," Kevin said. "It wasn't very good."

"Oh, no, what was it?"

"Someone called for Rob today," Jane interrupted, chilling them from their conversation, which was something Chick hadn't seen her do around Kevin before.

"Who was it?"

"I don't know, some Hispanic guy. But it was something about a job, and he wanted to know if I knew how to get in touch with him."

"What did you tell him?" Chick asked steadily, but his bowels were tightening.

"I just told him where he was staying," she said. "He didn't give me much information. But if it is a good job I wish you would talk Rob into taking it. He needs to settle down and start being reasonable again. Kelly needs it."

"I'll give him the message."

"Jane says you're going out fishing," Kevin said, looking a bit uncomfortable and trying to lighten the conversation.

"Yes, maybe. I haven't decided yet. When did this guy call?" he asked, looking back at Jane.

"This afternoon."

"I'll give him the message," he said again, and slid back his chair. "Good seeing you, Kevin. Good night."

As he walked away from them he tried to think what it meant. He knew damn well it didn't mean someone was calling up and down the east coast looking for Rob to give him a job. It had to be Rios, and he knew he had to warn Rob.

He found the little girl and told her it was time to go home. She was disappointed. She wanted to stay up all night and do lines and talk and fuck and be real hedonistic, maybe try something she hadn't tried before. That was what Chick had wanted her for too, and he was also disappointed when he pulled up in front of her house and let her out of the car.

He drove slowly back to Rob's motel and tried to think. He had five hundred dollars in his pocket and three quarter-ounces under the seat. They ought to ditch Rob's car and get out of town. Go to Baltimore. They should just go to Baltimore and do it. Be quick and cool, but do it. Turn it over, get the money, and go to Colorado or somewhere. Mexico, Rob knew Mexico.

He didn't get out of the car after he parked it in one of the tight spaces in the motel parking lot. He listened. The bartender came downstairs and emptied a bottle-filled can into the dumpster. Chick heard the glass crashing down the sides and skidding on the metal floor. The wind had gone east lightly and blown some salt mist on to the power lines. They crackled faintly, and every so often a small blue flame would jump away from one of them.

Finally he got out and walked up the outside steps. Rob's room was in the middle of the building on the second floor. As he approached on the breezeway he saw a band of

The Second Coming

yellow light shining under the door. He turned the knob and pushed it open, knocking softly, calling Rob's name. JP was sprawled face down and fully clothed on one of the beds. His breathing was deep and primitive. There was something about the way he lay there that reminded Chick of pictures he had seen of dead people who had fallen or jumped from very high places. He tried to wake him, but it was useless. He went back out on the breezeway and realized the Mustang was not in the lot. Maybe he had bolted. Still, if he hadn't, Chick had to warn him. He went back into the room to look for pen and paper. He looked on the bedside tables and the dresser, and tried to get into JP's briefcase, but it was locked. He opened a drawer and knew immediately he wasn't looking for pen and paper anymore.

His search was quick and methodical. He went through the drawers first, and then through the contents of the suitcase that rested on a stand at the foot of JP's bed, and a lumpy, deflated duffel bag on the floor next to the dresser. He found baggies and a spoon in it, but that was all. He checked under the bed and up in the bedsprings, and then he checked the mattresses for any signs that they might have been cut. He looked up at the ceiling, but it was tongue-in-groove pine and solid throughout. The bathroom and the small closet were also clean. After ten minutes he knew there wasn't any cocaine in the room. JP never moved. After one last look around, he left and walked down the breezeway to the stairs at the end of the building. He never wrote the note.

Rob was going to have to get out of this by himself. Chick couldn't warn him. If he did, he would have to stay and help. And he knew in this situation he wouldn't be any help. He was just being honest with himself. If Rob found him gone, then maybe he'd realize it was best for him to get going to.

He turned the ignition and backed out of the space. A big car pulled into the lot as he approached the road to make his turn. There was a man driving and a passenger next to him, but that was all he saw. His tires screeched as he pulled out on the street, and he looked into the rearview mirror and cursed himself.

He went back to his house and packed his sea bag. He couldn't remember what the tide was so he wasn't sure when they were leaving, but he knew there would be plenty to do to get under way if Harvey would have him. If he wouldn't, the five hundred dollars and the rest of the coke would keep him out of town long enough for things to quiet down. Rob wouldn't stay long when he found him gone. He was probably gone already anyway.

The bright lamps at the end of the dock cast a stark light on the rigging and booms of the boats tied to it. Chick was wired from all the coke he had done, and he had to walk carefully on the uneven boards to keep from stumbling. He saw dark figures at the end of the dock and on the boat itself.

"Harvey," he called when he thought he recognized the man's form in the shadows on deck.

"Ahoy!" Harvey hollered back. "Cap'n Pissgums here! Well, look who it be. It looks like old Billy Bones to me, girls. Billy, you old dark soul you, we didn't think you'd make it. Come aboard and lend a hand. We weigh anchor in an hour."

"Thanks, Harvey," he said, and stepped aboard. The man was smiling, but Chick didn't like the look he thought he caught in his eyes. "Could we go below for a minute? There's something I need to show you." He thought a few fat lines and the promise of more might help to smooth the passage for him.

XII

Rob was angry at himself, and he was angry at Chick. He was angry at himself because he had put Chick in a position where he could call the shots. The bottom line was that Chick had the connections. There wasn't anyone else. He had naively thought that he could keep Chick in check. But now it turned out that he was the one in check, and there were no other friendly pieces on the board. It was an end game situation like the ones he had tried to solve in those illustrated magazines in jail. "White to checkmate in three moves." Although he could avoid destruction for a while, he knew his demise was just a matter of someone else developing the proper sequence of moves.

The reason he was angry with Chick was not so simple. What had really bothered Rob at dinner was the girl Chick had brought. She couldn't have been more than seventeen or eighteen. She had tried to look as if she belonged, but most of the time her face had been a mask of confused and contrary feelings. At one moment she would cling to Chick with a knowing look of feminine possessiveness, and the next she would peer around the table with a stuttering, harried innocence. But there was another expression that followed the two, a look of sultry defiance which he had seen two days earlier and only a little less formed on his daughter's face.

Since he had seen Kelly at her mother's house he hadn't been able to get that look she gave him out of his mind. For those two days the first pages of "Lolita" with its rapturous repetitions had goose-stepped through his head. "Lolita, light of my life, fire of my loins. My sin, my song." He could stand away from her and not be her father and hear that. He didn't feel it, but he heard it. "Lo-lee-ta." He saw it in her. "Did she have a precursor?" Yes she did. "...a certain, initial girl-child. In a princedom by the sea.." He tried to remember more, but he couldn't. He only knew that there was something more that followed.

He was afraid to think of what Kelly knew to look at him that way. He wanted to blame Jane, but he couldn't. Jane's needs were basic and her methods were frank. To fault her was to condemn an honesty he knew he didn't have. He had never wanted the responsibility of a daughter, and sometimes he thought that was why he had left them. He would have felt blessed with a son...and safer. If a son grows up and turns evil or is flawed by some weakness, the evil or the flaw belongs to the whole world. But if a daughter becomes defective, the defect belongs to the father. Kelly, even at her age, was woman enough to give him a look to make him wonder. And she was subtle enough that her mother in the same room hadn't even noticed it.

He put JP to bed and went downstairs and got into his car and drove away. There was no traffic on the beach road. His headlights glistened on the moist pavement as he drove south. A few times he thought about returning to the motel, packing what little he had, and leaving. He knew he wasn't going to sleep again, and he wondered how long it would take until he relearned how. If he left tonight he could make two hundred miles in any direction he chose. But he wasn't leaving. Every ten minutes or so he'd pull on to a beach access ramp, scoop up some coke with his pen knife, and bump himself. He was becoming methodical about it. There was almost no head rush to it anymore, just the steady overall drone of his body rush and the warping effects of the streaking lights he passed under. There was no satisfaction or hope in it.

When he got to the traffic light in south Nags Head, he turned around and headed back north. Parked in front of a cottage a few miles south of the motel he spotted the car that belonged to the girl who had driven them to dinner. If there had been any lights on in the house he would have stopped. He continued north past the motel, repeating the

The Second Coming

same rituals, and only went back after a futile hour, or it might have been two. He walked to the beach and looked east for the faint coral kiss of dawn so he could sleep. But she was coy and wouldn't come, so he went back to the room disappointed.

JP didn't snore, but he moaned a few times in his sleep as Rob paced around him. Rob would have liked to talk, and a few times he tried to wake him. When he couldn't, he was forced to measure the distance from the door to the bed to the mirror in the bathroom to look at his alien self, and back again. He stopped at the desk periodically to do more lines. He was doing a prodigious amount, three or four lines each time, and he drank glass after glass of tepid water to slake his trembling thirst.

When he could stand it no longer he walked back to the beach. Finally, above the black water he saw signs that dawn was imminent, and the sun would rise again. He listened to the waves hissing up the beach and watched them slap the shells and flotsam into a frenzied dance. They rushed in and receded, rushed in and receded, each time gaining ground as the tide crept in. Sometimes he would shiver like he wanted to jump out of his skin. When that feeling came he would lie on his back on the sand and swear not to move a muscle until it passed. But most of the time neither his body nor his mind would obey him. Gradually people started coming to the beach, quietly and in awe, to see what the world looked like where the earth and the sea and the sky met and the sun burst forth to illuminate them for the first time. He rose and crept back to his room with his head down, and when he got inside he went to the bathroom mirror and stared at himself for a long time.

Finally he undressed and got into bed and forced himself to lie there though he knew he couldn't sleep. After a while, miraculously, he did drift into something almost like sleep, though it was an active enough state that he was aware of the light outside his quivering eyelids and the noises outside the door, and he still had a warped perception of time. He stayed in bed until he thought it was noon and then he got up.

He didn't know what to do with himself and it was driving him crazy. If Chick turned some of the stuff over they could leave that evening. They could spend one night in Richmond and one in DC, or else spend both nights quietly on the Eastern Shore, and go to Ocean City on Sunday night. He wanted to get out. He didn't want to see Jane again, or Kelly, and he had had it with JP, who was still sleeping on the other bed. He knew JP had reasons for acting the way he did, but he didn't care. JP's kind of weakness was what natural selection was for.

He dressed and got in his car and drove south toward Chick's house. There was more traffic on the road because of the approaching holiday, and the going was slow because he ended up behind a car whose occupants were sightseeing as they drove. He followed them listlessly, weaving back and forth slowly until, on one of his soft veers to the right, he saw in the driveway of a cottage ahead the car he had seen the night before that belonged to the girl Mary. He slowed and pulled his car off the road on to the scrubby grass in front of the house. Maybe if he talked to someone he could calm down.

He went up the front steps to the door and knocked, but no one answered. He thought about walking to the beach and checking there, and he thought about leaving her a note, but instead he walked to one of the lounge chairs on the deck and sat down. The sun was high and hung a little to the south and it shone broadly on the blue back of the ocean. He sat for a while and felt it tighten the skin on his face and warm the fold in his lap, and then he decided to leave. He knocked again one more time just to make sure no one was home, but again no one answered. On an impulse he tried the door handle. It wasn't locked so he pushed open the door and stepped across the threshold.

The Second Coming

The house was larger than it appeared from the outside. The front door opened into a living room with a vaulted ceiling and vertical skylights that bathed the rooms in a summery light. Against the wall to the right was a set of stairs that ran up to a balcony on the second floor. On the landing were two doors, bedrooms he guessed, separated by a hall he assumed led to two more bedrooms. Beneath the landing on the left was an open kitchen, and to the right was another bedroom, and behind them was a bathroom and utility room. He could see the back door at the end of the hall.

As he stood at the threshold he was suddenly reminded of when he was thirteen or fourteen and had gone through a spell of breaking into houses. It had started with a neighbor's house one day when he was alone and bored and sure no one was home. It was so easy that he did it again. A couple of weeks later he did one a block away. With repetition and practice he eventually became bold enough to enter any house that raised his interest. He never stole anything and never meant to. He would just walk through the rooms and look at everything. He would check their refrigerator to see what kinds of food they ate, and maybe eat a little of it himself. He would wander through their dens and children's bedrooms. But he would always end up in the master bedroom. He would enter it with a palpable nervous excitement, a sexual excitement. At first he would just breathe deeply and look at everything. Then he would begin to examine things more carefully. He would look at the titles of the books and magazines on their bedside tables and peer into their closets. Finally he would begin opening drawers and examining their wardrobes, checking out the kinds of lingerie the women wore, and looking to see what the man had hidden under his gardening clothes in the bottom drawer.

He never found what he was looking for, but he did gain knowledge of people and what they kept hidden. He knew a man who had a fat roll of large bills stuffed in a sock in his top drawer, and he found out the women who were into more or less revealing sexual lingerie. Some men had collections of Scandinavian pornography and one woman had a vibrator, though he wasn't sure what it was then. He had found it lying in an unclosed drawer next to her bed.

The most disturbing thing he found though was a stack of photographs a man had taken of his wife performing sexual acts with other men. At that age, Rob had imagined that a woman who would be into that would have a betraying look about her, an unmistakable hardness in her eyes or her laugh that she couldn't conceal. But he knew this woman. She was a friend of his parents who came to parties at their house. She shopped at the grocery store like other women, and worked in her garden in the afternoons. There was nothing revealing in her clothes or her actions or her words, or her husband's either for that matter. For Rob it was a tremendous lesson in the deception of appearances. It undermined his childhood belief that the hidden foundations of things were necessarily similar to their exposed structures. And he began to realize that many of the things he had not understood, and which had lately begun to bother him more and more, had the roots to their mysteries in those hidden dissimilarities.

He stopped soon after he found those pictures. It wasn't a conscious decision, and it didn't have anything to do with guilt or a fear of being caught. He just tired of the game. What struck him now was that he had only thought about it a few times since, and never in any depth. JP could have given him theories to explain his actions. He might have called the break-ins themselves a personal cabalistic initiation, or maybe corresponded them to some obscure aboriginal circumcision rite. He might have pointed out that the photographs themselves, and the consequent suppression of the memory of them, were graphic demonstrations of man's pass from his early reliance on homeopathic

The Second Coming

explanations to a more complex, though perhaps less satisfying, scientific view of things. To Rob it only meant he had taken his first bite of the apple.

He walked upstairs and across the landing and looked down into the living room. In one of the bedrooms he found a girl sleeping. She looked peaceful and comfortable and he was glad he hadn't disturbed her. She lay with an arm draped over her head, smiling at one of her dreams. Rob remembered being that age when you could sleep during the day, nap in the breeze and escape for an hour or two from the pressures and responsibilities that were beginning to envelop you. It was especially nice if you could find someone to share a big bed with you. The girl moved until she was half on her back and half on her side with the pillow under her neck and her head tilted back. Her mouth was opened slightly and her jaw sagged out of line, but she was still pretty. Her breath hissed slowly through her teeth, and her breast rose and fell gently under the sheet.

He heard a noise downstairs and walked back to the landing. "Hello," he called quietly when he saw Mary below him carrying her beach bag and chair.

"Hello...what are you doing up there?"

"Looking around," he said, and started to come downstairs.

"Isn't there anyone home?"

"There's a girl sleeping. I didn't disturb her."

"Do you usually make yourself so at home in other people's houses?"

"Not usually, but sometimes," he said and sat on the couch while she deposited her bag and chair in the utility room behind the kitchen.

"Why are you here?" she asked when she returned, speaking slowly and deliberately because she still hadn't regained her composure.

"I don't know. Just to talk to you at first. But since then I've decided I need to accomplish something important."

"And what's that?"

"I'm going to free Harold."

"Harold, the lobster?"

"Yes," he said, deciding suddenly and becoming immediately relieved because it meant he wouldn't have to track Chick down and hound him about getting out of town. "But I need your help. I can't do it alone."

"How do you propose to accomplish this 'something important' ?"

"I don't know yet. All I know is that it has to be done." She laughed, but she looked uncomfortable. He could tell she was intrigued, but something held her back. "You're not afraid, are you?"

"What do I have to be afraid of? I haven't said I was coming."

"How long will it take you to change?"

"Ten minutes, but that still doesn't mean I'm coming with you."

"Well, I'm going over to look at the ocean. That will give you a chance to shower and think about it. If you're not coming, just stay upstairs when I get back, and I won't bother you about it any more."

He smiled at her and walked out the door and skipped down the steps to the driveway. He crossed the street and went up the gentle slope of the path cutting through the sea grass and over the dune to the wide beach. There were three or four different Parrish blues fighting for eminence in the ocean and sky. The clouds had begun to gain a little voluptuousness in the early spring, and the breeze had white caps dancing far out to sea. A few people had stretched out blankets and were either fishing with their pants' legs rolled up, or else lying in their bathing suits flat against the sand trying to get the year's first bit of sun. He sat down and took off his shoes and let his toes work themselves into the sand. It was warm at the surface, but as he wriggled deeper the

The Second Coming

sand became cold and wet and heavy, like the first shovelfull of dirt thrown upon a coffin. He waited the prescribed length of time and a bit longer, and then he picked up his shoes and walked back.

Mary was standing on the deck when he returned. She had showered and her hair was slicked back. She looked a little mannish in the clothes she was wearing, until she moved. Then he realized that what she possessed, what had drawn him to her, was not a static grace, but one that lived in movement. She came down the stairs as he crossed the street and smiled shyly at him when they met in the middle of the driveway.

"Let's take your car," he said, glad that she had decided to come, but realizing it would have only cost him a shrug had she decided not to.

Neither of them said much on the drive to Roanoke Island where the Marine Resources Center was located. She was nervous and fiddled with the car radio as she drove. When she found a station playing a song she liked, she turned it up and sang softly along with the music. She had a child's singing voice, reedy and sweet.

The drive took a half hour. The last stretch of it was through an old neighborhood alive with the white of dogwoods and the pink of azaleas. The road forked, and though there was a sign with an arrow pointing to the left for the Marine Resources Center, Rob raised his hand and silently directed her to take the right fork that led into some woods. After they had driven a hundred feet he told her to pull the car over to the shoulder of the road. A hundred feet further there were more houses, but where they stopped was nothing but pine woods. Mary had a red scarf rolled into a bandana hanging from the rear view mirror. Rob took it down and unrolled it, and then got out of the car and tied it to the radio antenna. Then he turned and gave her a half-smile over the roof of the car. "Lighten up," he said, and they walked back to where the road forked and followed the sign toward the aquarium.

"You are afraid, aren't you," he said, but it wasn't a question, and he wasn't waiting for an answer. He didn't smile at her when he spoke, or look at her, but squinted up to where the sun was coming through the tops of the trees. His eyes stung from lack of sleep and his throat was tight with phlegm and cocaine. But suddenly he made a vague connection that there was something in the obvious renewal of life around him that came intrinsically from him. He felt that he himself, no matter how unworthily, had made some holy and ancient contribution to it. The feeling disappeared as quickly as it came though, and they strode together silently, kicking through the new grass.

The Marine Resources Center and Aquarium was a modest arrangement by anyone's standards. It consisted of one low rectangular building with an open courtyard at its center. Within the building the different sides of the rectangle held displays and aquariums and different artifacts indigenous to coastal North Carolina, as well as offices and laboratories for the staff, and a small auditorium where slide and movie presentations could be given, and where local and state experts could hold forth in their various areas of expertise. It was all arranged so that by making a circuit through the building a visitor could take in all the sights. The building itself was located on the Roanoke Sound. On the grounds were paths scattered with examples of fishing and surf rescue boats, and various net types and descriptions of netting procedures, and the lonely graves of some of the early Negro lifesavers from Hatteras Island. At the south end of the building close to the sound was a tall pole topped with a platform that a family of ospreys had been induced to adopt as their nest.

They ignored the exhibitions outside and walked through the entrance. Just inside there was a helpful-looking woman behind a chest-high counter strewn with a scattered array of brochures and souvenirs. She smiled at them,

The Second Coming

brimming with anticipation that they might ask her a question. They passed through the lobby and followed the hall to the right. It was lined with the nature photographs of some local exhibitor. There were many good shots, most of them of birds, beautiful in a diaphanous, misty way.

"How are the observations going?"

"I guess they're stalled right now. We're all waiting for the birds to do something."

"It looks like a waste of time to me, a gathering of a bunch of old farts with nothing better to do, and some college kids looking for a little extra credit and a week at the beach."

"Everyone's entitled to an opinion. Go on."

"Look who your leaders are. You have the colonel, who looks like he might have been something at one time, but now he's standing with one foot, and at least part of the other, in the grave. Then for a scientific expert you have JP Richardson. I've known JP for a long time and the only thing he's an expert in is introspective histrionics. He always felt like he had to figure it all out. But he never realized that if you don't find the answers, you still have your living to do. And maybe he would have found, if he had worked at it, that some of the answers he was looking for could be found in the very living of the thing itself." He shook his head. "And that's why you and I are here. We're going to actualize something. We're going to take an idea whose creator let it die as soon as he uttered it, and we're going to make it a reality. We're going to give freedom to a creature that has no conception of the meaning of it."

He was walking as he talked and getting more excited, until finally she stopped him by putting a hand on his arm. When she had his attention, she put a finger to her lips. But he shook his head and continued.

"And what about these birds? Everyone sits in that god damned room with their pencils sharpened and the lenses of their binoculars polished, marveling at 'how majestic' and 'how graceful' they are, waiting. When will they decide? What will they do? Meanwhile these poor stupid birds sit in the tree, preening themselves because something inside tells them to, and then they fly off to hunt for fish, because something inside tells them to. When they come back and perch on their branch again, too stupid to even be confused, you all take turns sitting in that room, waiting for them to 'decide.'

"I think that's what JP's been looking for, and probably what a lot of you want, some voice inside telling you what to do. Some of you want it so badly you actually hear it. But maybe that voice is just like the ospreys' instincts, just an accumulation of all the more timid voices that went before it. And maybe those voices were wrong. Maybe you should try some things that aren't so safe and just say 'fuck the voice,' and do what you god damn please." He turned and looked at her, and then past her at an old couple who were watching him nervously out of the corners of their eyes. "Oh, never mind," he said, taking her hand and leading her through the rest of the hall.

At the end of it was a small room with an exhibition devoted to old duck hunting methods. There was another corridor to the left of that room, and at the end of it was a shallow concrete pond filled with starfish, hermit and horseshoe crabs, all of which could be handled. At the other end was then entrance to the hall that led to the aquariums.

There they found there wasn't one large aquarium, but rather a series of segregated smaller tanks lining one wall, fronted with large individual viewing apertures like over-sized TV screens. Most of the fish were small, like spot and puppy drum, although there were a few larger species such as dog fish and grouper, and also some oddities like oyster crushers and blow toads. Rob and Mary walked slowly past the tanks until they got to Harold, who rested quietly in the bubbling environment of the last tank.

His body was not as large as Rob had expected, but

The Second Coming

his claws were club-like and massive. Above his tank was a plaque that read, "Harold the Lobster, Homarus Americanus, caught in a net off the Virginia Capes. Length 31", weight 24 lb., 6 oz., age approx. 120 years." He rested in his grotto, motionless and inscrutable, looking like the epitome of the immovable object. His antennae rose and fell lazily in the aerated current. Rob put his head close to the tank and tried to look up at the surface, but it acted as a mirror and reflected back at him. He took a step back and stood in silence next to Mary, unaware of the families and other small groups passing through the room. Finally he turned and went through the doorway into the next section toward some displays about Atlantic marine mammals.

"This will be easy," he said, suddenly relaxed and looking forward to seeing the rest of the sights.

"What do you mean?" she asked, pausing as he did in front of a large photograph. "How do we get to him?"

"We find that doorway," he said, pointing to the photograph. The photo and the text beneath it showed a view of the tanks from behind and explained how they were cleaned and maintained, and how their occupants were fed and cared for. From that angle they looked like a series of half-circular tubs with lids that could be opened in order to perform whatever job was required from a raised catwalk running behind them. There were tubes and pumps and gauges, and contrasted with the view the public got of the colorful fish and their painted backdrops, everything behind the scenes was a pristine white.

"But we can't just walk in there and take him."

"What time is it?"

"Two forty."

"There's a movie about the proposed raising of the Monitor in the auditorium at three o'clock. I'm sure most of the visitors here are looking forward to it. I'd bet the door we're looking for is behind that partition. If it is, that gives us twenty minutes to find the best hiding place in the building. We hang back when everyone heads for the auditorium, and when the coast is clear we duck into our hiding place and wait. The film lasts about an hour, and then there's another hour until the place closes, and then maybe another hour to make sure all the help has gone home. Then we have this place to ourselves until tomorrow morning."

She didn't argue with him, but she frowned so strenuously that he took her hand and walked through the rest of the exhibitions. A few minutes before three an announcement came over the PA system about the Monitor film, and people began to collect themselves and head toward the auditorium. Rob and Mary followed his plan and held back, looking at a large display of local and tropical seashells. When the last person rounded the corner at the end of the hall, he unlatched a low doorway in the side of the shell display, and with a bit more force than was necessary, he pulled her into the darkness and closed the door behind them.

They sat on the linoleum in the pitch darkness, squeezing each other's hands. Rob wasn't nervous or afraid, but he could feel the fear emanating from her. The excitement of their quick movements, coupled with the removal of their sense of sight, produced a sort of collaboration of their other senses which seemed connected through their touching hands. He waited, and she calmed slowly. After a few more minutes he could have released her hand, but he didn't. Because of the amount of coke he had done, and the fact that he really hadn't gotten any sleep, and especially because of the darkness, his mind began to work on a level that had less to do with concrete thought than it did with a confusing barrage of transcendent and contradictory images. They weren't thoughts he could arrange or precisify or conclude because his role in them wasn't critical or analytical. It was less important to discover what he was thinking than it was to feel the boundaries and synchronicity of what they were thinking

The Second Coming

together. In the end they both sat silently listening for voices and footsteps, but it remained quiet around them. Slowly their grips relaxed, and finally they released each other's hands. For some reason, though they were at least seventy five feet from the auditorium, Rob imagined he could hear the drone of the narration of the program, and he couldn't stop himself from cocking his ear to listen.

After he noticed the minutes lining up behind each other he found himself trying to remember what he had heard about sensory deprivation experiments. He had read recently where some health clubs and spas now offered the use of an SD tank as one of their services. Rob imagined some poor flabby sucker lying in a saline solution set at a temperature slightly lower than that of his body, benignly restrained in darkness and in silence, and told to relax. The effect was supposed to be a lowering of the frequency of brain waves responsible for the production of endorphins. Then he remembered what Robert Graves had written about one of the initiations of a Druidic priest. The novice too was left naked and in darkness. But his darkness was a coffin-like box filled with freezing water to a point where only is nostrils were left exposed to the air. When the water level was properly set, large stones were placed on his chest so he couldn't move. Then the coffin was sealed. He was left that way overnight and instructed to compose a poem of considerable length and in a difficult meter on a subject given to him as he was placed in the box. The next morning he had to be able to chant his poem to a melody he had been simultaneously composing, and accompany himself with a harp. So it was all relative.

The linoleum quickly became cold and hard and uncomfortable. The weather was so warm outside that neither of them had brought even a sweater they could have used to sit on. Rob became aware of an unwarranted feeling that although he was sure she was there next to him, his mind began to doubt the fact. He listened for sounds of her movement or breathing, and he felt an increasing urge to reach out and touch her so that he might re-substantiate her existence. He wondered if she felt the same thing.

Slowly he reached out his hand toward her. He strained his eyes to see it, but it was so lost in the heavy darkness he couldn't even accurately gauge the distance it traveled. He only knew that it moved slowly away from him. His arm began to extend, his shoulder tightened, and just when he had a panicked thought that it might be moving in the wrong direction, he felt the cool fabric of her blouse and then the subtle outline of her ribs. She put her hand on his arm and she was real again. He grabbed a handful of her shirt and pulled her to him, and when she was close enough he found her face with his other hand and kissed her. When she made no objection he kissed her harder and pushed her back toward the floor. As he pushed a bit of resistance sprung up in her, and as he pinned her down with his body she struggled, but there was no face or voice to it.

When she stopped moving under him he began to unbutton her blouse and her resistance became no more than a firm guiding hand on his wrist. He knelt above her with his knees between her legs and undid her bra from the front and swept it to the sides. He put his hand on her shoulders and drew them down her torso over her breasts and stomach until they reached the waistband of her shorts. Undoing the button and parting the zipper, he pulled them down, and then reached between her knees and parted her legs so that she lay open before him. He had undressed her without any feeling of excitement or arousal. Then, kneeling above her, he thought about reaching for the soft skin on the inside of her thigh and his pants did begin to tighten. He realized that just by touching her he could create her in the darkness in any form he wanted because for some reason he couldn't remember her face, and so even that most basic claim to individuality was taken for her.

She was still beneath him. He leaned forward and

stroked her stomach and when he felt the barest hint of down his pants became tighter still. He stopped long enough to release himself and then he began to explore her more vigorously. He found that mixed with his excitement there was also an element of violence. He began to handle her more roughly, moving her around abruptly, scratching her and pulling her up by her hair to kiss him, and squeezing her breasts and biting them until she began making little noises and twisting away from him. When she did, he lay fully on her and cupped his hand over her mouth and listened. But there were no noises outside from among the cowries and dogwinkles and conchs on the other side of the partition.

    She tried to close her legs but he kept his knees between them and reached down with his free hand, stroking her thigh until the thick muscle running through it began to relax. Rolling half over, he propped himself on one elbow so that all his weight wasn't directly on her and began to kiss her again, but more gently this time, going soft because she was so quiet and the initial excitement was gone. But then she kissed him back more urgently, stroking his arm and turning so that the buds of her breasts brushed lightly against his chest. It stirred him again, but he was just so sleepy. He rolled on his back and closed his eyes, as if it made a difference. She put her hands between his legs tentatively and began to pull and stroke him, and slowly and in stages it began to respond by itself. It seemed only incidentally a part of him, and he could almost sleep as it began to awake. He became less and less attached to his sensations or her movements. His arms fell to his sides and when they did one of them brushed against her free hand. She had it between her legs stroking herself, and he closed his hand over it.

    Only then did he become aware of the smell of her excitement and the dynamism of her movements. She tugged at his hips to center him better in their little cell. Then she mounted him and slid down until her buttocks rested against his legs. With her hands on his shoulders she raised and lowered herself, her breathing becoming raspy and uneven. Rob opened his eyes and tried to see her, strained to discern even an outline, but he couldn't. Then he suddenly thought of Augustine in the desert, or any of the other numberless ascetics living in caves in the mountains, or walled into cells in damp monasteries, and he began to experience their fear. He still couldn't remember her face, but now she had begun to create herself, and he thought she had become a succubus or thieving spirit come to wrest the life and grace from him. It was a crazy thought and to fight it he began to thrust back toward her, lifting his hips to meet hers. But it only made her growls less human. Her nails dug into his shoulders, and his aggressiveness was no longer any match for hers. She was alone, separated from him by darkness and the fact that they were strangers. He wondered if her face would deny it all once they were in the light again. She moved faster and faster until he knew she was coming as much as any man ever knows. Usually the excitement would have drawn him along too, but this time it didn't. He was almost relieved when she began to slow, but just as her movements seemed to cease, she began to move on him again. This time she drew him along with her, tightening her inner muscles as she drew away from him, and he swelled tighter and arched his back higher above the floor. Finally he grasped her hips and held her firmly and came deep within her. When he relaxed again, she kissed him. He felt her movements as she leaned forward blindly and found his face and cupped it in her hands, and then turned her head away and rested it on his shoulder. They lay together like that for a while, and then he slipped out of her like a fish. She moved off and away from him without a word, and she was so quiet it made him think of the succubus again. He still had sensations in the aftermath of what had happened, but in the damnable darkness and silence they seemed untrustworthy.

    Only gradually did his mind return to their initial

The Second Coming

reason for being there. He didn't know how long it had been since they had ducked into the darkness, but his inner clock told him it had been at least an hour, probably more, and he still hadn't heard any footsteps or voices.

"It won't be long," he whispered in a voice that hung in the air and seemed ghostlike even to him.

A few minutes later they heard footsteps and she quickly slid closer to him. They never touched, but he could feel the distance between them as if there were a chemical mechanism in his skin to gauge it. The sensitivity was so precise that he could tell when she inhaled and exhaled though he couldn't see or hear her breathe. The voices outside seemed loud enough to be understandable, but they were too deep or elongated, or else they collided with the blurred scuffling of footsteps. It seemed odd to him that they never heard anyone laughing. They dressed themselves and sat patiently, timing the darkness, waiting for what they imagined would be the hollow sound of large doors slamming and the ring of footsteps receding into the distance.

They never heard the doors slam, but they waited until long after they had heard the last sound before they ventured out. Rob pushed the hatchway open with his foot and put his head out, hesitating at the opening as he looked up and down the hallway. There was plenty of light to work by. The overhead lights were left on some low setting that kept everything in a brown but discernible shadow. Mary came out behind him and they walked down the hall in the direction of the aquariums. They passed the door to the room behind the tanks, and then through the aquarium room itself. The lights had been turned off in the tanks, but they could see flashes of silver and shadows darting among the rising bubbles. After making a complete circuit of the building and satisfying themselves that everyone had left, they returned to the room behind the tanks. It wasn't locked and Rob opened the door and walked up the few steps to the platform running behind the tanks. He found the light switch and lifted it, ordering her to close the door at the same time.

It was the first time he had really been able to see her since they left their hiding place. He was surprised to find the skin of her face undisturbed, and the faint pink on her cheeks could be attributed to no more than the excitement of their present enterprise. The only sign of their contact was the faint line of a scratch running down her throat toward her heart.

"He's in the last tank, isn't he?" she said, and then blushed deeper when she saw how closely he was looking at her.

They walked along the catwalk to the last tank. Like the others, it was covered with a large circular hatch with hinges running across its diameter and a rounded handle to allow one half of the circle to be opened. He lifted the hatch and they both peered down to the bottom of the tank where Harold lay hidden among the rocks and grasses of his lair.

"How do we get him out?"

"I don't know." Rob had thought the tank was shallow enough that he could reach down and lift Harold with his hands. But the water was much deeper than it appeared from the outside. He tested it with his hand. It was icy cold and the shock of it stung his fingers. Harold made no movement in acknowledgement of them and seemed nonplussed by their unexpected visit. Rob didn't know the mechanics involved in a lobster's sleep, but this one seemed to be resting peacefully inside his mottled shell. "We're going to need something to get down to him. Maybe if we prod him with something he'll use one of his claws to protect himself and we can pull him up by it."

"How about this?" Mary asked.

She had found a finely-meshed net with a long aluminum handle leaning against the opposite wall. Rob took it and reached into the tank and tapped gently on Harold's carapace with the meshed end of it. Harold didn't move. Rob brought it forward to the largest of the toothed claws and tapped that too, and then he brushed it across his antennae and still nothing happened.

"Harold, you old son of a bitch, you better do something soon, or I will eat you."

"Maybe the water is too cold for him to have the energy—"

Before she could finish Harold turned, and with a speed and agility Rob did not expect, he clutched at the net with his large claw and tried to wedge his bony feet among the rocks to give him better leverage to crush whatever was intruding into his domain. Rob realized that if he let Harold get himself set, he might wedge himself so firmly that they wouldn't be able to get him out. He gave the net a quick jerk upward, dislodging Harold from the rocks and bringing him to the surface.

"I hope he holds on," Rob said. In a sweeping arc he lifted him from the tank and set him gently on the floor of the catwalk and held him there by placing his foot firmly on the middle of his back. "I wish we had some gloves."

"I already looked," Mary said, shaking her head and wiping at the water that had splashed on her ankles. "How are we going to carry him?"

"I'm not sure, but it looks safe if I grab him here," he said, pointing to a place at the top of his abdomen, behind the claws and above the point where his blue-green legs were slow-dancing on the floor. "He's heavier than I thought so when we get out of here, I'll hide with him in the bushes while you get the car. He'll be safe once we get him in the trunk."

"How do we get out of here?"

"At first I thought we might have to break a window. But then I noticed you can open the windows back by the feelie pool from the inside. What they've done for security is remove the handles that crank them open and closed. All we need to get out of here is a pair of pliers. I'll bet you a plate of lobster thermidor we'll find some in that tool box." She opened it, found a pair, and held them up for him to see. "Ready? Here goes." He reached down and got a grip on the animal just in front of its forward legs. "I wish we had some gloves," he repeated, and lifted Harold with his one hand and used the other behind the tail to steady the load. He nodded for Mary to lead the way to the door. "Don't forget the light."

They went down the steps and out the door and headed toward the windows in the back. Harold had made bubbling noises when they first removed him from the water, but now as they made their way down the hall he actually blew bubbles from an opening beneath his black stalked eyes and antennae.

"Do you think he's alright?" Mary asked, walking next to Rob, taking funny little crossed steps and holding out her arms as if she could help.

"If weight has anything to do with health or stamina, he'll be fine."

"Do you think we should really do this? Shouldn't we have brought some wet towels or something to wrap him in? What about the sea water? Isn't it going to be a lot warmer than he's used to?"

"Look, if you want to defrost him, or decompress him, or de-anything to him, that's up to you. My only job is to set him free." He began to walk more quickly as he approached the corner that led to the windows where they could make their escape. "Jesus!" he said, holding the lobster out to the side as it evacuated some fluid from its system. When he was finished, they moved on. Just as they got to the corner Rob saw a reflection of moving lights bouncing from one of the framed pictures on the opposite wall.

"Wait!"

They kept their backs against the wall and watched as the reflections of other lights joined the first. As the beams

The Second Coming

approached and shined more brightly, the shadows became sharper and more distinct. Rob fell to his knees, and with the lobster under him and his head to the floor, he edged around the corner. When he realized the lights were still outside he drew his head back again.

"I think it's the fucking police."

"What do we do? How did they know we were here?"

"I don't know, but they must be here for us." He put Harold on the floor and held him with his foot, his long thin legs trying to run on the tile. "Go back to where we were hiding. Right now! Make sure no one sees you and don't come out again until morning, no matter what you hear. When they've opened again, when you think the coast is clear, then come out. If anyone sees you, act like you know what you're doing, straightening up or something. Are you listening? Come out, and leave quietly and walk to your car. If anything looks different from the way we left it, don't go near it until you know for sure what's going on. If it looks like it's been tampered with, find another way back to the beach and wait. If you don't hear from me by noon, report it stolen. But if you have to do that, make sure you have a good excuse why you didn't know where it was."

"What are you going to do?"

"Act drunk if they catch me, but don't worry about that. Get going."

She hesitated, but then she heard voices and footsteps and she knew they were in the building. She looked into his eyes, and then turned and ran back to their hiding place.

Rob knew they would see him immediately if he crossed in the lights and tried to get to the window. From the sounds of their footsteps they were only forty or fifty feet down the hall, and there were probably others outside. His only chance was to retreat back to the tanks and try to open the emergency door on the other side of them. If he could get out that way, and if they didn't have it covered, he could run around the back of the building to the sound, and with any luck wade out into the deep water before they spotted him.

He picked up Harold and ran a dozen steps before he dropped him again. He heard him slide along the floor and clatter into the wall. He rounded the corner and was at full speed within a few seconds. The doorway was dark as he skidded to a stop in front of it, and the door itself was locked. He shook it a few times, and kicked at the bolt, but it wouldn't budge. There was a pane of wired glass running vertically next to the door, and he looked for something to break it with. But there wasn't anything. On a sudden impulse, he turned and swung at it with his fist. The glass splintered, but the wire didn't give. He tried to kick at it and more of the glass broke, but he saw he wasn't going to get through the wire. He rigged a sling in his shirt for his bleeding hand and ran toward the front door past the shell display, hoping he could find another way out. But he heard footsteps and voices coming from that direction too, and he knew he was caught. He walked back toward the exit again. His hand hurt and he withdrew it from his shirt to look at it. Blood flowed through the bright splinters of glass on the knuckles, and there was a deep cut in his palm which contributed to the flow down the back of his hand, and from there, in raised rivulets, toward his elbow. No wonder blood-letting had been such a popular remedy, he thought, as he watched the blood fall in thick black drops to the floor. He felt relaxed, almost sleepy, and the sounds of the approaching footsteps seemed hollow and dream-like.

Suddenly there was a uniform coming around the corner, and a gun was raised and pointed at him. It wasn't a policeman, but a park ranger. When Rob looked at the man's face, he saw more fear of the gun in his hand than anything else. He thought about raising his hands, but he let them fall to his sides instead.

XIII

Emma awoke knowing she had dreamt about the colonel, but she could remember nothing of the dream. She let Ben sleep and dressed and went alone to have coffee in the dining room. Then she decided to walk to early mass at the church, which was conveniently only a half mile from the motel. There were no sidewalks so she walked on the edge of the road, except when she was forced by an approaching car to step off the shoulder into the deep, dusty sand. There were only a few other people in the small modern chapel and the priest spoke quickly and clearly. Because he omitted the sermon, she was back in the sunlight within thirty minutes. Instead of returning by the same route she crossed over to the beach and walked on the shoreline back to the motel.

It was a glorious morning, too beautiful, she thought, to fall on the day the Savior had died. Emma had always felt she had a realistic faith, but sometimes she still found herself looking for more concrete signs that her beliefs would bear fruit. She thought that in the years like this when Easter came early that Good Friday, in the morning at least, should wear a dark and foreboding face, and be swept by winds strong enough to suggest that winter was still a force in the world.

She would love to hear Gert's thoughts on that. They were to work the evening shift from two until sunset, and for the first time she almost wished she didn't have to go. She had been determined to be realistic about Cal Wheeling's health, but now that reality was becoming less and less acceptable to her. She thought about when she was younger and how she had viewed her grandparents and others who were the age she was now. Almost without exception she remembered them as being old, and not only in the way they looked, but also in the ways they acted and moved and spoke. But Emma didn't see herself as old in any qualitative sense. Neither had Cal Wheeling been until she saw him on this trip. But now he had aged suddenly and starkly. And because she didn't want to understand what was behind it, the rapid transition had frightened her.

As she approached the motel she saw James with his new gear casting a line out past the trickling shore break. He had taken a ferocious new interest in surf fishing. Gert complained that when he wasn't actually on the beach he spent most of his time at the bait and tackle shop near the motel, pumping the proprietor for advice and information. Emma knew that Gert's complaints were half in jest, and she thought she knew her well enough to know that she was really glad for the relief.

"Any luck?" she called when she got close enough to hail him.

"Not so far," he said. "But you can see them out there. If I had a longer rod with a bit more flex I think I could get out to them. The man at the shop said they should be coming in any time now, and when they do I'm going to be ready for them." He nodded emphatically in their direction. "Where have you been?"

"I went to mass. Today's Good Friday," she said. "Where's Gert this morning?"

"I think she's waiting for you. Don't you two have a shift together?"

"Yes, but not until two o'clock."

"I think there's a problem. Someone called for you to say someone else didn't show up for their shift this morning. I'm not sure exactly. Gert took the message. But I think they wanted the two of you to come in early."

"Then I better go see what's up," she said, and turned back toward the motel. "Good luck with the fish."

She passed the dining room, but didn't see Gert there among the tardy breakfast diners, so she went upstairs and knocked on their door.

The Second Coming

"I'm glad you're back," Gert said when she opened the door. "Things are getting curiouser and curiouser. I saw Ben in the dining room and he told me Miriam Wheeling had called to say that JP hadn't shown up for his shift this morning. Apparently the colonel was very upset about it and asked her to call you. I thought you might be at church so I went up myself to check his room, but there wasn't any answer when I knocked on the door. I called Miriam and told her I'd be glad to come in early, but then I remembered I didn't have a car."

"We can both go in early. I don't think Ben's planning to use the car. And if he is, we'll get him to drop us off. I'll call Miriam right now. What time is it?"

"Almost eleven."

"Can you be ready in fifteen minutes?"

"I'm ready now."

Emma called Miriam, and Miriam again explained that JP had not shown up, although his observation mate had. But because the colonel was having a bad morning, very bad was how she put it, she had been unable to convince the man to stay and take responsibility for the shift himself. The most she could get out of him was a pledge to stay until noon so that she might have a chance to find someone to replace him. Emma assured her that she and Gert would be there within the half hour. When she went down to meet Gert it was a little before eleven thirty.

"Gert," she said as they drove, "I don't know quite how to explain this, but I have a favor to ask you. I'm sure you know today is Good Friday. When I was a girl in parochial school we were taught what a very solemn day it is, and as an exercise to underline the solemnity, the nuns encouraged us to observe the hours that Christ was on the cross, from noon until three, in silence. Of course, as a child I wasn't very good at it. But it's something I've continued to do since then, and it's something I rather look forward to because it gives me a chance to meditate on my life and faith and the importance of the day. I know it might be difficult under these circumstances, but I hope you will be patient with me."

"I'm not trying to insult your impulses, Emma, but does the church still encourage that sort of thing?"

"Even with all the changes the church has gone through, I can't remember anyone saying anything about it one way or another, although I might not have listened if they had. I was thinking about some of the things you've said, and you were right when you said that the church had taken away some of our unconscious reasons for loving it. It's been hard for me to accept some of the changes. Some of the innocent and simple things, like this exercise, were what inspired awe and a sense of being inculcated into some mystery when I was growing up. And to some extent, even beyond what we were intellectually supposed to believe, that was the attraction."

"Although that's always been a point of contention, from what I've read. Even dating from the earliest dogmatic struggles between Peter and Paul, the question was whether the religion was to be one of initiation or of conversion. On the one hand you had Peter who believed Jesus was the unique fulfillment of the Hebrew prophesies, and the salvation he promised was to be a gift to the Jews exclusively. On the other you had Paul, who because he had never met Jesus, was converted by the word and not the personality. He saw the impersonality of the word as a gift for all. And because he ultimately won the struggle over that point, it was he, and not Peter, who was the architect and builder of the 'Catholic' church. If left to Peter, the church might still be arguing about whether a man with an uncircumcised penis is capable of salvation."

"Aside from all that," Emma said crisply, again offended by Gert's habit of reducing her most important beliefs to repulsive formulas, "I hope you'll respect my wishes."

The Second Coming

"Of course I will," Gert said. "That may be all either of us has to do anyway. More and more lately I get the feeling the birds are not going to stay."

Miriam had been right in saying the man who was to observe with JP didn't want to stay in the house by himself. In fact, he came down the stairs and said goodbye at the same time Miriam opened the door to admit them.

"I think Cal's coughing bothered him," she said after he left. "And after I saw how much it was bothering him, I began to worry about myself, that I may be getting too used to it, I mean. Cal said he wanted to talk to you, Emma, but he's sleeping now."

She had something to do in the kitchen so Emma and Gert found their own way upstairs. They didn't see the birds at first. But then Gert spotted them flying high above the trees wheeling in tight circles in the air.

"What do you suppose they're doing up there?" she asked Emma.

"I don't know. I don't think I've ever seen them that high, have you?" she asked. Gert shook her head. "Look at this. He didn't leave us a single note. I wonder how long they've been up there?" They both leaned closer to the window, with their necks turned awkwardly in order to keep their eyes on the birds. After about ten minutes the pair gradually began to wind lower, passing each other slowly in their downward spirals until they were circling just above the tree. "I'm a bit embarrassed about this now, Gert, but it's almost noon. I know it's not fair to you. I usually try to make sure I'm at home or in church so I don't bother anyone. I hope you understand."

"Of course I understand," she said, and smiled kindly. "Don't be silly, and don't worry. A little silence would probably be good for me."

After another few minutes the male swung around the tree for the last time and landed on his usual limb. The female didn't follow his lead. She continued to whirl above him. Emma became mesmerized by the invisible patterns it drew in the air, the way it banked into a turn with its slightly crooked wings, and lifted its head and shoulder to one side to plan its path through the curve. She couldn't see that it flew for any particular purpose. Its actions didn't seem to have anything to do with hunting or courtship display, but they didn't seem completely aimless either. Finally the bird began to lose altitude and then suddenly broke off its circle and flopped to rest atop the manmade platform. Both Emma and Gert leaned forward in their seats at the same time. Gert turned to her and was about to speak, but she remembered in time, and instead scribbled furiously in the notebook.

    She had turned to Emma with a look that was at first incredulous, but then it quickly melted into a knowing smile. When Emma saw that transformation in her expression, she knew in an instant why she was glad she hadn't chosen a life like Gert's. All her life Emma had had friends who looked at her as if she were less intelligent somehow because of her beliefs. Emma had recognized early that Gert had dismissed the possibility of the two of them sharing an intellectual friendship. When she found out how strong Emma's faith was, Gert assumed, as so many others had, that it was an escape from her intellectual obligation to search, as if faith were an end in itself. So few people realized what a hard and continuous decision it was. In fact, in some ways it increased her responsibilities because it made her incapable of yielding to the tempting reflex of casually dismissing the unfathomable and sometimes horrible turns in life by shrugging them away to fate. Because of her faith she had to see and feel more of what was terrible in life and still be able to place her trust in the good that was over all. Who was really more responsible? Gert put so much stock in knowledge. But if knowledge alone was the key, then everyone was locked in a race that no one could win. 'Neither the most potent dialectic nor the boldest imagination can ever produce that irresistible force of

The Second Coming

conviction which dwells in the soul's power to surmise.' She had read that somewhere and never forgotten it. It was that irresistible force of conviction that carried her faith, and it was a force that went beyond knowledge or ken. Its very sublimity pointed to the power of its architect.

The female bird stood at the edge of the artificial nest, examining it carefully to make sure there was no hidden danger. When she was satisfied, she began to re-arrange some of the sticks that had been placed in it so they might better suit her needs. Far more material was needed to make it a proper nest, and Gert and Emma watched with more and more impatience for one or the other bird to begin collecting it. But they both seemed content to remain where they were. Once the bird had landed Emma expected that the manmade nest would either be quickly rejected or adopted, and that if the female made the decision to stay, it would be followed by a flurry of constructive activity. And if she opted to leave, they would probably quit the area altogether and settle themselves somewhere else.

With these and many other thoughts Emma and Gert sat in silence. A few times Emma felt the strain and agitation the silence caused in Gert who was so used to giving vent to her thoughts. But though she sometimes struggled, and sometimes almost forgot, Gert managed to keep her tongue in check. At first it was hard for Emma not to find a little satisfaction in Gert's struggles. But she realized those thoughts were unkind, and a distraction at that. She guided herself to concentrate on Jesus' sacrifice, and the meaning behind it. Though she still watched the birds and still heard Gert moving in the chair beside her, at the center of her being she was contemplating a mystery that gave meaning to the life she had chosen to lead. Before she knew it, it was after three o'clock. In fact, by the time she looked back at the clock on the wall it was almost three thirty.

"Thank you, Gert."

"Don't thank me. That was marvelous. I don't do

that nearly often enough. It was so relaxing. It was hard at first because I'm not used to it. But once I lost the urge to share my thoughts, they took a distinct inward turn, and after a while I got to the point where I don't even know if I could have verbalized them. But what about these birds?"

"I don't know."

"I had the feeling we were on the verge of a real breakthrough, but now they seem as indecisive as ever. The wait for them to act is certainly becoming tedious."

A few minutes later Miriam came in and told Emma that the colonel had awakened and wanted to talk to her. "This has been another hard day for him," she whispered as they walked down the hall. "And it's getting more and more difficult for me. He wants to stay here, but I almost can't take it anymore. Please talk to him, Emma. Tell him to be reasonable before it's too late. I don't want something to happen to him here and have people think I didn't take proper care of him." There were tears in her eyes, and her voice quavered with frustration at her inability to give him any relief. "He'll listen to you."

"I'll talk to him, Miriam," Emma said. She put her hand gently on her friend's shoulder as they reached the dark door at the end of the hall.

"Emma," the colonel greeted her as she entered the room. His voice was a faint croak that fought its way up from deep in his chest. She went to the bed and took the hand he held out. His skin hung loosely on him, and his eyes had retreated further beneath his jutting brow, which was now his only remaining prominent feature. "Thank you for coming. That damned worthless Richardson. The school is going to hear about this."

"How are you feeling, Cal?"

"How do I look?"

"I'll leave the two of you alone," his wife said from the door. "Be good now, Cal."

"Yes, dear, I'll be good. I don't have much of a

The Second Coming

choice now, do I?" Although Emma didn't think he spoke loud enough for her to hear, she nodded as if she had and pulled the door closed behind her. "She doesn't know what to do with me any more. I've gotten so irascible that I've made impossible for her to be kind to me. But she doesn't know any other way to be."

"She's always taken good care of you."

"Yes, Emma," he said, looking her straight in the eyes. "She has. But now the problem is that she wants me to go quietly, and I can't because I'm not ready. There are still things I want to do, and if I go to some damn hospital, they're not going to let me do them. They aren't any big or important things, I know I'm beyond that, but I want to finish what I've started. The most important thing is that I want to finish with these birds. I don't give a damn what they do any more, I just want them to do it. I started this, it was my idea, and by God, I'm going to finish it."

He squeezed the words out until he was overcome by a long flat cough. He pointed to the bedside table and a group of medicine bottles set in a jumble like the high-rise buildings of a third-world city. "The one on the end," he choked out. She opened the bottle and began looking for a spoon, but he signaled impatiently to her and finally reached out and grabbed the bottle from her hand. He took a long fierce draught and fell back on his pillows. Emma could barely make out the insubstantial curves of his body beneath the blankets.

"This is codeine," he whispered. "Don't ever let anyone tell you that narcotics are evil." He looked away toward the bookcase on the opposite wall, and she tried to follow the line of his eyes as he squinted at the books.

"Things have not turned out as I planned," he said after a few minutes, in a voice that was soft, but fairly well under control. "Have you ever heard of Frederich II Hohenstauffen? He was the last of the true Holy Roman Emperors, a poet, a naturalist, a precursor of the Italian

Renaissance, a man Nietzsche called the first European. He was probably the one medieval ruler most responsible for separating church and state. This may sound funny, but when I was younger I used to think I was one of his incarnations. I read a lot when I was a boy, and when I was sixteen or so I read his biography. I was amazed at some of the parallels between our lives. His father died when he was three and his mother when he was five, and so did mine. In Frederich's case he was sent from Germany, where he was born, to Palermo, Sicily, where he grew up. As was often the case with royal children in those days, his mother had made arrangements with the pope to act as his guardian and be responsible for his education and upbringing. But the pope was busy with other things and no formal system was ever set up. Frederich was educated by a number of different people in a number of different subjects, apparently at his own initiative.

"I too was sent south after my mother died. I was born in Pennsylvania, but both my parents were originally from North Carolina. My mother had a cousin in a small town in Carolina called Carrboro, and he was contacted and agreed to take me. I can remember being put on a train in Philadelphia wearing a new woolen suit and cap with my name written on a tag and pinned to my lapel. To this day whenever I embark on something new I get the same tingling on my skin that that woolen suit caused.

"My cousin was a minister and he turned out to be a dilatory sort of cleric who was also something of an inventor. His wife was a quiet woman who was continually pregnant or taking care of small babies. When I arrived there were three sons and a daughter, and three more sons came after I became a member of the family. I'll have to amend that. I never became a member of the family really. I was cousin Al. That is, I was cousin Al until one of the smaller ones insisted on calling me Cal, and I've been Cal ever since.

The Second Coming

"My mother's cousin, like many people who don't have it, was very interested in money. That was why he was so keen on his inventions. He had the feeling that if he could just come up with the right thing, his problems would be gone forever, and he could fully devote himself to his religious calling. His sermons were protracted pleas for alms, and he knew every bit of scripture that could loosen the purse strings of the faithful. So it wasn't a surprise that he was more interested in the stipend that came with me than he was in my education or well-being. But in a way that was a blessing because as long as the check came on the first of the month I was left alone."

He paused. There was an involuntary contraction in his chest, but no cough.

"As it turned out Carrboro was only a few miles from Chapel Hill. When I was fourteen I discovered the university library. I had already read the few books that were in the house, and everything I could lay my hands on at the small school we went to. In both cases most of what I found was religious and devotional. I had an urge to discover the natural world and the texts of those books seemed more geared to hide answers than to provide any satisfactory understanding. I was already watching birds, and as I was handy with a pencil, I had begun sketching them and making notes. I would go for long hikes in the countryside and record the birds I saw, and sketch them, and phonetically write out their songs. I knew the names of some of them, but gradually I began to find birds I didn't know, and I noticed differences in birds with the same names. I did some rough dissections on birds I found dead for one reason or another, and I have to admit I shot a few for that purpose. I began to develop a general working knowledge of them and their environments and habits.

"But I'm getting off the track. As I said, I discovered the library at Chapel Hill. What I remember most was the almost magical feeling of one book leading to another. A question would send me to a book which would answer it, and then raise another question, and pass me on to the next book. Sometime during the process I got on historical biographies, and that was where I ran into Frederich. Aside from our beginnings, there were other similarities, our shared interests in birds and philosophy, our kindred open-mindedness in environments where that was often considered heresy, and most important was our shared good luck. A study of his early adult life is like a paean to good fortune. He seemed to have an efficient and fortuitous angel looking over his shoulder. Of course, it wasn't just luck. It was also a matter of placing himself in opportune positions, and a willingness to gamble, and then an ability and determination to consolidate his gains. Anyway, I was determined to follow his example and I convinced myself that his blood somehow flowed in my veins. I finished high school and applied for and got a scholarship to Chapel Hill. But the war broke out in the middle of my sophomore year, and because of a clerical error, I was drafted. I entered the service as a private soldier, went through basic training, and was shipped off to North Africa. Two months later, I was on a troop transport heading for Sicily, Frederich's kingdom.

"That was where things got eerie. I won't say I recognized places, because I didn't. But in Sicily I got the feeling that things were exactly where they should be. More than that, some places gave me distinct feelings about things that were about to happen. My unit was sent into the hills in the interior to subdue some scattered pockets of resistance that were raiding our supply lines. On one patrol we had to pass through a narrow ravine, and when we did we were ambushed and pinned down by fire from the ridge above. Our retreat was cut off and we didn't know what lay ahead, so our lieutenant decided we should remain where we were and hope another of our units would come and rescue us. Though we couldn't move, we felt relatively safe in our position because there was good cover.

The Second Coming

"Unfortunately they had a mortar and they began lobbing rounds at our position. It seemed like our only escape was to retreat over open ground the way we had come. Suddenly, I knew there was a way out ahead of us. I convinced the lieutenant to let me give it a try. I had to cross a stretch of bare ground, but at the end of it was an overhang which would provide cover if I made it that far. I collected myself and took off. I must have taken them by surprise because they only got off a few shots, and none of them landed close.

"Once I made the overhang I followed it around. By keeping close to the wall I was effectively hidden from observation from above. I followed it until I came to a narrow trail cut into the rocks leading upward, and I knew that was what I had been looking for. I had known it would be there. As I climbed I wondered if it had been carved by the Saracens who had lived there so many hundreds of years before, the Saracens the young King Frederich had been forced to subdue, and who afterwards became the core of his personal guard, and the basis for the legends that he kept a harem and preferred the company of Moslems to that of his Christian brothers."

The colonel smoothed the blanket on his lap. Emma saw him returning, reliving it.

"The trail wound its way upward, and in a matter of minutes I was at the top. There was enough cover that I was able to make my way to a position behind the enemy. There were only four of them, and I remember feeling lucky that they were Italians. I threw a grenade that killed two of them outright, and then I shot the other two in the ensuing confusion. Everyone thought it was a heroic action on my part, although bravery had nothing to do with it. Nevertheless, I was awarded a medal for valor, and a promotion, and most importantly, I was transferred.

"I was sent to Palermo and assigned to a supply division where within a short time my organizational abilities led to another promotion, and then another, and finally I was given a commission. I was transferred to another supply depot on the Rhine. That was in January of '45, and I stayed there until the end of the war.

"I had no attachments in the states so I volunteered to remain in Germany after the war on the condition that my commission was transferred to the regular army. I was there during the airlift of '48 and '49. In fact our unit was at one of the main junctions of incoming supplies, and many of the newsreel shots you saw back in the states were taken at our base. After the airlift I did one tour of duty in the states, and then went to Korea.

"I met Miriam when I returned from Korea and we were married. Shortly afterward, although it didn't have anything to do with her, I began to have problems. I had always had more work than I could handle. Supply during a conflict is an extremely challenging occupation because of the fluidity of location of your supplies as well as those you need to supply, and the fact that inventories invariably become useless. So for a good supply officer it becomes a matter of mnemonics and logistics. It's exhilarating because the material in your charge can well mean the difference between life and death, victory or defeat. Unfortunately, that sense of urgency does not carry over into peace time, and the job can very easily become a matter of shuffling paperwork and moving things around that don't necessarily need to be moved. After Korea I began to feel things slipping away from me. I was passed over for lieutenant colonel. I began to drink too much. It seemed that where once I had been so fortunate, I now began to see the other side of the coin. Of course, I still had my interest in birds, and I had ideas of writing a history of the airlift. But they were not enough to cloak the lethargy I felt in my professional life."

He stopped speaking, and for a moment they both sat quietly. She thought he might begin coughing again because she could hear the growl of his breath struggling through the

The Second Coming

liquid in his lungs.

"'Stupor Mundi,' that was what they called Frederich, even in his lifetime, 'The Wonder of the World.' When my twenty years was up in '64, I retired. I never did make lieutenant colonel although they retired me honorarily as one. I don't remember who first called me 'the colonel,' but I remember being embarrassed by it." He paused again. "I can see you're getting impatient with me," he said, and she knew she was, though she thought she had done a better job of hiding it.

The things he had been saying were so out of character. She had only heard him speak of his past in terms of accomplishment. She had never expected that he had ever done anything but what he wanted to do.

"I won't be much longer, I promise. The point I'm trying to make is that my life has not gone the way I expected, or the way it should have been destined to go. If I may hark back to Frederich, another quality we shared is a liberal outlook on life, and living, and dying. He was a terrible tease with the philosophers, both Christian and Moslem, who came to his court. But now, when it comes down to the crunch, my beliefs are proving to be ineffective. I've been afraid for my life before, especially during the war, but there was always enough of an element of chance that I could deal with it. But now that element of chance is gone, and I know it. I could feel this time coming, and that's why I've pushed so hard for these observations. I wanted them to be my legacy. It's funny, really. Here I am, a man who chose for his life model one of the most enlightened and erudite rulers in history, one of its most civilized minds, and I'm ready to settle for a plaque on a wall at the state university. And it doesn't even look like I'll get that."

"But Cal, the female went to the new nest today."

"Did she? And I'll bet you had faith that she would all along, didn't you? That's really why I wanted to talk to you. My way hasn't worked. I'd love to call a priest and make a clean breast of it and know a little peace in the end, but that won't work either. It won't work for me because I won't surrender that much of myself to it, and I don't think it will work for you. I think the only reason it has so far is because you won't allow yourself to see certain things.

"I'm going to tell you something I swore I would never tell you. It's the truth and to me frankly it's rather tame. But to you it will probably seem terrible and cruel and unfair. I want to think I'm telling you for your own good. But because of the way I feel I'd probably tell you even if it wasn't, because I hurt, and the pain is so bad it's making me want to hurt someone else. That may not be the noblest impulse, but it's the most honest. It hurts more than anything I've ever known or imagined It's killing me, but it's killing me too slowly, and I'm afraid I won't be able to hold everything in I need to hold in. So maybe if I let this out it will act like a steam valve and relieve some of the pressure.

"But what do you mean, Cal?" she asked. But she didn't want him to answer. She was hoping he would become the old Cal she knew, and hoping it so much that she wanted to close her eyes and wish the one in front of her away.

"I'm talking about Miriam and Ben," he said, and let the sentence hang there. "I never understood how you couldn't have known."

"Couldn't have known what?"

"About Miriam and Ben, and Miriam fucking Ben and Ben fucking Miriam, at their age, under our noses. And not only that, but them thinking they loved each other and being ready to risk everything." Emma knew she must be as pale as she felt because when he continued he spoke more softly. "At first I didn't guess it because I wouldn't have given either of them the credit for the ingenuity. I knew they enjoyed each others' company, but they weren't kids. They were both in their fifties, for christsakes, and I thought we

The Second Coming

were all enjoying each others' company. But I got a feeling. I noticed that when you and Ben were in town Miriam found more and more reasons to stay away from home. Even that wouldn't have been suspicious, except that when she'd return she would become overly solicitous to my needs. You know you live in a funny world when kindness begins to draw suspicion. I didn't connect it to Ben. I just knew something was going on.

"Finally I set a trap and caught them in it. When I did a funny thing happened. After the tears and recriminations and finger pointing, things took a turn I would never have expected. Once it was out in the open it didn't take them long to see how unrealistic they had been. What is love anyway? It's what you make it. As long as no one knew, it was natural for them to build it as large as they could. Once they were found out though they both realized they weren't ready to give up what they had, and so the most important thing for the three of us was to make sure you didn't find out. I, of course, was expected to understand. But we all knew you wouldn't understand how a husband who claimed to love you could be so base, or how a friend you thought you could confide in could take those confidences and use them to her advantage. We were all so intent on protecting you that we became friends again, and eventually stronger and better friends than we had been before."

"Why are you telling me this, Cal?" she asked as evenly as she could. "It's not just to hurt me. I know you think you have some important and overriding reason, so what is it?"

"I told you part of it, because I'm afraid. I used to not know if there was anything beyond this life. More than that, I didn't care. But now as I'm getting closer to the end I know there is more, but I don't want it and won't accept it, because it's not on my terms. You already have accepted it, but for reasons I don't think are valid. I resent your complacency, and I want to shake your faith."

"How is this going to shake my faith?"

"By taking something very important to you, your marriage, and telling you it's not what you think it is, and maybe never has been. And if something as basic as that is not what it seems, then how can you trust the structure of your faith when its foundations are even more precarious?"

"There is only one thing wrong with this attempt at enlightenment of yours. I know about Miriam and Ben. I've always known. I just understood there was a mutual conspiracy of silence about it. I forgave them both a long time ago. I'm disappointed in you, Cal. I would have thought that you of all people..." she began, but she didn't know how to finish. She stood and went to the door. "When are you going to stop all this foolishness and go to the hospital? Miriam has done everything she can for you. You have to know how much it hurts her for you to continue to refuse help."

Once she was in the hall she could breathe again, but that was all her mind would allow her to do. She felt her insides had begun to dry up as soon as he said that word. Of course she hadn't known, and never would have guessed. And though he had told her now, she didn't know if she could believe it, although every bit of her intuition told her it was true. But why did he have to use that terrible word? She leaned against the wall in the darkened hallway amid a welter of conflicting emotions and questions, trying to breathe quietly so no one would hear her. Suddenly she was terrified that Miriam might come upstairs to check on them, and she couldn't have faced her, so she walked as quietly as she could back to the observation room.

"She's still there," Gert said when she heard her come into the room. "Once or twice I got the feeling the male might join her, but so far he hasn't budged. Are you alright? You look awfully pale."

"I'm fine. It's just so hard to see the colonel like that. He's so weak."

The Second Coming

It was almost dark. They sat in the room using the remaining light, watching the female osprey as she preened herself on one of the ribs at the crown of the man-made nest. Occasionally the bird would raise a plaintive call to her mate who would return it with a slight variation, but he never left his perch in the old tree. Emma sat like a stone while Gert tidied up the place, and remained in her seat until Gert told her it was time to go.

She was able to say goodnight to Miriam quickly and easily by saying she had talked to Cal, and hoped she had done some good. She found herself speaking in the same voice and using the same words she would have used if nothing had happened, because she was able to use the habit of their old relationship as an anchor. It was only after she and Gert were in the car and on the way back to the motel that some anger began simmering in her.

She planned to confront Ben as soon as they were alone, but when she tried she found she couldn't. When she remembered everything of the colonel's conversation, she realized that he had told her almost nothing. She didn't know where or how, and most importantly, she didn't know when. They had known the Wheelings for almost fifteen years, and they had seen them three or four times a year for that whole period. She tried to recall any obvious clues in her memory that she might have overlooked at the time. Before she knew it she was reliving every excursion they had taken together and every meal the two couples had shared, but all her efforts were fruitless. She had never caught them whispering, and she could only remember a few times they had gone off alone together, although the memory of those times now filled her with a peculiar dread of the unmalleability of the past. The problem with her inability to confront either Miriam or Ben was that her own equilibrium suffered. She went to bed bitterly, and after Ben had fallen asleep next to her and she could feel his warmth and hear the well-recognized pattern of his breathing, she stayed awake a long time wondering if he had ever reached for her in bed after he had been with Miriam.

She hated the light of day on Saturday. She did not want to awaken, and after she had, she didn't want to get out of bed. The thought of trying to have a normal conversation or just putting one foot in front of the other scared her to death. Her skin felt loose and heavy, as if the last bit of youthful tension had gone out of it. Her frame of mind had taken an unconscious turn in her sleep, and when she woke on Saturday she felt compelled to move in a different direction than she had the night before. On Friday night her feelings were overwhelming ones of hurt and self-pity, with only momentary stabs of anger. But by Saturday morning, after the percolation of sleep and dreams, all the hurt had settled itself into a brooding, sullen indignation. Every old memory that surfaced came under a new scrutiny, and each had to be stamped with approval or disapproval in the light of her new knowledge. The knowledge of one indiscretion led to a querying suspicion of others.

In the bathroom after she got up she was struck with a thought that bore the faint outlines of a refugee from her dreams. What about Gert? Had those suspicions she had harbored all winter been as silly and unwarranted as they seemed then? With all Gert's well-maintained indifference, it was still obvious that if she wanted something, concerns about the prerogatives and rights of others wouldn't long stand in her way.

Emma had always known that Ben had the potential to wander. But she had thought him too cowardly to take the ultimate step. She had counted on that cowardice and built a life around it. Could there have been others? Before she went down to join him at breakfast she had a procession of their female friends through the years parade in front of her memory. But for one reason or another, none of them seemed to fit. The thought was not as comforting as it should have been though, because in most ways Miriam

The Second Coming

didn't fit either.

She and Ben had previously arranged that after breakfast on Saturday morning they were to be part of a group that had chartered a boat to go offshore to find a rare tern that migrated north this time of year. It took a path along the Gulf Stream about forty miles out, heading for its summer nesting grounds in Greenland. They had attempted the trip three years earlier, but the day of their charter dawned as a stormy, cold one, and most of the group had backed out. She and Ben and a few others had been determined to go, and they did, but it proved to be a terrible mistake. The farther away from shore they got the higher the swells ran, and by the time they reached the Gulf Stream their forty-foot boat was dwarfed by seas running so high that even if they could have stood on deck, they couldn't have spared a hand for their binoculars, and there were no birds of any kind to be seen anyway.

When she remembered they were to go on the excursion, her first thought had been to bow out and let Ben go by himself. But something prevented her from doing so. She sat quietly through breakfast, answering his questions in monosyllables, wishing she could find a way to effectively broach the subject that was so much on her mind, and realizing she was absolutely at a loss as to how to begin. Ben rambled on about the excursion, confident they would have much better luck this time. The weather was clear, the winds were calm, and some of the birds they were looking for had been spotted a few days before so the captain already had a course charted. She finally resigned herself to going, but she realized her decision was mostly based on a terrifying fear of being left alone. At least if she went she would be occupied, and perhaps a moment would arrive when she could approach him.

The boat was moored at the marina at Oregon Inlet, twenty miles south of the motel. They arrived at the dockside and met the rest of the party at nine o'clock. The chartered boat was long and sleek and had a large comfortable cabin with a covered steering station above it, and an ample, open deck behind. In the summer it was chartered to game fishermen looking for billfish and wahoo and tuna. It had just been brought up from a winter in Florida, but there were no fishing charters to be had yet, so the captain had agreed to take them to make a little money and keep the boat in good running condition. He was on the bridge warming up the engine when they arrived, and the mate stood on the gunwales ready to help the passengers aboard. The day was already warm, but the party knew it would be cold off shore and so they were bundled up, or else they carried their coats with them. They all had binoculars slung around their necks. Emma thought she noticed a small derisive smile on the mate's face as he helped them aboard and directed them where to stow their gear. His look had become a familiar one to her over the years. They were, after all, chartering a boat to take them an hour and a half out to sea just to try to get a view of a small bird.

  When the last of them was safely on deck, the mate undid the lines and cast them off. They pulled out into the channel, and the captain steered by the buoys through the shoals toward Oregon Inlet. They passed under the bridge and then followed the markers out to the open sea. The mate made coffee and instructed them in wearing their life preservers and in the operation of the levers and pumps in the head. When he finished most returned to the deck to enjoy the morning. Ben and another man climbed the narrow ladder to the bridge, and the rest of them relaxed in the sunlight, sipping their coffee and breathing the salty air. A small woman, very much older than Emma, with a peculiar sad smile in her down-sloping eyes, approached cautiously across the rolling deck.

  "Mrs. Corcoran," she said familiarly as she made a grab for the rail next to Emma. "I guess I haven't quite gotten my sea legs yet. How are you this morning? I guess

The Second Coming

you don't recognize me. I'm Adele Rainier. We took this trip together a couple of years ago when the weather was so ghastly. Do you remember now?"

"Yes, I do. How are you?"

"I'm fine. I'm slowing down by degrees, but I still manage to get around."

"And how is your husband?"

"Robert died last summer," she said. "Oh, you don't have to look at me that way. It's better for us both really. But that's why I wanted to talk to you. Robert was great friends with Colonel Wheeling, and I wanted to ask how the osprey observations are going?"

"It's hard to say. From the standpoint of what we were expecting them to be, they've been a disaster. And of course, the colonel has been ill."

"Yes, I've heard. How is he?"

"He's quite weak, and he seems to be getting weaker, I'm afraid."

"I'm sorry," the woman said. "You know, it's funny. Robert died very suddenly, and if I would have had a choice then, I don't think I would have chosen for him to go that way. I would have wanted the chance to say goodbye properly, and put everything in order, so to speak. But now I think I've changed my mind. It must be very hard for Mrs. Wheeling...I'm sorry," she said again. "I guess I must be rambling. It's a marvelous day we have this time, isn't it?"

"Yes," Emma said, and then the horrible weight, which had been lifted momentarily by the surprise of meeting an old acquaintance, fell upon her again, and she suddenly felt as if she were going to cry. She looked away from Mrs. Rainier past the bow of the boat. There was barely enough wind to break the surface of the blue-gray water ahead of them, and only the small swells gave a clue to the movement beneath its surface. The sun shone off it as if it were striking against a lazily animated plate of glass, and where the swells softly topped themselves it shot them through with brilliant crystals. Only the prow of the boat cutting through caused any sign of disturbance, and as she looked at the stern she saw that their churning wake followed them only until the relentless calm overcame it.

It was a beautiful scene, as beautiful as any she had ever seen, and in recognizing it she became aware that she was becoming guilty about her sorrow, and that in turn made her angry because she knew she deserved a bit of self-pity. Hadn't she sacrificed enough to be able to claim that small reward? But even thinking that, she couldn't stop feeling guilty because the whole thing somehow didn't seem real to her. At another time it might have been something to thrash out, to scream and cry over. Now it was just a challenge to the stability she needed at her age, and a faintly dog-eared one at that. She just wanted to forget it, that was all, but she couldn't.

It took an hour to get to the color change in the sea water that marked the border of the Gulf Stream. Once they passed over it the ocean seemed much more alive. There were many more birds in the air and also more convincing signs of life beneath the surface. Ten minutes after they passed into the stream a basking shark was spotted to starboard, and all eyes turned toward it. It was large and dark and hung suspended just beneath the surface, straining the water for its food. To Emma, it seemed dead.

Finally they began to see the seaweed and Sargasso the birds they were looking for were known to collect around. When it came right down to it there were only very subtle differences in markings between these birds that never made landfall on the continental United States and other similar terns that were familiar on the eastern coastline. But Ben and Emma, like most of the others, had made the trip in order to add this to their 'life' lists.

The men took turns as lookouts on the bridge. There were short bursts of excitement as different possible sightings were made, but it was not until the end of the

The Second Coming

second hour that a pair of the birds they were looking for were positively identified. For a few minutes Emma lost herself in the excitement with the others. Afterward though her sorrow returned, and along with it came collected numbing feelings of futility.

They had chartered the boat for a half-day, and after the group had finished observing and photographing and discussing the birds, the captain had the mate bring out the tackle and bait a couple of lines and the party began to take turns trolling. There were fish visible in the water, but though the captain skillfully swung through the spots where they seemed most concentrated, no one managed to get a strike on either line. After an hour the mate got the signal from the captain and the two lines were brought in and the boat was turned for home.

When they were in the parking lot at the marina Ben finally asked her what was the matter. She had been acting strangely all day, he said, and he wanted to know if it was something he had said or done, or if it was just the condition of the colonel that was bothering her. Emma had hoped there would come a time when she could just let the words and feelings rush out of her. But she still didn't know what to say or how to say it, and she wondered if she would ever find a way.

"I'm alright," she told him. "I'm just a little unsteady from the motion of the boat."

They returned to the motel and the draining entropic worm of habit took over her actions. They both took a nap before dinner and to Emma's amazement she was able to sleep. They had their evening meal in the dining room at the usual time, and she only ate a little less than she normally would have and Ben didn't notice. After dinner they watched TV in bed and they eventually both fell asleep with their clothes on. Emma's bladder woke her and she went to the bathroom. When she returned, instead of putting on her night clothes and making Ben comfortable as she usually would have done, she decided to go have a look at the stars.

The night was just barely cool, and even under the breezeway she could tell the stars were out. As she walked to the stairway that led to the beach path she detected an astringent hint of smoke that faintly stung the tips of her sinuses. She didn't think it was late but the whole scene was deserted of life until she went down the outside stairs and passed two well-dressed men coming up. One of them raised his dark face and smiled at her, and she saw the glint of gold in his teeth.

Sitting on a bench in the motel gazebo at the edge of the dunes, she watched the stars and listened to the ocean and tried to empty her mind and forget. A young couple walked by arm-in-arm, carrying a blanket, whispering to each other and quietly laughing, and made their way down the beach to the south. After they passed she realized they might have been a little drunk. She stayed a short time longer, but suddenly she became cold and a bit frightened so she took the key out of her pocket and went back to the room. Ben was snoring quietly. She adjusted the covers for him and put on her nightgown and crawled into bed. The very familiarity of the act calmed her, and she was thinking just that and rehearing the voices of the couple on the beach when she fell asleep.

She woke the next morning, and it was Easter. For as long as she could remember Easter was the most important day of the year for her, much more important even than Christmas or her birthday. When she was a child it was because of the new dress and bonnet and the brilliance of the lilies and other flowers and decorations in the church. It was the one day of the year that had initially drawn the essence of her femininity to religion. As she grew older she had come to understand that the strength of her faith was inextricably bound with her earliest remembered sensations of that day. It was both a beginning and an end of her year, and she had learned to use the day to meditate on her past

The Second Coming

and plan her spiritual path for the future. But this morning was much, much different.

Ben was at breakfast when she awoke, knowing she would not eat until after mass. She got out of bed and impulsively pulled the new, carefully-wrapped dress from the closet and laid it on the bed. As she did she began to cry. She could think of a hundred reasons not to, but she couldn't stop herself. She stood in the middle of the room above the dress, sobbing convulsively and feeling chagrined because though she felt every bit of the sorrow that came out with the tears, there was still something contrived and forced about it. Slowly she was able to stop herself by degrees, and in the midst of the reveries that followed, someone knocked on the door. It was Gert. Her first thought was that she didn't want to deal with Gert or her psychological observations about anything. She was about to tell her so, but Gert spoke before she could.

"You might think this is a strange request," she began, and she seemed a bit embarrassed trying to find her words, "but I'd like to go to church with you this morning. What a beautiful dress! Now I'll be honest and tell you I haven't been struck by the paraclete or anything. But the fact is I was struck by something, and it happened the other afternoon when you forced me to be quiet for a while. It was something I wasn't used to, and I found I rather enjoyed it. Sometimes I'm so busy explaining my thoughts to myself and everyone else that I don't take time to listen to everything I'm saying. Anyway, I've developed an admiration for you and what I've come to see as the integrity of your outlook, and I would be honored if you would allow me to accompany Ben and you."

Emma looked at her for a moment, searching her face for some sign of mischief. But in her eyes was a very marked look of sincerity. That was the only word for it, and for a minute she didn't know how to respond.

"I won't be a bother."

"Of course, Gert," she said, coming to herself. "I'm sorry. We'd love to have you. This is my favorite day of all, and look how beautiful it is out here." She stepped past Gert and looked to the east at the cloudless sky. "You know, I think I can count on the fingers of one hand the number of times it's rained on my Easter parade. It's been that few. Mass is at ten. Can you be ready by then?"

"Yes, Emma. Thank you."

"I'll send Ben for you when we're ready."

As Gert turned to leave, Emma looked again at the beautiful morning and determined that she would change her mood. Then she stepped back in the room and set about getting ready in earnest.

Ben came in while she was dressing and dressed himself and then sat at the edge of the bed while she put on her make-up. When she was almost ready she sent him to fetch Gert. They met at the car and drove the short distance to the church.

The church was striking in the morning light, although the arrangements of the flowers were ill-conceived as they often were in churches in resort areas. The priest however wore his best vestments and did not rush as he had on Good Friday. During his sermon he spoke about the joy and promise of the day, and as Emma listened she gradually became aware that she disagreed. Joy was not the object of life, not this one anyway. Its object was to find and give meaning to the works and acts that composed it. More than her faith, more than love, it was work that had given most meaning to her life. She realized that she had not been used as she had found herself thinking in the last few days. She had given, and given freely, and it was not for her to judge how well her gifts had been received, or to try to judge the worthiness of the recipient. It was just up to her to continue giving where she thought her gifts would be most beneficial. That was the answer if she could conquer her weaknesses and her expectations. And that was why she believed,

The Second Coming

because of the moments like this when she could feel His spirit within her. She looked over at Ben and waited until she caught his eye, and when she did she smiled at him and tried to convey with the smile the beauty and certainty she felt returning to her heart.

XIV

JP came out of his sleep more at the beckoning of his mephitic breath than anything else. He didn't know what time it was, except that it must be afternoon. He had tried to open his eyes at different times in the morning, but the trumpeting pain had always quickly closed them again. Now he knew he was awake for good, so he dredged himself from bed and stumbled to the bathroom. The tepid water gagged him so he splashed some on his face and the back of his neck until it cooled, and then he drank as much of it as he could. After toweling off, he looked at himself in the mirror. The pain caused by the constricted blood vessels had re-etched the dormant vertical frown lines that reached up from between his eyes. The other lines on his face, especially the newer ones at the corners of his eyes, made him seem much older than he was. It was not character they added on awakenings like this, but only further evidence of his dissipation.

He tried to think how he had gotten back to the room, but he couldn't remember. Rob wasn't there to tell him, and there was no note to say where he'd gone. He went back into the room again and fell on the bed, but he knew he wouldn't be able to sleep. As he lay with one forearm draped over his face to keep the light out, he began to remember snatches and disconnected episodes from the night before. When he did he got the familiar cubbish feeling that he had said things he shouldn't have said, and he cringed when he remembered he had done things his tequila-soaked worm of a brain told him he wanted to do, but his normal sober sense of civilized decorum would have prevented him from attempting. It all had to do with the kinetics of desire, he thought, and then realized what a stupid fucking zombie rationalization that was to make on a morning after.

At the beginning of the evening he had wanted the

The Second Coming

girl Mary, or the cocaine in him wanted her. But he quickly realized she was leaning her attention toward Rob so he began to hit on the beautiful tall girl. He thought he had started well. He usually started well. But gradually the alcohol began to outdistance first his discretion about subject, and then his physical ability to speak, and finally the desire itself, although he had the feeling that near the end of the evening he had made a final desperate and graphic stab.

He didn't care what the girls thought. What worried him was what Rob and Chick thought. They were the bosom friends of his youth, and because of it they were still tied up with his dreams. He drank to forget his disappointments, but he couldn't explain that to them anymore because he had cried wolf so often in the past they no longer had the patience to listen to the particulars. He couldn't explain how much he hated to be alone, that he constantly ached for someone to share his life and give him a little strength when he needed it. Or that how each time he thought he had found that person, the fear of trusting a strength outside himself caused him to step so carefully that invariably he would falter, and then try to cover his stumbling with hyper-criticisms. Finally he would torpedo the whole thing, if it lasted long enough, with a haughty and regal façade of pride which he used to hide the crumbling masonry of his basic animative fear. Then after they were gone, he would blame them for not recognizing it.

And what about his job? He had promised himself to stick it out no matter what. He correctly looked on it as his last chance to prove to himself that he was capable of a sustained commitment. He had kept his determination the first year, and had managed to keep it for most of the second. But by the beginning of the third year though it was suddenly gone. Suddenly wasn't the right word though. Like so many other things, he just hadn't recognized it packing. He still had two more years until he was granted tenure, and then only as an instructor. Although his department head had been understanding initially, there had gradually developed friction about JP's teaching method and emphasis. Only recently it had been made clear to him that while his "antics" had been tolerated for the indoctrination period, they no longer would be, and he would soon be expected to toe the line like everyone else. Though the language was couched in the paternal concern of the head of the biology department, it was an unequivocal challenge to his methods, and one he couldn't ignore if he expected to keep his job. While it was hoped that the effect of the chastisement would be to nudge him back into the fold, what did happen was nearly the opposite. He began to spend more time socially with his students in an attempt to lobby for their support, and he raised the level of his histrionics to the point where even they did not take him seriously. But ultimately he just tired of the game. He gave up.

Suddenly lying on the bed he felt like a French seigneur at Agincourt, his horse shot out from under him, and with it gone any hope of finding the chatelaine of his vassal heart. He was lying on his back in a muddy field, unable to rise because of the heavy armor, unable to move, waiting for the pike to be shoved between the plates of his armor.

It was his own fault. He had turned it all inward and expected to find the answers there. He smiled remembering that during school he had chosen as his credo, 'Prophets are always disagreeable and usually have bad manners, but it is said that they occasionally hit the nail on the head.' He found it funny now because if he remembered correctly it was a quote from Carl Jung's psychological study of the Book of Job.

It had all come to a sort of head in his third year of college. Rob and Chick were gone by then and had taken with them the familial acceptance that allowed him to form his most accessible ideas. He hadn't recognized how gently they had tethered him, and that they had known him well enough to allow him only as much rope as he could handle. Without the weal of their counsel he decided to switch his major. He jumped from English and history, where he was comfortable and safe, to biology. His reasoning was simple. He planned to study medicine. He secretly decided to model himself after Albert Schweitzer, pursuing various interests in the arts and sciences and humanities. He didn't think he would have any trouble with the curriculum, and he didn't. But what did happen was that with all the study and lab work, he had little time left for reading and writing on his own. He decided to follow Balzac's dictum that a cultured man should educate himself in the subjects that interested him between the ages of twenty and thirty, and so he resigned himself to look forward to the time when he could plot his own course of study. Slowly though, because he had no creative outlet, in its place he developed a cynicism, a niggling cynicism. He did make it through his undergraduate studies, but as he began his graduate work and faced the reality of many more years of study before he could complete his formal education, other subtle changes took place within him.

He lost interest in medicine because he found he lacked the requisite proportions of humanism and ego. Instead he found himself more drawn to the study of pure Biology. But the more he immersed himself in those studies, the less satisfying they became. After two years of graduate work he decided not to go further, nor to re-apply to medical school, and he escaped with an MS degree, though he knew with that he could only look forward to teaching or the most rudimentary lab work.

In an act that further underlined his escapism, he moved to the beach and took the job at the Marine Resources Center. Jane was there and that helped, and Chick was too, off and on. He was very much overqualified for the position, but he hoped to make enough money to live quietly and resume his studies of history and literature. Soon though he ran into the problem that the little public library was inadequate to his needs. Though he found he could order titles from the state library in Raleigh, the delays in their arrival were sometimes too long to keep the interest trained in his wandering mind.

He was also seduced by the lifestyle at the beach. The seasonal influx and increased activities of the summer provided him with a continuous string of distractions. While in college he found he possessed an adroit Falstaffian glibness that was particularly apparent in a bar environment, and was actually heightened by the first two or three drinks he had. His problem was that he rarely stopped after a few drinks. Though he developed more of a tolerance to the alcohol over the years, the tolerance itself was eventually followed by a mental dullness and then other changes in his personality. When he drank he would become by degrees voluble, then acerbic, then physically aggressive, and finally maudlin. After a few years at the beach he was still able to hold his own during the transience of the tourist season, but more of the locals avoided him because they were never sure which aura he would be emanating, and what besides the booze triggered his changes from one to the other.

When it became apparent that he didn't have the constitution to be a great artist, he changed tacks again and became determined to perform well at his Marine Resources Center job. But that didn't last either because he couldn't convince himself there was enough challenge there to warrant the effort.

Finally, through the help of an old professor, he was offered the job at State. His first impulse was to refuse the offer because not to do so was essentially to admit defeat. But then quickly, and with much less consideration than he should have made, he took the position. It was a heavy blow to his self-esteem and he had to use what he thought was an honest humility to take it. He still silently hoped that if he were diligent and directed some of the good habits of

The Second Coming

discipline would rub off and he would be able to get on his creative feet again..

As usual his most implacable enemy was time. There were never enough hours in a day. At first it took longer than he had anticipated to maintain his new schedule, preparing lessons, writing and grading tests, conducting labs. He was conscientious enough at first to give his students the time they deserved. But then, after he had brought his teaching hours within reasonable bounds, the administration began to make the first rumblings of their dissatisfaction with his teaching methods, and creatively he was still seized with a numbing intellectual drain, so it was all still going no where.

He sat on the bed, sick of feeling sorry for himself. Sometimes, in just the right frame of mind, he got a glimpse of how other people must see him. He saw from the circumstantial evidence how they might think of him that way. But he had been there, and lived it all first-hand, and there was more to it than showed on the surface. At one time he had thought that it was all a matter of will, but now he knew how small he was in the face of so many larger circumstances.

He wondered where Rob was...and then he remembered. He had missed his shift! He was supposed to have been at the colonel's house at ten o'clock, and from the angle of the sun coming through the curtains he knew it had to be at least two. His first grasping thoughts were for an excuse, and he felt like a child trying to think of one. But there weren't any excuses. He knew he should get up and go to the phone, accept the responsibility, and make the best apology he could. And he knew how much it mattered that he do it. But he lay on the bed for a long time not moving, trying to make something out of the shadows from the moving curtains that swept across the ceiling tiles.

He knew it was the drinking, and he got a feeling that didn't come to him all at once, but rather through the progressive stages of guilt, that this was his last chance to strangle it before it had complete control of him. He had to keep things at the surface where he could see them, because as soon as he let them take those few dark steps down toward forgetfulness they were lost to him. He saw that all his sensitivities had become the enemies to his resolution. He could remember as a child how quickly and unexpectedly he could be brought to tears, and the willingness of his companions to exploit the weakness.

Then he remembered once, on his sixth birthday, he had saved some balloons from his party and hidden them in his closet. He was playing at something else a few days later when he suddenly remembered them and ran to the closet to retrieve them. But when he opened the door he found them limp and shriveled, with the life gone out of them, and he sat in the closet with the shoes and loose toys and cried, cried at the death of balloons. Now he got the hint that it was change that had made him cry, and his inability to control it. Almost from that moment he had unconsciously begun to hone his will to either change things of his own accord, or else make himself immune to the changes he couldn't control by substituting ambivalence for compassion. In theory it worked, but as he grew older he found he couldn't always tolerate the shrunken feeling that followed the external changes without the aid of something to drive the spooks away, and that was where the drinking came in.

It was a thought he was afraid of because when he really saw it from that far within himself, saw it with a rare honest lucidity, he didn't know if he could stop. He knew a hangover wouldn't stop him because he had already sworn a dozen times before that one would. He knew that the shame of the memory of his behavior wouldn't stop him either, because he didn't have that much pride left. Even the woman who had left him, the one he had told Rob about, would not have been able to stop him. He knew that now. But he still had to be careful about that. Though it had been

The Second Coming

over two years since she left, he still sometimes thought it was too early and too dangerous to think about her.

He couldn't even properly remember her face anymore. It had faded slowly until it was no more than a misty and confused reconstruction of disjointed features and expressions. After she was gone he had been forced to make some sense out of it all and justify the things that had happened. As usual in the face of an emotional upheaval he was able to pick up his writing again. For a few months he was able to lose himself in it and exorcise a few demons. When he did pick it up, he bound it dangerously to his guilt about the unborn child. He began to look upon his writing as an act of creation and spurred himself on with the idea that the results were the offspring of his mind, and that the act of creation and the disciplined work of collation that followed were somehow substitutes for the aborted victim. It never struck him that the resulting parthenogenic innovations would never assuage the core of his guilt.

Gradually though he began to renew some of his confidence in his abilities, and eventually he built himself up to the point where he could show the stories to his friends who encouraged him to try to get them published. Although he hesitated at first, eventually he did secretly sent some of them off. But they were all returned, some of them obviously unopened, and gradually he stopped sending them. Slowly too he stopped writing, and even got to the point again where he didn't flinch when his friends asked him how it was going. He hadn't written a thing since then. The guilty child of his imagination was stillborn.

It all eroded in the end, from the mountains to the dolmens of kings to stones made smooth in a stream bed. Eventually the edges disappeared so that time could pass more smoothly over the outlines.

He was too much of a coward to call the colonel to apologize. He knew he had disappointed him, and that the flaws the colonel had suspected in him were in the open where they couldn't be denied. He was more upset because the colonel reminded him so much of the ghost of his departed father. With his shriveling head and hollowed cheeks he had become like the memento mori of a medieval philosopher, the skull reposing with empty eyes on Erasmus' desk. And the reminder had come at a time when he was feeling such strong feelings of uselessness that the coincidence frightened him.

    He thought about many more things as the shadows lengthened in the room, about broken promises and lost loves and diffusion. Even with the passing of so much time the hangover didn't ease much. Eventually it was dark, and he purposely sat in the darkness. He wondered where Rob was, and when and if he would return. But as night wore on, it seemed less and less important.

    He didn't know how long the sun had been down and there was nothing in the room to tell him. He had never taught himself to pace around a room, preferring instead a sedentary percolation of thought in a comfortable chair, but he turned on the light and tried anyway. After he had crossed and re-crossed the room a dozen times he stopped in front of the dresser mirror. On the dresser top was the blade he and Rob had used to bump themselves in the room. When he was young he had written a lot of poetry about suicide. Even as he had written it he had recognized that there was something overly-dramatic and staged about the whole idea. He gave vent to the feeling, not because he ever had any intention of committing the act, but because it put him in touch with something to write. His only first-hand experience was through Leslie and the story of her husband. While JP could sympathize with some of his inner confusion and torment, when he was really honest and looked at those who had been left behind, himself peripherally included, he couldn't see it as anything more than a shallow, impotent egotism. To those left behind it would always be viewed as an act symbolizing failure, sometimes fear, and always the

The Second Coming

most palpable self-indulgence. Only for one's self could it be genuine, if indeed it was, because afterward you were safely beyond genuineness.

He picked up the blade. Could he do it himself? He knew the proper mechanics. It was better to draw the blade up the arm toward the elbow than across the striations of the palmaris longus muscle. He imagined himself doing it. It stung a little from the residual salt on his skin, but it didn't hurt. He saw the skin separate and the blood come up quickly and flow over the cut's boundaries. But it didn't spurt as he expected it to. The warmth of it brought on a pleasant, lazy feeling. Then, even in his imagination, he knew he wasn't going to die. And he felt silly when he saw himself going into the bathroom and wrapping his sticky forearms in one of the white motel towels. He found when he finished that imagining the act was almost as self-indulgent as actually performing it.

He changed his clothes and went down to the dining room, hoping it was late enough that no one from the observations would be there. As the restaurant staff cleaned up and reset the tables for breakfast, he quickly ate a late dinner. Afterward he went back to the room and waited for Rob, but he didn't come. Finally JP undressed himself, and though he was apprehensive about the possibilities at first, after a few minutes in bed he fell asleep.

The next morning, as early as he thought reasonable, he called the colonel to apologize. He spoke to his wife, but the colonel himself couldn't or wouldn't come to the phone. As JP couldn't think of a message he could trust to be properly translated, he asked if it would be alright to try again later. After the phone call he went down to the dining room and ordered the largest breakfast he could. He felt sure he would see people from the observations, but again he didn't. Afterward he went to the gift shop adjacent to the motel and bought two pens and two spiral notebooks. Then he went back to the room, situated himself, and began to write. He wrote for an hour and a half unhurriedly, filling page after page in one of the notebooks. When he felt like he had completed his immediate thought, he put down his pen and read what he had written. He was dissatisfied with almost all of it. But instead of balling up the paper and throwing it away and giving up as he had done so many times before, he took the other notebook and began to transcribe what he had written, working changes and adding and deleting things. When he finished the second version he read it over, and this time he scotched almost all of it and concentrated on the few lines which struck him most vividly. He spent most of the early afternoon working on it, and eventually he felt like it was finished. He got up from the desk and went to the bed where he nestled against the pillows and re-read it one more time.

'His face was one long protracted curve, round as the moon, and white, eyes set shadowed in the cratered mares with no discernible light of their own. Lips touched with a lavender glow, curved with the same flow, but colder and with an iridescent cruelty, as if no single color could hold that vibe. One bestial curse after another hissed through those clenched teeth...but no heat. His ears pressed tight against his head, stone-cold-cauliflower-marble white. His hands, soft and irksomely handsome, but oh so stiff dead. They never danced with the venom in his head.'

Jesus, it sounds like Captain Beefheart channeled through Gertrude Stein. The face was familiar though, but he couldn't place it. At first he thought it was a conjuring up of a face from history, but he could bring it into no closer focus than Yahweh or Zeus. He then wondered if it might be an unconscious rendering of his father. But he quickly dismissed that idea because the vision had such an obvious power. The only thing he was sure of was that it was the form of some super-image his mind had called up, and there was a distinctly vengeful cast to it.

Finally he put it aside and worked through the rest of

The Second Coming

the afternoon on other things, not necessarily in a specific direction, but with the buoyed feelings in this new incarnation of his creative spirit. He wrote without urgency or desperation, and while he worked he began to dream and plan. He thought about how much trouble it would be to juggle the writing and his teaching. But he was able to remain positive because he could remember and anticipate the traps he had fallen into before.

When it turned dark outside he stopped. He went into the bathroom and shaved and took a shower. Refreshed and relaxed, he thought about calling the colonel again, but he decided it would be better to go in person the next day and take his medicine like a man. He went down to dinner and afterward, instead of going back to the room as he had planned, he found himself walking up the narrow staircase to the lounge. Once there he found a few of the diners from downstairs, as well as the usual noisy crowd of college kids drinking beer. As soon as he walked in he ran into the tall girl from dinner two nights before. She was leaving with a man about JP's own age. They all said hello, and he asked where her friend Mary was.

"Mary left this afternoon. She said she wasn't feeling well, and she was sick of the beach any way. Sometimes she gets like that."

As he watched them go down the narrow stairs he wondered if Mary had missed any shifts, and he made a mental note to check his schedule when he got back to the room. He found an open seat at the bar and was about to order a scotch from habit, but he stopped himself and ordered a club soda instead. When it was served, he sat on his stool swirling the lime around in the ice with the plastic swizzle stick. Even before he had taken his first sip he was wondering how quickly he could finish it and order the scotch, and he wondered what the bartender would think of his resolve if he did. He buried the thought, but he knew it was still there swimming just below the surface. He had thought he would just sit quietly in the bar thinking about his writing and his new enthusiasm. But he had undervalued his desire for a drink. If he was going to stay there any length of time he would have to find someone to talk to. He certainly didn't want to talk to any of the college kids because on a night like this their prattle would be sure to bring his cynicism to a quick and bitter head. Bartenders were usually just as bad because most of them would try to draw him into a game of world-weary one-up-man-ship, and before he got to the point where he would beat them at the game, he would have to drink enough to prove to them it was no accident. So it appeared he was going to have to settle for the taut silence.

He finished his soda water and was about to leave when a woman came in and took the seat at the end of the bar. He watched her out of the corner of his eye as she ordered a drink and tried to guess her age. His first guess was that she was his age, thirty, but almost immediately he decided she was older. She seemed relaxed, but she had just enough of a smile on her face that he knew she felt out of place among all the beer-drinking students. She had probably been looking for a nightcap in a quiet bar and not realized that this Saturday was the last safe blowout for the students before they had to collect themselves to hit the books again a few days later.

There was no way to go over to her at first, and in fact she wasn't casting him any 'come hither' glances, so he waited, ordered another soda, and glanced casually toward her every few minutes. Finally the couple occupying the seats between them paid their bill and left. Before their seats could be taken he slid over and took the one next to her. He had planned to introduce himself and begin a conversation from there. But once he was in the seat next to her and they shared a quick smile, he was so nervous that he couldn't talk. He had felt her contract when he first invaded the space next to her, but with the smile she had relaxed a little. With the

The Second Coming

lengthening silence though, she began to shrink again, not from fear, but from annoyance that he was acting so oddly.

"I'm sorry," he said finally. "I guess I'm not getting off on the right foot. When I sat down I intended to strike up a conversation immediately, but then I started thinking about something else...anyway it just sounds worse if I try to explain it. My name is JP Richardson," he said, and held out his hand.

"I thought I'd seen just about every come-on before, but I don't think I've ever been so obviously approached and then so completely ignored. Is it supposed to gain you some sort of psychological advantage?"

"No, I was just thinking of something else."

She looked at him and smiled so that he saw the tips of her teeth arranged neatly below the line of her lip. "Is it my imagination, or is everyone else in this bar ten years younger than we are?"

"It's not your imagination. It's Easter break and a lot of college kids who can't get to Florida come here."

"A friend of mine recommended this place, the beach I mean, but what in the world are you supposed to do with yourself? The ocean is frigid, the beaches are windy, and from my count there are never more than ten scrubby trees to be seen at any one moment. And as for the night life, the bars are miles apart, the drinks are weak, and when you finally do get approached, the man who approaches you forgets his come on."

"Where are you from?"

"That's a good start."

"OK, what do you do?"

"I own a pet shop."

"That must be interesting."

"It was interesting when it was a hobby," she said, and he noted that she had a peculiar way of drumming her fingers on the edge of the bar, and that it didn't seem to have anything to do with nervousness. "But then my husband and

I split up, and now I'm supposed to make it my livelihood."

"Does that mean you don't make enough money at it, or that you don't find it challenging enough?"

"Let's put it this way. I've had to move to less expensive apartments three times in the last two years, and I spend a lot of time teaching the cockatiels to say, 'Here kitty, kitty.'"

He laughed, and then asked if he could buy her a drink.

"I know what you mean about this place though," he said. "A lot of people hate it here, especially people from cities. I'm not sure exactly what the mechanism is, but it seems to have something to do with introversion and extroversion, and the need for an ability to let the place happen to you. Sometimes it is boring, but I don't think that's the whole reason for the dissatisfaction."

"It's the whole reason as far as I'm concerned, but maybe I'm missing some of the nuances. Why don't you tell me what the attraction of this place is for you?"

"I can try. First of all, I won't contend that there are any more activities than you have found. The attraction or the message of this place is not action. What I've found, and I've been coming here for a long time, is that it has more to do with apprehending the evidence around you, a lot of which can be very symbolic, and then making use of the peace of the environment to meditate on what the symbolism means to your life back wherever you live it.

"For instance, just take the physical structure. What you have is a long stretch of barrier islands, sand bars really, thrust out into the Atlantic, completely unprotected from the wind and rain and surf and all the eroding aspects of the great ocean, taking the full brunt of whatever the sea can throw at them in order to protect the low and otherwise unprotected tidal lands and delicate marshes behind them. And how do these fragile islands fight against this overwhelming force? They respond by allowing themselves

The Second Coming

to be shifted. When the wind blows they let it sweep up their grains of sand and hurl them down the beach. But eventually the wind tires and they fall. They allow the waves and currents to shift tons of their sands, but eventually the seas calm and the sands settle again. They simply and repeatedly allow themselves to be reformed and reshaped. But the wind and waves and currents are fickle. Half the year they drive the Banks south and the other six months they drive them back north. So there is a consequent stasis. It's Buddhistic, really."

"That's an interesting way of looking at it."

"Then look at history. For centuries the only inhabitants were Indians. While they were certainly not responsible for any great historical contributions, they probably lived fairly well. They had plenty of protein from seafood and access through trade to the produce from the interior. Of course, they were periodically set back by storms, so they were probably somewhat nomadic. But I'm sure they learned, like the Japanese because of their experience with earthquakes, to make their structures simple and light so they could be easily replaced.

"Then came the white man. You've heard of the Lost Colony? It was the first settlement of English-speaking people on the North American continent, a venture financed by Sir Walter Raleigh. It is believed to have been located eight miles west of here on Roanoke Island. The settlers disappeared mysteriously, but they left us with a very attractive legend of the first English child born in the new world, Virginia Dare, whose name was found carved into the trunk of a tree.

"For the next three hundred years the area's settlers came from a different stock. The pirate Blackbeard plied these waters, and I'm sure descendants of his crews could still be found living here. Land pirates flourished by showing lights on the dunes and running ships aground on the sand bars, and then salvaging the wrecks. Some of the survivors of those wrecks must have settled here, as well as castaways and mutineers, and deserters from both sides during the Civil War. Go to Wanchese, the fishing village on Roanoke Island, and listen to the local voices. You don't hear the southern accents you expect, but rather the cadences and inflections of England's ports. The local people probably wouldn't like to hear me say it, but I've always found a sort of primal wildness in them, a vitality like you find in Australians who come from similar stock. It's the potential for sudden violence on the one hand, and the ability to see through artifice to the simple grain of truth on the other.

"Then you come to flight—"

"The Wright brothers."

"Yes. When I was a boy I always had the impression they were a pair of tinkerers who had almost accidentally discovered the secret of flight. I guess it's because the story always mentions that they owned a bicycle shop. I used to picture them trying to rig a chain and pedals up to a propeller and topping the contraption with a crude set of wings. But the truth is that they were two of the keenest minds of their age, physicists, self-taught experts in aerodynamics, brilliant and careful experimenters, and indefatigable in the pursuit of their goal.

"Anyway, because of the First Colony and the first flight they call the Outer Banks the 'Land of Beginnings,' but I guess I've gotten carried away."

"No, I enjoyed it. But I do have one question. If that's what you meditate on the first time you come here, does it leave you anything to think about or do the next time you come?"

She had a few more drinks while he sipped his soda, and gradually she grew less sarcastic and bristled less at his questions and comments. As she relaxed her face began to sag a bit around the corners of her eyes and beneath her chin, and he noticed a little heaviness in her arms above the

The Second Coming

elbows. Her voice softened, and more and more she smiled a little smile that had probably once been developed for an effect, but now had been used for so long that it had developed the special polish of an old pretension.

He still had the urge to order a drink, but he didn't. When he first began talking to her he didn't have any plans to try to seduce her. He was just looking for some casual conversation to take his mind off things for a while. But the more they talked, the more attracted he became, especially as she let her guard down and spoke more openly about herself.

It turned out they were the same age, and she finally told him her name, Daphne. They had both gone to parochial schools, and later listened to the same music and experimented with the same drugs. They shared stories about their best pot highs, and the first time each of them had done acid, although he didn't know if he believed she ever had. They told each other about the most wasted they had been on downs, he on reds at a Zappa concert, either the best or the worst place for it, and she on bootleg Mexican quaaludes, but she couldn't really remember where. She said she didn't like coke much, and he agreed. But it got him wondering again where Rob was, and if he had been back to the room yet, or if he might be there now if JP brought Daphne back with him.

Gradually the bar grew noisier and the college men began challenging each other to beer chugging contests. While their companions alternately taunted the opponents and grunted obscene chants, the combatants raised pitchers and pulled the liquid down to the suds.

"Would you like to go somewhere else?" he asked when she seemed to be tiring of the place.

"Is there any other place worth going?"

"Not really, I guess, and I don't have a car anyway. But maybe we could get a bottle of wine and go back to my room. At least it's quiet there."

She looked at him boldly and frankly as if she were

trying to gauge something in him, and then she smiled and nodded toward the entrance. "You buying the wine?"

As he ordered a bottle from the bartender she got up from her stool and wandered toward the stairs. She left her tab on the bar in front of him. He didn't have a corkscrew in the room so he had the bartender open the bottle for him and re-cork it, and after paying the tabs, he joined her at the alcove at the top of the stairway. He guided her as they went because she was a bit unsteady on her feet, and when they got to the room she allowed him to support her as he unlocked the door.

Rob wasn't in the room, and there were still no signs that he had been there. Daphne sat casually on one of the beds and ran her eyes over the room. JP reopened the wine and poured each of them some into the sterile, plastic-wrapped cups. He was already rationalizing that he could drink some 'for medicinal purposes.' He had bought a chardonnay thinking it would be the least offensive of any choice he could make. But as he handed her cup to her he wondered if he should have asked her first what wine she might have preferred, or if she even cared for wine at all.

He sat next to her enjoying their proximity and the shared excitement. It wasn't intimacy, but it had a touch of a prelude to it. He realized when he was ordering the wine that he was hoping its effects, in combination with the harder liquor, might make her more amenable to his desires. But when he finally found himself alone in the room with her, and he himself hadn't had anything to drink that might have loosened him up, he was afraid to be too interested. Before long they were lying back on the bed kissing each other. He became a little aroused in spite of himself because she was a good kisser. As someone had once put it, she had one of those mouths 'made humid for kissing.' She responded languorously to his touch, but with just enough forwardness that he thought she might be ready for more. But because he had not at first intended to seduce her, he was slow to

The Second Coming

increase the scope of his caresses.

"This could go on all night," she said, jarring him back. Then she stood and began unbuttoning her blouse. Underneath she had on a soft black bra that made him think she probably paid a lot of attention to her lingerie. But when she unhooked her skirt and let it fall, he saw that she wore nothing to cover the dark triangle between her legs. Even so, he was no longer aroused. Not only that, but the more he thought about it and realized how uptight he was, the more embarrassed and further uptight he became. By the time he had taken off his own clothes it was apparent to both of them that something was wrong. And though he tried to be flippant about it, there was just enough of a hitch in her attitude to push him past the point where he could hold out and hope it was just a temporary thing.

They got in bed together and her skin felt cool and powder dry. But those sensations were lost among a thousand others climbing over each other for ascendancy in his teeming brain. Her lips and skin, the smell of her hair, the shifting focus of wrinkled sheets, and then patches of muted darkness and tracing antic light…but nothing.

She was patient at first, and soothing, recognizing the potential for the erratic in male sexual behavior. But life is short. With something like the increasing velocity of a falling object, things began to approach a different kind of climax. In a final desperate attempt to salvage his self-esteem he decided to attempt the only alternative he could think of, to pretend he didn't care. As soon as he made the decision his mind became rife with the dramatic possibilities. Where moments before he had been hoping to play out one drama, he saw in another more potentially gratifying mental possibilities.

"I'm sorry," he said, rolling away from her, staring up at the ceiling and spinning the pause out. "I'm just tired of fucking people I don't know."

When he began speaking, she rolled on to her side

and propped herself on her elbow to listen to him. As the words came out he could see genuine concern in her eyes, and that more than sex she had probably desired a real simpatico between them. And there was an instant when he could have stopped himself, but that moment passed. After he spoke it took a minute for it all to register. But as soon as it did she sprang from the bed and began gathering her clothes.

"I know it's not fair to put this on you. It doesn't really have anything to do with you. I'm sorry."

"I think you take yourself a little too seriously, JP," she said, struggling and finally slipping one of her arms into her blouse. "You know, there's only one thing worse than a barroom philosopher, and that's a bedroom philosopher. I get tired of fucking people I don't know too, but not half as tired as I got fucking some of the people I did know." She was crying silently, wiping her nose with the back of her hand like a little girl, and the tears were running in black streaks with her mascara down her cheeks. "Is this so wrong? Is it? I didn't want anything from you...nothing." She said, and her voice trailed off. She zipped her skirt, trying to stuff her bra into her purse and wedge her feet into her shoes at the same time. She stopped crying. "Good night, JP. You ought to be more careful though. Sometimes we know each other better than we think."

He knew he should feel guilty, but he didn't. While he was speaking he tried desperately to yoke his words to some real necessity or justification. But with the sound of the slamming door still echoing in his ears, he could get no further than thinking that maybe it was something he could write. He had listened to her words, not as they were directed to him, but as a necessary counterpart to the dialogue he had started. He saw the downy hair on her skin as she passed in front of the lamp, saw the glistening tears on her cheeks, watched the starts and stops as she dressed, heard the door slam, and her footsteps receding down the

The Second Coming

breezeway. He saw and heard and felt it again and again after she left. It only happened to be written. Nothing properly happened to him except to be written.

He lay nude on the bed, composing and arranging sentences to describe his feelings and hers and all the underlying feelings that were the basis for them. He thought about his cruelty and decided that it was one with every other meanness in the world. No matter what the degree, they all came from the same source, and the laws to prevent them were only set up to protect the weak and deflect the wills of those powerful enough to exert themselves. 'Laws are only measures of man's ethical frailty, insatiable accomplices of sin and death.' Who had said that? And what about Goethe writing that 'he had never heard of a crime of which he didn't feel capable himself,' a statement that at first seemed to JP to be intellectual grandstanding, until he allowed himself some of the darker sadistic fantasies he himself had indulged in, and he was never so sure again. And then thinking about Daphne again, he remembered James Joyce. 'Pity is the feeling which arrests the mind in the presence of whatsoever is grave and constant in human suffering and unites it with the sufferer. Terror is the feeling which arrests the mind in the presence of whatsoever is grave and constant in human suffering and unites it with the secret cause.' But JP had never been united with the human sufferer, and he was afraid he wouldn't recognize the secret cause, so it was all a confused yellow jumbo. And when he got to the point where one quote led to another like this, he sometimes ended up with the feeling that half the thoughts in his head needed to be footnoted.

He was on the bed for what seemed like a long time, and his mind continued to bounce frenetically. He finally got up and put on a pair of jockey shorts and went to the desk to get his pen and notebook. There was a full cup of wine on the dresser and he instinctively picked it up. No, he thought, no. He heard footsteps outside, lovers who had been watching the ocean breathe beneath the moon, he fantasized. But then there was a knock on the door. Why had she returned? As he went to the door, he looked around to see if there was anything she had forgotten. He was a little apprehensive about what he should say to her. Maybe it was Rob, he thought. But no, Rob would have a key.

He opened the door, but it wasn't Rob or Daphne on the other side. Instead there were two silhouetted men framed in the doorway. Before he could ask them what they wanted they were on him, and his first thought was that he couldn't write it because there was too much fear too suddenly. It paralyzed him and froze in his limbs and his larynx. They pushed him back into the room and one of them hit him below the ribs and something hot went into him and lifted him off his feet. He fell back on the edge of the bed and the other man kneed him between the legs, but it barely mattered because he couldn't breathe anyway. Something ripped into his abdomen again and it all began to sting. He saw a face above him, but he couldn't describe it because he was crying. He heard voices that sounded like snakes hissing through clenched teeth. But then they were far away and distorted like they were coming from the end of a long tunnel. And he wondered, if it was the language of death, why did it sound so much like Spanish? He tried to speak but something smashed into the side of his face, and it hurt, but it didn't hurt him. Then everything was dark and still and quiet, and he realized that perhaps he could write it after all.

It had all stopped. It was as repetitive as a skipping record and as numbingly mundane as something from Proust. Please God, he thought, even if I do deserve it, don't let me die with someone else's words in my mouth. Even so he couldn't stop thinking about it. And just when he thought he had a grasp of what it all meant and what they were trying to do, everything began to enter again and enter all at once, no differentiation, no choice. But he wasn't going to die, not

The Second Coming

yet. He was stepping back. Everything was stepping back into the previous moment's footsteps and erasing the footsteps in front of them. It looked real. It wasn't visually distorted, just somewhat slower than it should have been. And the sounds played backward too. It was wonderful. For an instant he thought maybe he could get out of it, let it retreat to a safe moment in the past, and then stop it and send it forward again. But how far back would he have to go? And could he really trust himself to do things differently? It was all silly, and it was moving backward too slowly. But the sounds playing backward, they were the silliest of all.

XV

The moment was peculiarly relaxing, but within seconds two more people had come around the corner, one of them in the uniform of the Sheriff's Department. He approached Rob cautiously with his service revolver held firmly with both hands in front of him. When he got five feet from Rob he signaled for him to lie down of the floor.

"Down, motherfucker, down!" he yelled.

As Rob went down slowly to his hands and knees the deputy came up behind him and shoved him down hard on the tiles by putting his knee in the small of Rob's back. It was a technique he probably hadn't had the chance to use yet, and he was going to make the most of it. A cowboy, Rob thought. When he was flat on the floor the deputy stood and tapped Rob's foot with the toe of his boot to get him to spread his legs, and when he did the man gave him a vicious kick to the inside of the thigh. Rob yelled out and was about to get up in spite of the guns when another group of three men came around the corner.

"Alright, alright," one of them said. "Murphy, help him up…and everyone put the guns away." The deputy and another man picked Rob up and held him under the arms in front of the man in charge who also wore the khaki uniform of the Sheriff's Department. "What's your name, son?"

Rob didn't answer, and he felt the cowboy's grip tighten under his arm. He was worried about the girl and whether she had done what he told her to do and hidden herself. He thought he should do something to keep everyone's attention…like punch the fucking deputy…but he had to be wary not to make the sheriff suspicious. Ultimately though, he just didn't want to be responsible.

"Where's your friend?" the older man asked as if he were reading Rob's mind.

"I'm by myself."

The Second Coming

"We know you're not alone," the man said, and more people arrived. By now there were about ten people in the hall, most of them in uniform. They'd probably all shit if they knew how much coke he had back at the beach. Another man in a park ranger's uniform came around the corner holding Harold out in front of him the same way Rob had. The lobster's claws dangled and his legs rotated slowly, and he was still bubbling around his mouth parts.

"Look, it was a dare," Rob said. "Some friends and I got drunk, and they dared me to do it. There isn't anyone else."

"Williams," the sheriff said, turning and locating the man in the back of the group. "I thought you said there were two."

"I said I thought there were two," Williams said, and Rob realized he was the ranger who first came around the corner and found him. "It might have been a shadow. I'm not used to this and I was flustered. We've looked every place anyone could have hidden and we haven't found anything."

"Well, was it one or two?"

"One, I guess. Like I said, I was a little jumpy."

Rob almost wanted to laugh, and he did smile slightly. The sheriff caught him and quickly his patience dissolved. He was in charge, and he wasn't amused.

"It's only me," Rob repeated.

"Call the magistrate," the sheriff said. "After you do that, get him to the doctor and get him cleaned up." Then he turned and started to walk away.

"What's the charge?" the cowboy asked.

"Criminal trespass and vandalism to begin with, and if you're creative, I'm sure you can come up with something else. Check the cruelty to animal statutes."

The group broke up after the sheriff left. The deputy handcuffed Rob and led him limping outside to the parking lot where there were still a few cars with their blue lights on.

He could hear distorted conversations coming in over their radios. He was put in the back of one of the cars, and he had to wait there while the deputy talked everything over with the other deputies and hangers-on next to one of the other cars.

It was a short drive to the clinic where a nervous nurse washed and disinfected his wound. The doctor came in to examine him, and decided Rob needed a few stitches in the heel of his hand where he had the deepest cut. From there he was taken to the magistrate's office which was located next to the jail at the back of the courthouse.

The magistrate was a big, florid man with a prominent paunch which tightened the fabric of his shirt and stretched the connections of his buttons. It looked like he had been disturbed during his dinner because he had a large, moist stain from tomato sauce on the front of his jacket. He was incredulous when the deputy first began explaining things, but once he understood the facts he was all business. Rob answered his questions as he filled out the forms, and submitted quietly to the fingerprinting. He didn't want to call anyone and refused to post bail. He was told that if that were the case he would have to wait until Tuesday to stand before the judge. By this time the magistrate's assistant, who was also one of the jail keepers, arrived, and he and the arresting deputy led Rob down the hall that opened from a door behind the magistrate's office. At the end of the hall were three cells. They were all unoccupied and clean, and looked like they had been recently painted.

Rob had done everything they told him to do. Nothing had bothered him except the occasionally throbbing in his hand and the tenderness of the knot on the muscle on the inside of his leg. But as he walked down the hall in front of the deputy and the jailer, Rob became aware of how much he didn't want to go into one of the cells. When they directed him to the one on the right he hesitated at the door. Like the others it was clean and everything from the walls to

The Second Coming

the light fixtures was covered with new layers of gray enamel paint. There was a window looking out on a small fenced yard with a large overhanging willow tree in one corner. Suddenly more than anything Rob didn't want to be locked up, and he was ready to call to the beach to find Chick or JP, or even Jane, to see if they could come up with the bail. But then he smiled to himself and thought 'what the hell,' and went in and let the door be closed behind him.

After the jailer and deputy left he walked around the cell. He looked over the titles of the small selection of grimy paperbacks on the table next to the bed. Then, sitting in the straight backed chair, he tried to discern the subtle differences in the grays and blacks outside. Finally he went over to the bed and stretched out on his back with his hands entwined behind his head and looked at nothing in particular on the ceiling. He was tired, but it was much too early to sleep, so he lay there and tried to gauge the strength of the springs beneath the mattress cover. He had learned a little about how to exist behind bars, enough to know that the best jail time was spent asleep. There the hours were guileless and touched each other and huddled together, and then spun themselves out in dreams and unconscious dodges until you woke and were somewhere further down the line. But he had a lot to think about, and it was a long time before he could relax his mind enough to sleep.

He was awakened the next morning by a buzzer located high on the wall above the door. A little later his door was unlocked and a breakfast tray was brought in. He hadn't paid attention the night before, but now Rob saw that the jailer was an older man with a craggy face and hair swept back and turned silver because of the oil he put in it. He was missing a few teeth on one side of his mouth, and when he talked his cheek on that side puffed in and out like a bellows.

"This is probably the best jail food you could find anywhere," he said as he put down the tray. "We don't make it ourselves. They cook it at the restaurant across the street and send it over, and the state pays them by the meal. It makes it easier because we don't normally do enough business to warrant having a kitchen and hiring someone to order and cook the food and make it 'cost efficient.' The state is big on that. They're all good women over there, but sometimes I honestly think they make better food for the prisoners that they make for us folks who have to earn an honest living to pay for it. That food's good, ain't it?"

Rob nodded.

"It's good alright. I can see that myself. After breakfast you can do whatever you want as long as you do it quietly. I'll bring lunch at noon and then you get an hour outside unless it's raining, but it ain't going to rain today. Hell, it hasn't rained since September. Why should it start now?"

After he finished explaining the rules he left. He came back a few minutes later and Rob heard him across the hall talking to someone else so he guessed they must have brought someone in during the night, and then he remembered what he thought had been a dream. There was no continuity to it, just footsteps and disembodied voices.

Rob ate the food and it was good, though maybe not as warm as it could have been. When he finished he arranged the straight-backed chair so he could look out the window. There wasn't much to see except the dangling tendrils of the willow being heckled by the breeze into a seductive dance above their shadows on the lawn. The jailer came back again after a while to fetch the tray and explained that the restaurant also took care of washing the dishes, but the dishwasher would cuss if the yolks were sticking to the plate.

"It was good, wasn't it?" he asked, and Rob nodded. "If you do something bad enough to keep you here for a while, you could get fat in this place."

After he had gone Rob heard more talking across the hall, but he ignored it until he realized the jailer had gone

The Second Coming

away and the voice was calling for him. He reluctantly got up and went to the door and looked through the barred window. There was a black man in the cell across from him. His head was large enough to fill the window in his door. Even across the hall Rob could see the broken veins and jaundiced whites of the man's eyes. Maybe it had something to do with the fluorescent lighting. The man had one arm slung out the window. His hand was long and tapered and the skin was smooth as Rob followed it from the wrist, until he saw on the fingertips there were large cracks and the skin was gray. Rob thought he must be a concrete finisher or mason, and the lime had dried out the skin like that.

"Hey, man," he said, but when he continued Rob couldn't understand a word he said except 'muv-uk-uh,' and he couldn't tell from the cadence of his speech whether he was asking him a question or telling him something.

"What?" he asked, and the man repeated himself, but Rob still couldn't understand what he was saying. He wasn't going to make him repeat it again, so he just nodded his head and moved away from the door.

He spent the rest of the morning avoiding the door because he still felt the presence of the man across the hall with his arm dangling out the window still waiting for a chance to explain himself.

Rob knew Chick and JP must be going crazy trying to figure out where he was. If they hadn't found his car in front of the girl's house, they probably thought he had split. He also thought about the petrified look on the girl's face. She could only have gotten into the shell display with a second or two to spare. They were lucky the ranger arrived by himself before anyone else. The center should be opening to the public soon, and he wondered what she would look like when she came out, and if she would be careful to make sure no one saw her. The things he remembered about being in there with her no longer seemed real. Or the teeth in the memory seemed loose or broken, unable to chew the meat of it, much less swallow and digest it. He hoped she remembered what he had told her about returning to her car.

After lunch the jailer led him outside for his hour of exercise. It was warm and the breeze had calmed so it was just filtering through the trees. Sunlight fell in the whole yard except for a few jealous patches beneath the willow tree. He walked around the perimeter of the yard, kicking cigarette butts as he went, and finally he stopped and leaned against the chain-link fence. It was only ten feet high and there was no barbed wire or any kind of discouragement at the top. He could have been up and over it in a few seconds. But there was no place to go after that, nothing to blend into. The black man was gone when he was led back inside. He guessed he never would find out what he was trying to say.

A couple of hours later he was fetched again and led to a small room off the hall near the magistrate's office and given a towel and soap to shower with. He was told he would be left alone unless he wanted to shave, and in that case the guard would have to stay and watch him. Rob said he'd wait on the shave. When the door was closed behind him he undressed and went into one of the stalls and turned on the water as hot as he could stand it and stood under the stream without moving until there was a knock on the door to tell him his time was up.

A different man came with the tray with his dinner. He was taciturn and preoccupied, and not disposed to be friendly or talkative like the other jailer. The food looked good, but Rob didn't eat much of it. He was tired and worn out and vaguely afraid of the approaching night. Though he hadn't slept much the night before, there was still too much incentive to remember. After the jailer retrieved his tray he walked around the cell for a while, through sunset and dusk until well after dark. When he tired of that he crouched down and looked through the stack of paperbacks next to the bed. They were mostly Agatha Christie and Rex Stout murder mysteries, along with a few trashy sex novels. There

The Second Coming

were a few books with the covers torn off. He picked one out of the pile and opened it to the title page. It was "Lolita," which made him smile at a number of levels. He was about to open it and begin reading when he heard the heavy door at the end of the hallway open, and he listened as someone was led in.

It was too early for bar fighters or drunk drivers. But the voice he heard was loud and belligerent, and unheeding of the other quieter voices trying to soothe and calm him. The grunting expletives continued until long after the key had been turned locking him into the cell across from Rob.

An hour and a half later another man was brought in, this one coming timidly, and was put in the remaining cell. For the first time Rob wondered what would happen if there were any more arrests. It was a Saturday and it was still early. He was suddenly nervous because even thinking about sharing a cell reminded him of Rios, and he didn't want to remember him. Fucking rabbit!

He picked up "Lolita" and opened it to the first page and began to read. He quickly came to the part he couldn't remember. 'You can always count on a murderer for a fancy prose style!' He froze as soon as he read it. Then he closed the book and put it on the table and looked out the window at the shape of the willow tree in the moonlight. JP had once told him about willows and their extensive root systems. He couldn't remember why, but JP had volunteered information about how they choke pipes underground and entangle themselves around buried cables and strangle the roots of other trees in their search for water. They buckle sidewalks and loosen foundations, and have been known to undermine swimming pools in their blind acquisitiveness. He was still thinking about it, visualizing what happened underground, when the guard came in dragging a creaking, fold-out cot.

"What's that for?" Rob asked.

"For your new boarder."

"Can't you put him in one of the other cells?"

"No, son. This isn't the Hilton, and don't complain yet because the way things are starting out tonight you'll be lucky if you have to share this cell with only one other person. Sometimes it gets like this even when the moon isn't full."

Ten minutes later they brought the man in. He was so drunk it took two of them to support him. Rob saw right away that he wouldn't have to worry about conversation because the man was too far gone to be able to talk. He spent the first five minutes retching into the toilet, and he had the dry heaves after that. When he finished he sat on the floor, his head bobbing. His eyes gradually focused, and Rob pointed to the cot. The man stumbled over and fell heavily on it. He mumbled something repeatedly and emphatically to the wall, and the sound of his own voice seemed to lull him because after a few minutes he was snoring, and he slept soundly after that.

The interruption was not enough to stop Rob from remembering. In fact, the way the drunk lay on the cot was like a boon to his memory. Slowly it became clear again as if he was focusing on it, and he saw it as sharply as he had seen it a dozen times before.

Rios. He thought he had killed him when he hit him with the statuette, though he had held back at the last moment. He had never hit anyone that hard before or heard a noise quite like that. He was trembling so much he couldn't run, but he finally made himself sit on the edge of the new couch, and tried to slow the rate of his heart and his breathing. But it was difficult as he watched the pool of blood become larger on the carpet beneath Rios' head. He didn't know how long he sat there, but it must have been quite a while to accommodate the lengthy procession of images. But it was the same realization now which had jarred him then.

Rios' hair was too fine. It was beautiful. Rios had beautiful hair, clean and shining and iridescent, except on the

The Second Coming

side where it was becoming matted by the thickening blood. And lying there he didn't look like himself at all. The way he had fallen he looked smaller, like a child almost. He looked calm and peaceful...and innocent, without evil, or the potential for it.

Rob got up from the couch and walked over and stood above him, finally recognizing the almost imperceptible rise and fall of his breathing. He wasn't dead. And if he wasn't dead, he might have been dreaming. Rob knelt and put both hands around his neck just below the margin of his beautiful hair and began to squeeze. He squeezed until the skin on Rios' neck above his circumscribing hands began to turn blue and then gray, and he kept squeezing until his arms ached and his whole body shook with the effort. Finally he felt something collapse and Rios shook a little. But he didn't stop until he knew Rios was dead and past dead. Then he let go and went through his pockets and picked up the package and got into Rios' car and drove away.

He remembered it all as he had done it...without guilt. He didn't have any fear of retribution, whether judicial or spectral. He wouldn't have defended himself. But he would have liked to explain what he felt as he did it, and what little beauty he had seen in the black hair and the epitomized form. He thought about it for a long time, well into the early morning hours, and as neither resolution nor absolution were his aims, he could think about it all calmly. When he did finally sleep, his dreams were intrinsically lazy and benign.

The friendly jailer, whose name was Johnny, woke them early the next morning. The man from Rob's cell and from the cell next to them were led away before breakfast. They didn't return. That left only Rob and the man in the cell across from him who had raised such a ruckus the evening before. When Johnny came in with Rob's breakfast he explained in whispers that the man had beaten his wife pretty badly and threatened her with a shotgun. And if that wasn't bad enough, her brothers, who were out on a trawl boat, had found out about it and sent a threat by radio that they were going to take care of him when they got back to port. As Johnny picked up their breakfast trays, he announced with some excitement that the magistrate was still there after signing the releases for the other two prisoners and he wanted to talk to both of them so they had better clean themselves up. Fifteen minutes later he returned, unlocked their cells, and led them to the office where the magistrate sat behind his desk signing papers and stamping them with an official seal.

"Good morning," he said without smiling, and motioned for them to sit in the two chairs that had been placed before the desk. When they were settled and the jailer had retreated to a spot behind them, he took off his glasses and began speaking slowly. "My wife is a religious person. She always has been. You know that, Rusty," he said, looking at the man, who shrank when his name was spoken. "And because today is Easter she feels it is her duty to do something for someone. This morning I told her I had to come to the office before church to sign some releases, and she wanted to know if there was anyone in the jail I wasn't signing a release for. And I had to tell her that, yes, there was. Needless to say, Rusty, she was very upset when she found out you were here, and heard what you had done. She and I have known your mama and daddy for almost forty years, and we've known you and Mae since you were babies. It's just not right what you did no matter what the reason was and, trust me, I will get to the bottom of it. And now, to make matter worse, you got her brothers issuing threats over the short wave radio, and I don't need that kind of headache. But for right now she wants me to be charitable and forgiving. So if you can promise not to make trouble with Mae or anyone else, then I'll wave your bond and release you on your own recognizance." He pointed at him with his glasses again. "You better iron things out, boy,

The Second Coming

and do it fast. And remember, if you stir anything up or get into any mischief, then the judge is going to be asking me for answers, and if that happens, it won't matter how long I've known you or your family.

"Now, Mr. Wheat, you are a different case. The economy of this community relies a lot on the tourist dollar, and so we try to be careful how we treat people who come here to visit and enjoy our area. But every so often we get someone like you who feels like he has to take his fun a little further, whose dares become breaking and entering and whose practical jokes become vandalism, and I don't like that one bit. I tend to think the court is not going to view your offense as seriously as I do, and you will probably get off with a fine and a slap on the wrist. For that reason I would like nothing better than to keep you here until the date of you court appearance, and maybe even try to get a continuance to keep you here a little longer. But that would be neither fair nor charitable, and because of my wife's wishes I intend to be both this morning. Therefore if you will make the same promise as Rusty I will also release you on your own recognizance and expect to see you here on Tuesday. Will you both promise?" They both nodded their heads. When they did he pushed forward two batches of papers. "Sign these and collect your belongings from Officer Swain, and I will see you both bright and early on Tuesday." He collected his papers from the desk, and for the first time Rob realized how uncomfortable he looked in his Easter suit, and that he had shaved himself so closely that he had a rash on the fleshy part of his neck above his collar. "I hope the two of you realize how lucky you are, and how close your guardian angel is."

Ten minutes later Rob was out in the warm morning sunlight. Everywhere he heard birds singing, and everywhere the sun shone powerfully. There were only a few motionless clouds, and they were high and thin against the sky behind them. There was a dull brown of smoke to the west.

He walked down the main street of the town to the road leading to the causeway which would take him back to the beach. Once he got to the road he walked for a while with his back to the traffic before he turned and put out his thumb. It didn't take long to get a ride all the way to the girl's house. His car was still parked out front, but hers wasn't there. He thought about asking at the house about her, but instead he retrieved his key from under the bumper and got into the car and drove away.

He drove straight to the motel and went up to the room. He knew something was wrong as soon as he opened the door. There was blood on the rug at the foot of the bed. He looked around outside to see if anyone was watching and listened carefully for any sounds in the room. When he was satisfied he went in and closed the door behind him. JP was lying on the floor between the bed and the door to the bathroom. He was on his stomach in a lot of blood. Rob was afraid to turn him over, but he recognized the pallid gray color of his skin. They must have mistaken JP for him. That was the answer he wanted to believe, but it didn't satisfy him because they must have realized someone else was staying in the room. He got his satchel and bag and looked around the room to make sure he wasn't leaving anything else that was his. As he walked around the room he kept repeating to himself, "JP is still my friend. JP is still my friend," though he didn't feel anything.

This was not the way it was supposed to be. Everyone had this dream. You win the lottery. You find a suitcase full of money on the side of the road. You find the gold at the end of the rainbow. "JP is still my friend," he thought again, and then he began to get angry that someone had done that to him. Then he felt sorrow, then fear for his own safety, then sorrow again. It was all very much on the surface though, especially the sorrow, as if each feeling were just a prick on the skin.

The Second Coming

There was nothing to be done for JP. That was obvious. Rob took his things and went outside and closed the door behind him. There was a maid's cart in front of the room three doors down. He quickly turned his back and went the other way and walked to the car with his head down. As he got into the Mustang the maid came out and moved one door closer to JP. He wondered why she was going to be the one to find him. JP would have wondered the same thing himself.

He drove to Chick's house. There was no one there and no note under the loose brick in the steps where he said he would leave one if they got out of touch. Rob knew he had blown their timing all to hell, but with that much coke on the line he would never have expected Chick to lose contact. Maybe he had been to the motel and found JP too.

From there he drove to Jane's house. He had to say goodbye and try to explain things, and he had to see Kelly one more time. But there was no answer when he knocked on their door either. He knocked again and waited, and then tried the door. It was unlocked, so he opened it and walked in.

It was Easter so maybe they had gone to church. He knew Jane didn't believe, but maybe her new boyfriend did, and maybe she thought it would be good for Kelly. If Kevin was a believer she would go to church with him, at least for a while to try to please him. But as far as Rob knew Kelly had never been in a church, and the idea of her going scared him. He looked around the living room. There were cigarette butts in the ashtray and in the kitchen there were dirty dishes in the sink. He walked to the back of the house and the two bedrooms. Jane's was to the left, and he looked in, but he didn't cross the threshold. Instead he turned and walked into Kelly's room. For some reason he had expected it to be frilly, but it wasn't. There was no dust ruffle hanging from the edge of the bed, and there were only a few stuffed animals and dolls. She had posters on the walls of unicorns and pouting, bang-your-head musicians wearing tight black pants. Though the room was at the corner of the house there was only one window, and it looked out on the yard with its scrubby weeds and bushes and then the street. He had had a better view from his cell in the Manteo jail. It was a depressing little room in a depressing little house, and it couldn't have provided much substantive food for her daydreams.

But what were her dreams? At different times he had dreamed of coming and taking her away, kidnapping his child from her mother and living on the lam, showing her the different parts of the country he had seen, or maybe taking her to Mexico or Central America, or even out into the Pacific somewhere, showing her his way and hoping she could see it through his eyes.

He looked down and saw the stuffed bird he had given her lying half-buried under the rumpled sheets of the unmade bed. He picked it up and looked at its simple stitched-on face. He held it to his chest in the middle of the quiet room, but it felt cool and artificial. He looked at the face again. Then he turned it over and took the razor blade from his pocket and slit it down the seam in the back and pulled it open until the stuffing began to flow out. He pulled it out in handfuls until he found the white, sealed plastic bag he had hidden inside. It had been the only safe place he could think of to stash it...and he had meant to replace it...but there just wasn't time now. He dropped the limp animal on the bed, put the package inside his jacket, and left the house and went back to the car.

He still had to get rid of it. He couldn't wait for Chick now, and he couldn't go to Baltimore by himself. It had to have been Rios' cousins or his brother who had gotten to JP. Whether they thought they had gotten the right man and were satisfied, he didn't know. They might still be looking for him. They might even know he was in the Mustang.

The Second Coming

He would head west. Lately he had thought he might go to Nashville or Memphis, somewhere away from the ocean. He could stay there until he figured a safe way to get rid of the coke, and then dump the car and take a bus anywhere he wanted to go. What was the name of that girl who lived in Albuquerque?

The Second Coming

XVI

Of course, she would never be able to believe it. But like the afternoon she spent sharing the silence with Emma, it did have an appeal for her. Gert knew she had always been too hard on people whose faith rested on externals. It probably had to do with the conclusion she had come to that even the froth of her intellect and the residue of the things that boiled up unconsciously were somehow more valuable than anything outside herself that she could put her faith in.

Emma had appeared especially uplifted during and after the service. It was obvious that it wasn't just a blind hysterical response. There was something else to it. Emma had tapped into something, the mystical part of it. Gert was impressed that she could still see it at her age, and in spite of everything else she must have seen during her lifetime. She had worried about Emma because she had seemed so forlorn over the weekend. She knew the severity of the colonel's illness must be preying on her mind because it was so much on the minds and in the conversations of the others in the observations, even those like Gert who hadn't known him before. But now here Emma was on Easter morning, radiant, powerful, and obviously reborn, and Gert was jealous that her friend could so fully enjoy the psychological benefits that came with the strength of her beliefs.

She was jealous because she could not view the world with the same innocence as Emma did, and it bothered her because she was usually so proud of the fact that she didn't. In fact, though she had been sincere about her reasons when she asked Emma if she could come along, there was still something jaded in her attitude which was ready to smile inwardly at the whole thing once she got there, but that knowing smile never felt comfortable on her lips. The crux of it was the interpretation that Emma's innocence wasn't a product of what she had seen or done or felt. It was a product of what she knew or allowed herself to know, but it was on a non-intellectual level because everything was filtered through a pre-operative sieve. It was something that allowed Emma to look at the evidence, even irrefutable scientific evidence, and reduce that evidence and its conclusions to a tenderness there was no argument against. Emma was not stupid, and everyone had their own special mechanisms, so why did Emma's bother her so much?

    She probably would have felt better about it if she had been closer to Emma's inward struggles. It had to be hard for Emma after what she had told Gert about her upbringing, which Gert viewed as just this side of hysterical, to believe as well as she did in the face of her religion's forced retreats. How did the reality of the scientifically-constricted world affect her? An awe-inspiring relic like the Shroud of Turin had been proven by carbon dating to be a fake. Several saints had been abandoned or demoted, including St. Christopher, who was the patron saint of the unavoidable pursuit of travel. Could Emma still pray to St. Blaise when she felt that lump swelling in her throat? Dead saints were not the only victims. The pope had been shot, and he was now forced to make his speeches behind bullet-proof glass. While in those speeches he reiterated the church's various doctrinaire stands, Emma had to see that the church would eventually have to change its position on birth control, because the groaning planet could not hold out much longer under the strain of all the mouths it had to feed. It was retreating on all fronts. The ideas of the infallibility of the church and pontiff were cracking. There were embezzlement scandals in the papal treasury, outlaw priests and bishops preaching birth control or admitting their homosexuality, or leaving the church altogether to marry or pursue other interests. As nuns grew older and died their convents were emptying because no one heard the call to replace them.

The Second Coming

Of course, a lot of it had happened before. There had been scandals and heresies, schisms and the Reformation. It wasn't the first time Rome had been sacked. But now communication was just too good for belief to be as strong as it needed to be, unless you refused to accept some of the evidence. There was a required reactionary narrowing of consciousness that resembled the calcification of age. Only the dinosaurs and militants and those with the most effective squints now believed as well as they should.

Fraser had used a good analogy at the end of "The Golden Bough" where he wrote that magic and religion and science were just progressions of thought. Though science had presently begun to supercede its precursors, it might be a mistake not to think that at some point in the future science itself might be overtaken and replaced by some intellectual system entirely unforeseen now. She loved the image he had drawn of the web woven by the three different threads, the black thread of magic, the red thread of religion, and the white thread of science, and the way he tracked man's progress to higher levels of consciousness and understanding by means of following the threads. First there had been man's childlike attempts to formulate the world based on assumptions derived from his primitive observations, and the homeopathic system they engendered, like to like, everything corresponding, everything having a soul. But gradually the most observant man saw the fallibility of that system when after further observations he realized that most things didn't correspond except peripherally and tangentially. There were many times when he realized that he did not have control over the events around him. From initially seeing himself as possessing an arsenal of great manipulative powers, with repeated failures he became aware of the ancillary results of his magic and how small he was, and how powerless. It was then he turned to religion and allowed himself to be wrapped in the arms of a being much more powerful than himself, but somehow having the same essential spirit. In order to subscribe to that system though he had to believe that nature itself was subject to the will of the deity and could be manipulated according to that will. The more he observed though, the more man saw that some laws, and especially the laws of nature, were not mutable, but rigid and precise and possessing a definite punctuality in their operations. So the deity, if there was one, must hold back his hand and step behind a curtain of the perfection of his works. Fraser, with his analogy, took us from the black thread of magic and gradually checkered it into the red of religion, and then entwined that red with the white of science and left us there, moving toward the concise purity of science, but not quite there.

    His book was finished in the early twenties, Gert thought. In the face of further developments and discoveries, how would that thread look now? Fraser would have had us think that the red of religion would have been further bled from it, and in a sense it had. But with some of the strides made in depth psychology and the discovery in the unconscious of collective memories from the time before religion when the mysteries of life were often only explainable by grasping at magical straws, if we looked at the conscious and unconscious mind as a whole, would the thread now be checked with black and white, or was it just becoming gray? And how long would it be before our abandoned religious orientation put its peculiar stamp on the collective unconscious? Science had taken chance, which Gert thought was the basis of all man's questioning, and had thought to reconcile it through the austerity of statistics. But Rhine and his Russian counterparts had begun to show that the laws of probability were in some ways malleable to the will of the unconscious. So in a sense, what goes around, comes around. Maybe that was the key. Perhaps the thread wasn't linear, but circular like the uroboros, the snake chasing its own tail, and that's all our attempts at knowledge were.

The Second Coming

After the service she wanted to get in the car and drive somewhere. A few times during the past week she had chafed at the inconvenience of not having ready access to a car. She had always loved to drive. Ben was glad to let her use it. After he gave her the keys, she went up to the room to change her clothes. James wasn't there. He was fishing. It was odd because as long as she had known him the thing she found most remarkable about his personality was his seemingly absolute inability to be consumed by anything, whether it was work, or the stock market, or a sport like golf, which he played sporadically, or any sort of intellectual pursuit, or Gert herself. He had never had a hobby. It had been an easy rationalization the times she had been unfaithful to him because she thought that even if she were found out, his possessive urges were not strong enough to ignite any feelings of jealousy. She had known he would not be interested in bird watching or the observations, and she had surprised herself when she talked him into coming. That surprise had been magnified many times when he became so taken with surf fishing. There was a new, unfamiliar expression on his face when it was animated with enthusiasm.

She easily found the road that led back to the colonel's house. When she made the turn on to it she noticed a funny color to the sky on the western horizon. She didn't know who would be on duty at the house, but she didn't think they would mind if she checked in. No one at the motel seemed to know what had happened to JP Richardson, but no one had seemed too surprised or concerned except the colonel, whom Emma said had been livid. There was no guard to challenge her at the gatehouse entrance to the colonel's development so she drove through and took the winding road around and over the canals back to the house. There were three osprey nests in trees off the road on the way back, and she drove slowly past each, craning her neck over the steering wheel to look up and see what they were doing. Two of the nests were unoccupied, and she could only just see the heads of the pair in the third.

There were no cars in the driveway at the colonel's house. She parked and walked up to the front door, but no one answered when she rang the bell. Her initial thought was that the colonel's health had taken a serious turn and he had finally been forced to go to the hospital. But she would have thought that under those circumstances someone would have called the motel, or at least left a note on the door. She went around the house past the empty garage to the west lawn and looked up at the tree and the man-made nest. It was obvious that both sites had been abandoned. She looked up at what she could see of the sky within the rough circle of trees around her, hoping to catch sight of the birds on the wing because she knew she would recognize them if she saw them, but they were nowhere to be seen.

She looked up at the empty tree again. The sky certainly was odd beyond it. It had looked smudgy on the horizon before, but now a massive, mutated brown cloud had risen from the west and was coming over the tops of the trees toward her. Wisps and feathers of a preceding brown already sullied the sky above her.

She got in the car and drove back to the beach, still keeping an eye to the sky on the chance that she might yet see the birds. She switched on the car radio. After the song that was playing faded into its ending, an announcement was made that the fire that had been burning in the marshes to the west had gained strength because of the dry windy weather and had begun to spread rapidly. While there was no immediate or foreseen threat to life or property, a great deal of smoke was being pushed toward the coast by the prevailing westerly winds. She had thought about doing some more driving, maybe going down to Hatteras Island or visiting the Wright brothers' monument, but instead she drove straight back to the motel. Emma answered the door when she went upstairs to return the key.

The Second Coming

"How was it?"

"You know, it's a funny thing," Gert said. "I drove back to the colonel's house to see how things were going, and there was no one there. Have you heard anything?"

"No, and if anything serious happened to the colonel, I'm sure Miriam would have called me. No one from the observations was there either?"

"No, no one at all," Gert said. She was about to add that she was sure the birds were no longer there either, but something made her decide not to. It was suddenly no longer important to challenge her faith. "Let me know if you find out anything."

She went back to the room, and then decided to walk to the beach to see if James was having any luck with his fishing. It felt good to feel her legs tightening as she trudged through the sand on the back side of the dune. As she approached the top she began to hear and see what seemed like thousands of gulls wheeling and diving into the boiling water just off shore. As she got to the crest she saw there were dozens of fishermen on the beach casting their lures out into the water and reeling in fish almost as often. It took a moment to pick James out from among the other anglers, and when she did she walked down the soft slope of the beach toward him. She realized as she got closer that the roiling in the water was not caused by the breaking waves, but by the thrashing of hundreds of fish blitzing in a savage, indiscriminate slaughter. To the north of where James was fishing a school of larger fish suddenly rushed toward the beach, breaking the surface, their backs flashing like the blades of knives, and chased a group of flipping, twirling, smaller silver cousins up on to the sand in front of them. A group of barefooted boys, whooping and yelling, with their unbuttoned church shirts flapping in the wind, rushed over with buckets to scoop them up off the beach. When she reached James she found him straining against some invisible quarry beneath the surface. It had bent his pole almost double and was charging back and forth in smaller and tighter reaches trying to rid itself of the hook in its mouth.

"This is great, Gert," he cried when he saw her. "This is the blitz! This is what I've been waiting for!"

His face glistened with perspiration, the veins stood out savagely on his neck and temples, and his eyes flashed with blood-lust. All around him were large fish flopping on the beach, slapping at the sand with their broad tails, quivering. Some of them must have weighed ten or fifteen pounds. They were all gorged, snapping hungrily even in the choking air, vomiting parts and bloody pieces of other fish and sending plumes of sand skyward with their tails, panting to their red gills, silently gagging.

She realized it was getting darker and she looked up at the sky above her. It was turning orange and gray, and brown and gray. All the blue had gone out of it so it looked like an old sepia-tinted photograph. The sun had shrunk and become an ineffectual orange ball. Gert looked back at James and saw him cursing at the thing on the other end of the line, and suddenly she realized again it was Easter Sunday.

What would they have thought of these signs a thousand years ago? They would have thought it was the Second Coming. The flagellants would have ripped the sackcloth shirts from their shoulders and begun to scourge themselves. Mothers would have stripped their daughters, shaved their heads, and taken them to the rivers to anoint them. The wealthy among the righteous would be cowering in their apartments and private chapels, hoping they had spent enough on their plenary indulgences. Others not so righteous would be wailing and gnashing their teeth. The confused would be seeking Joachim of Flora or some other prophet to interpret the signs and tell them the answers. The unrepentant would run riot, raping and pillaging and rutting in the streets in a final blind orgy before their damnation.

The Second Coming

But all, no matter what their station or state of grace, would keep one eye to the east for signs of the approach of the terrible army of the lord.